About the author

Truth be told; the first reason I wrote this book was, purely and simply, for fun. My publisher said "don't send me any more books about dragons" and one day I said to myself, "I'm bored, I think I'll write a book just for fun. Hey, I know what would be fun, a book about dragons!"

Well, the book gained sentience, told me it wasn't done, and has now escaped. In truth I am proud of it for all it has achieved, my Frankenstein's monster, my Pygmalion, my robot uprising. I don't know where this book will end up, but it seems to know, and that is enough for me.

Second, I wrote this book to help my young nephew consider what he was becoming – a young man. I have no sons, yet, but am proud to be a male. I have spent most of my life surrounded by women, conflicting gender ideology, and cloth doilies. I still have so much to learn, so I thought I might put some thoughts down on paper hoping I might learn something more from it, and hoping some of what I've already learnt might be shared with the next generation. I love you, nephew.

But you asked about me. Well, I am 42 now, genetically engineered by breeding to be a teacher, in love with my wife Samantha, and committed to my three daughters. I enjoy a deep Christian faith, and am kept busy during work hours with touring science shows and curriculums.

One day I will be rich enough not to, and then I'll probably keep doing it – just for fun.

- by Dr Joseph Ireland, aka, "Dr Joe"

Dragon Riders of Pearl

by Dr Joseph Ireland, aka, "Dr Joe"

PhD Science Education

Edited in Melbourne by Adroit editing.

And the unparalleled Carl Antuar.

Published by Creating Science

Current edition, printed by Lightning Spark 9780648494140

28 mar 2019

First published January 2014 ISBN-13: 9781495327292

25 January 2014

Second edition January 2, 2017, 978-1541366886 edition 2.4

16 August 2018

Visit www.DrJoe.id.au

Cover illustration and design copyright © Dr Joseph Ireland 2014. Created on Daz studio and Adobe creative cloud.

Inside Illustrations by Samantha, Joseph, Emily, Karlie and Sarah. Illustration and design copyright © Dr Joseph Ireland 2014.

Target age: Young adult readers.

More wonderful titles by Dr Joe & Creating Science:

Delightful high fantasy for the thoughtful young reader

Choice, set free

1: The Quest of the Tae'anaryn

2: The Tae'anaryn and the Wizard's Apprentice

3: The Tae'anaryn and the Paladin's Squire

4: The Tae'anaryn and the Enchantress's Chrysalis

5: The Tae'anaryn and the Spear of the Troll Prince

An engaging science fiction adventure that introduces real science concepts to readers.

Space Chase 1: Arrendrallendriania

Space Chase 2: Elizabeth

Space Chase 3: Daniel

Space Chase 4: The Mechanizer

Thrilling young adult science fantasy adventure.

The Dragon Riders of Pearl

The Dragon Riders of Pearl 2: Seven Worlds

The Dragon Riders of Pearl 3: Return of the Plague

The Dragon Riders of Pearl 4: Rage of the Dragonmen

And for the budding scientist:

Creating Science – Dr Joe's book of science experiments and activities

Dr Joseph Ireland

To:

My parents

Robert Ernest Ireland

And

Julie Margaret McGuire Ireland

Who taught me more about being a man,
than I could have ever known by myself.

And with special thanks to;
Anne McCaffrey – who started something beautiful.

Contents

Dr Joseph Ireland

The night before disaster

The alarm sounded.

Pure fell silent. She was not ready. The noise cut through her reverie so sharply that it took her a second to realize what was happening, and when it did, her heart leapt in her chest so much that it hurt.

She was not ready.

The toy figurines scattered across the floor like shattered glass as she scrambled to stand up. She knew she only had a few seconds to grab her evacuation bag before the escape capsules would light up the sky, tearing new holes in the blackness of space.

But the noise was so loud she couldn't move.

"Pure!" A voice roared. It was her older brother. "By Drallah's light you're slow. Go. This isn't a drill, the Perish are coming!"

She looked up at Courage. He was in his late teens and had looked after her and her mother since their father had died protecting another world years ago. Since then they'd moved to this beautiful cloud wreathed world, Pearl, funding a magnetic farm on the outer moon. Her brother was a soldier now; tall, powerful, and a respected defender of the law on their world. A world that had known peace for hundreds of years, as had most of the galaxy. Until the arrival of the Perish.

"Go, go!" He roared again.

But she was too frightened; she only had wit to grab her plushy dragonling from the floor.

Courage muttered something unkind under his breath, leapt over, scooped her up in his arm and snatched her evacuation bag from the locker inside their family room. "Go, it's probably just a small outbreak or something. Stop worrying."

He placed her in her mother's arms, and together they ran down the streets to the rapidly filling evacuation capsules. In spite of his scared, angry face, Pure reached out to hold him for fear that they would never see each other again.

He read her thoughts. "You're never alone, kid, my spirit is with you. And …"

His voice faded in the throng, but she held on to his hand as long as she could. She allowed her mother to rest her tearfully into the capsule next to her own. They'd only just sat down and activated the warding stones when they felt and saw the first Perish beasts approaching. They were misshapen blobs of mindless suffering; a disease that was capable of infecting every life form imaginable. Her people had invented countless means of defending themselves, but the Perish continuously evolved. They took any, and turned them into monsters.

She watched him run down the street towards the Perish that were laying waste to their once great city. Her heart raised in hope as his dragon alighted to the ground in front of him. It was proper protocol to bow before a dragon, but war was excuse enough to ignore formalities. The dragons had been humanity's allies since they'd been found on a faraway world thousands of years ago; with skin as strong as steel they could brave the emptiness of space without fear, and their minds were a match to any human's wit. Dragons and humans had forced back the hordes of the Prill, defeated the might of the Landwraith, and overcome the terror of the Tendrail hunters. But even dragons weren't immune to the Perish.

Her brother and his dragon took to the air, the dragon incinerating a flock of diseased locusts with a single fiery breath. They headed right to the center of the writhing foes, charging a beast that looked like a sickened and twisted elephant. It thrashed about, levelling buildings with its diseased enhanced trunk. Beasts did not live long once the disease took hold, but it increased their ferocity and strength tenfold. Courage and his dragon collided with a roar, ploughing into it head on. For a moment it staggered, then swept out at them with its rotting limb. They ducked. It turned for another blow, pulling back its fetid trunk, preparing to swing much lower this time. It had always been that the dragon and his rider shared one mind; Courage and his dragon charged the elephant as it swung about, throwing it off balance, then they leapt forward and snapped its leg. They didn't need to finish it off; Perish consumed their own fallen with mindless ferocity.

The capsule gave a lurch and Pure knew they'd be out of reach of the monsters soon, waiting for the rescue boats to find them. Pure let her tears fall freely as she watched her brother and the others fight back the horde. He'd sounded so confident, but they were so many… with all her heart she wished for nothing more than the chance to see him once again.

The howling ruin

Rayn pushed the sweat from his brow, and watched the cavern. The hessian backpack felt heavy on his shoulder, the ivory hilt of his little knife slippery in his grasp. He would be a fool not to admit he was afraid, but a dare stood unfulfilled.

He turned to his younger sister. Well, half-sister. "Whose dumb idea was this?" He asked.

"Yours," Jayd reminded him.

"Oh, yeah," he muttered.

"Don't back out now. You said you'd come if I did, and now I'm here; you're going in first!"

It was a dare. And no future wiseman of the Celtwyld tribes backed down from a dare, not if he was a man, and not if he didn't want to be branded a fool for the rest of his life.

Rhoc, his closest friend, gave a guttural roar of agreement. Rhoc cared little of what others thought; he was already a fool. He could not hear and thus could not speak, though he was very good at reading lips and body movements. Even so, everyone assumed that since he couldn't speak it was because he was too stupid. But Rayn always seemed to know what his friend wanted, and that had spared him many indignities.

Rayn swallowed hard. He looked out again at the cavern that was quickly proving to be the demise of his manhood. It was the howling ruin, a perfectly round cavern that looked like a giant worm had gorged its way through solid stone in the pretime. The cave was large, only just as tall as a grown man; about right for him. When the colder winds from the west blew across the mouth of the cave it could be heard to moan, as though a demon was suffering for its eternal wickedness somewhere deep in the cavernous depths. Every adult of the village had made them swear since youth to never enter or go near the ruin, and many would make a ward-evil sign just at the name of the place. It was dark and evil, and nothing good waited in its depths.

So what am I doing here? he wondered.

Jayd poked him in the back once more.

Or am I just another fool?

"Why do you delay?" she asked, smiling wryly. Jayd was the weakest yet wittiest of them all. Rayn's father had remarried years ago, and Jayd was born shortly after. They had grown up together, even though she looked nothing like him. She must have taken after her mother, which probably explained why the two women got along so poorly. She acted nothing like Rayn either: no dignity, always playing, always looking for rules to break. It was as if she was just looking for an excuse to misbehave, as if she never got enough attention or was looking for a kind of attention she never got; especially his attention. And she was always willing to get him into trouble just to get it.

← Jayd always seemed more willing to cause trouble than she could handle.

1 Jayd

Just like the kind of trouble he'd be in if their father or her mother ever found out about the dare to enter the howling ruin.

Rayn clutched his little knife, the one his father had made for him. Its blade was no longer than his hand, but it was sharp and sturdy.

"I fear not spirits or demons or cursings for my blade is blessed by a good wiseman and my soul forged in Divinity's bosom!" Rayn boasted in an old pledge, and walked forwards. As if to answer him the wind blew strong and a thundering sounded from the depths of the cave.

"And what of dragons?" Jayd asked him, fear clinging to the edge of her mischievous voice.

"Dragons?" Rayn hesitated. None had seen a dragon in over a hundred years. There were legends of great warriors who slew the beasts

Dr Joseph Ireland

in far off lands, and of maidens who enchanted them, but all was such confusion that it was impossible to tell if they held a grain of truth. There were even legends saying that men and dragons once rode as one, before history began. That by dragons, men once travelled beyond the clouds.

Bah! He thought. *What do legends matter while a dare stands unfulfilled?*

Silently the ruins waited.

Rayn looked out at the darkness. A darkness that once many a warrior must have faced in the long night hunting a dragon. He too would gladly wait out a night of fear in the forest if it were to slay a dragon, or just to see one.

And with that thought he found courage again. If he died here, he would die knowing more, and having faced his fears. That was better than to die in ignorance or cowardice. He would prove his courage and wisdom to the world, and never be thought a fool.

He stepped towards the ruin.

"You're not really…" Jayd grinned in disbelief.

"If you're afraid, you can both stay here." Rayn pointed to them and then the ground, teasing her and trying to sound sensible at the same time.

Rhoc pounded one fist into another. Rayn knew he could be counted on to go wherever he went.

Jayd, however, hurried to catch up.

"I'm in," she said, not willing to be left outside either.

They faced the darkness together.

***

The tunnel sloped down, right into the darkness. He pulled a torch from his back pack and lit it with the tinderbox. Their footfalls stirred up dust that hadn't moved in centuries, apart from the occasional insect, but it soon seemed even the beasts of the underworld avoided this place. They continued down a hundred paces more.

"Look," Jayd whispered, "a light."

Rayn held away the torch to stare into the darkness. Sure enough, a faint light shone from the depths of the ruin. It was sure to be unnatural, for it glowed blue, like the brightnight that came at the beginning of each month. For a moment he paused, not sure if he should follow. Making the sign for the Divine protection over his heart, a sign he'd learnt carefully since he was very young, he chose to face the unknown and whatever peril it might bring, and swore again to see such through to the end.

Another hundred paces or so they came to the strangest sight. It was a coffin, or it *looked* like a coffin, yet it was made of sleek silver with strange dark markings along the sides. It was so large it could have made the tunnel, melting through the stone like a hot wedge through ice. Yet the coffin had sunk deep into the stone somehow so that only the top was still visible. There was a window in the top, and inside, there was a girl.

She looked strange. She was young, about their age, but tall. She had gently pointed ears and terribly long, blond hair.

"What is she?" Jayd wondered out loud.

Dr Joseph Ireland

"I have no idea," Rayn replied. The girl was distractingly pretty. She lay there so peacefully, the air so serene around her that it was hard to believe that anyone had come to fear this place.

"Is she dead?" She asked.

"She doesn't look dead, just asleep."

Rhoc looked concerned, and with a grunt indicated that they should leave. He made the sign to ward off evil, specifically against the risen dead.

"I don't think she's cursed," Jayd said, looking closer.

Rhoc pulled her away.

"He does have a point, however: this is a tomb. This is her grave. Mother was right; we should not have come here. We should leave before we disturb her spirit any longer."

But Jayd was incorrigible. She twisted out of Rhoc's hand and popped her face right up to the coffin, leaning right up over it.

"She really does not look dead," she argued.

Rhoc gave a concerned grunt, and Rayn wholeheartedly agreed. He had seen enough.

"Stop this, Jayd, you'll not get us in trouble again. We've seen enough. We should never tell anyone what we have seen. We should leave here *right now* and take nothing with us. This is her grave!"

"Somehow, I don't think–" Jayd began.

She never did finish. Rayn would have never admitted it, but he was afraid: he was terrified. That he'd made himself walk all the way down into the howling ruin was proof enough he was man, but to desecrate the graves of the dead? No one was fool enough to do that.

With a rough hand he grabbed Jayd by the arm in order to pull her away from her sacrilegious curiosity…

… and in the process brushed against a glass panel on the side of the coffin. There was an unexpected, shrill peep, like a bird. They held their breath, and Jayd looked over at him with a mixture of fear and excitement in her eyes.

Trust her to find something enjoyable in all this.

Suddenly the coffin lit up with blue and green lights.

"*Demonry!*" Rayn panicked. "She must have been a demoness!"

"Time to leave," Jayd muttered as she threw herself away from the coffin.

Rhoc was already out the door.

Suddenly a bright, golden light, that reminded him of the presence of the Divine, shone from inside the box. The entire top split away from the base. It was opening up.

"Run!" Jayd screamed.

But Rayn couldn't run. He just stood there, transfixed to the spot. Suddenly the casket lid shimmered, and in some way he couldn't explain, began to disappear. The girl within took a deep breath then cried out.

She was alive.

In spite of himself, in spite every fear of his heart that she really might be some kind of demon, or cursed. In spite of the fact that he'd just sworn to Jayd that he'd leave here and never take anything from this place, he ran to her side.

"Are you alright?" he asked in concern, too afraid to touch her.

She opened her eyes; a riveting shade of blue.

Dr Joseph Ireland

"I…" she said, and passed out.

For a moment they stood there, speechless in silence. It was a girl, hidden in a strange coffin at the end of the howling ruin. She must have been there since long before his parents' birth, but why? Was she hiding? Or was she placed here long ago and simply forgotten?

Or was she another demon sent by the Divine to test the obedience of the faithful?

The others looked at him.

"We take her home," he declared.

The child

The town was in an uproar.

No one had dared to touch the pretty girl since they'd brought her, unconscious, back into town. To be honest, Rayn had hoped to be treated like a hero.

Instead, he was the villain.

She was lying still, completely unaware, on a bed in the large town hall where they held the communal meal each night. They'd laid some blankets over some logs, so unfortunately it looked like they were preparing her funeral bier. No one seemed to be able to agree what to do.

"She is a demon. Mind not her fairness!" someone exclaimed.

"Nay, but an angel to reward our obedience!" another called.

"Enough!" The wiseman of the village shouted. He was the councilor, the storyteller, and the healer. His word was the final law in matters of family and council. He was Rayn's master and tutor, and truth be known, Rayn's truest friend. "How can any of us hear reason with such noise?"

People slowly fell silent, muttering their own thoughts.

"Tell us again, how you found her," he said to Rayn, his voice serious. The wiseman was the highest authority in the village, after the chief, who sat silently watching the people's fear.

Rayn paused. He'd already told the story a hundred times but none seemed to like the telling and so seemed to want to put words in his mouth each time he told it anew. But he tried, nonetheless. "I... as a dare, I went into the howling ruin-"

"See, he brings a curse on us all!" someone shouted, voice raised.

"Silence! Let the boy *speak*," the wiseman roared.

Rayn continued, "I took Jayd and Rhoc with me. We went along and found what looked like a bed."

"You mean coffin," Jayd corrected.

Rayn had been very careful not to use that word.

The village erupted in shouting. Several citizens approached the bier with lit torches and had to be forcibly held back. He just wanted to slap Jayd over the head for the chaos she'd caused. The dead did not rise often in these parts – they were always careful to cremate those that passed on. But some curses were so powerful they would bring those incorrectly buried back to life to hunt the living. To mention a coffin!

Jayd just rolled her eyes. She *liked* causing chaos.

Finally the shouting died down.

"And we found her," Rayn continued, "and when I touched her bed-"

"You *touched her bed!*" His step mother shouted in disbelief. It was a profound evil to touch a maiden's bed; that was only permitted by her parents. Rayn realized too late what he'd just said and cringed, but everyone else seemed too shocked to say anything.

"It..." He took a shuddering breath. "It was an accident! I was trying to stop Jayd from touching it," he shouted, trying to blame her.

There were loads of rules how boys were supposed to treat girls, and all of them seemed designed to keep the two as far apart as possible.

No one spoke, so he continued. "And when I did the entire... thing... changed shape, and then she woke up. I thought it best not to leave her in the darkness after we had awoken her, so I took her and Rhoc helped me carry her here. Now we need to take care of her or she may die for real!"

"Then let the demoness die, you filthy, perverted son of a liar!" A woman shouted.

His step mother replied with something awful and strong men were needed to hold the two women apart.

Rayn looked at the beautiful girl. She seemed ageless. She was dressed in the purest white with no decoration but a simple pearl necklace and a headband with a diamond that glittered with iridescent beauty. The chain that held the headband on was so fine it could not have been made by any human hand, and yet for all their roughness it did not slip from her brow on their journey here. Her form was pure and perfect, unmarred by any misshaping or disease, unlike most of them. Truly she was a thing of Divine beauty, so why did they not treasure her appearance as a blessing? Could they not see that Divinity had brought her to bring them good tidings or a bountiful harvest or a sign of its blessing?

That was when Rayn saw something that caused his breath to catch in his throat. It was Hak, the town trapper. He was hulking and tall, with a black scruffy beard and matching hair. He was always boasting how he'd slain a dragonling one summer, single handed, as a young man.

He'd always claimed he'd taken the head as a prize, but was obliged to leave it behind when pursued by a pack of wolves. He'd taken a tooth from its head then, wearing it as the dagger at his hip. But a few would whisper that dragonlings lost their teeth every few years, and he'd just as likely picked it up on the road to Ferriswold. None said so to his face though, for no man in the village alone could match his great strength, and none would match the width and weight of his broadsword, Dracobane, which he wore constantly and claimed he'd forged with quicksilver and demonbile, granting it miraculous speed and sharpness. A sword he swore had not been unsheathed since the battle with the dragonling.

A sword which was unsheathed right now.

No one seemed to notice, or if they did, they did not care. Hak was walking the steps toward the sleeping maiden. He had drawn Dracobane, point downwards. He looked at the pretty, young face, his own visage dark and murderous.

Rayn knew exactly what he was planning to do. He was going to plunge his sword into her heart. It was the only sure way to test for demons. If their heart bled, then they were surely human. If it did not, it was because they were a demon. But no one could survive a punctured heart, or so it was told. So the test for demons was always fatal.

"STOP!" Rayn roared.

The room was in uproar and the only one who seemed to hear was Hak himself. He looked up at Rayn and smiled a cruel smile.

"He's going to do it," Jayd said. He realized she'd been watching at his side the whole time.

2 Hak and Dracobane

Dr Joseph Ireland

Hak raised his blade high and a few more noticed, but none were near enough to stop him. He was about to slay her. Rayn did the only thing he could do: he pled with the Divine.

Perhaps it was just pure random luck? Perhaps it was that the Divine really did hear his wishes? But the very moment the trapper was about to strike, was the very moment the white maiden woke up.

One can only imagine how the scene presented itself to the young woman. Waking up somewhere strange, in a room full of hostile people, a huge hairy man standing over you ready to put a sword into your heart to see if it stopped beating so that he could declare you innocent...

It was little wonder that she screamed.

People cried out and leapt back. Hak stumbled like something had hit him. The good wiseman ran and held him back.

She looked about in terror, and cried out again. She stumbled from the bier and cringed against it, looking at them all, a look of horror and bewilderment on her face.

No one said a thing.

Rayn sensed his moment. Everyone else was frozen with fear. This was the time to be great. The time Divinity had called him to.

"It's all right," he said to her.

She looked over at him and said something he didn't quite catch, in a language he didn't quite know, though it seemed familiar. Some stopped their ears, fearing evil powers.

"It's all right," he told them, walking closer to her.

She said something again then spoke to everyone. No one moved. Suddenly she lifted her head up, and shouted to the clouds. Calling, calling someone's name.

"She seeks her ancestors," someone muttered.

Rayn drew closer, and she suddenly grabbed a stick, threatening him with it as one might with a knife. It was a clumsy, inefficient weapon that she clearly had no idea how to wield.

Rayn paused. "Don't worry, I'm not going to harm you."

He knew the men around him had their hands on their weapons and if she made any sudden movements she could face a dozen blades through her body before she could draw her next breath.

She said something again. It sounded like a question.

He reached out and held the end of her stick so that she could not use it against him. He stood there, talking as one might to a frightened animal, trying to soothe her fear with his voice even as he held her eyes with his and stepped slowly towards her.

Then she looked down at her own hands and gave a cry of dismay. Her hands leapt to her face and she cried again. Something about her own appearance was very distressing to her. Perhaps she was a demon, forced into human form after all?

With bitter weeping she collapsed against him, and he held her in his arms. In her dismay she fell to her knees, surrendering to the situation. The sound of her cries filled the room.

Jayd walked up and joined them in the embrace. She looked out at Hak, as if angry at him for the way he'd welcomed this stranger to their village.

"See? She is but a child," the wiseman advised, "stay your hand, good man, Hak. Have pity."

The trapper then spoke, his words dark and full of anger. "Mark my words, *wiseman*, you will live to see the day you regret what you suffered to live today. You have unleashed a demon on this world..." He stormed out, a few of the harder souls going with him.

But Rayn sighed with gladness.

The white maiden would live.

The wiseman's apprentice

In darkness, there is hope; and in light, there is truth. Rayn repeated the blessing as he lit the last of the street lamps, reaching up with his sheltered candle and pushing the mottled glass cover closed against the wind. It had been a good day, the night wind was cool and the day had been fair.

But the birds had fallen silent early this day, as if expecting an evening of portent.

Rayn had pushed this nervous thought from his heart several times as he reached up to light the lamps. It was his chore as the wiseman's servant and apprentice since he had been ten years old. It was what he'd wanted all his life, and as the last lamp burst into flame he promised himself once more that he, unlike some of the others, would never tire of the chore of lighting the street lamps every evening. It didn't matter that nobody walked the cold streets of town after dark for fear of meeting an ancestral spirit, or worse. But they might have need to risk the darkness anyway, and knowing that a wiseman's apprentice had lit the lamps would bring them comfort. This year, now that he held the sash, he could not only light the lamps but also bless the children. In two years' time he would be eligible for his robe and could administer to the sick and anoint the weapons. And should the village wiseman then ever take ill or, perish the thought, die, he would acquire the staff and be eligible to declare marriages or execute death sentences, both of which paid well. Not so well that he would be the wealthiest man in town, but well enough so that he and his future wife could live good and decent.

He smiled to himself, for whom to take as a wife? No one could choose a wife for him, not since the grand council of wisemen three generations ago had declared marriage so solemn that a man must choose for himself and not have his parents decide for him. But few ignored their parents' advice even many years after that announcement.

The rhythm of his pleasant thoughts was broken as the laughter of youth came from the village hall where the communal dinner was being prepared. His chore complete, Rayn decided it was time to join them.

He smiled as he entered; the white maiden was making Hallow and Eveningsong, the young children of the village wiseman, laugh. She enjoyed their company and while the meat was cooking she narrated a clever story using two pieces of cloth, upon which she had used charcoal to draw eyes. Whatever the story was actually about was lost on him, but the broken narrative didn't seem to bother the children, and he laughed at their delight.

Their eyes met, and she smiled.

He found himself blushing. He could not bear her glance long. How the past six months had flown by! They had grown close and she spent most of her hours with him and his family, learning their language, helping with chores. That she was intelligent was obvious, and the wiseman assured him she was learning their language faster than any in the past. Rayn tried to ignore the glances of the other men who watched her and the smiles of those who treated him as though he was already

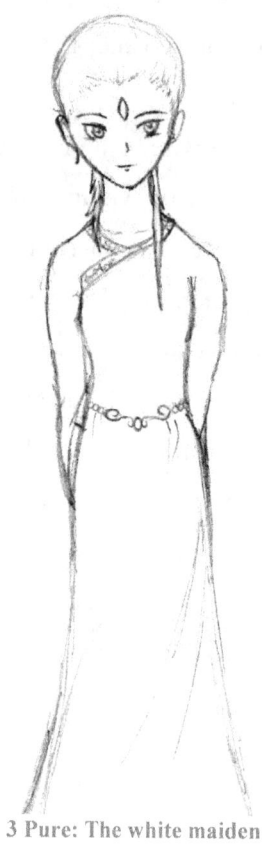

3 Pure: The white maiden

betrothed to her. It was annoying but Rayn swore to protect her and so was by her side as often as the chores of the apprentice wiseman would permit.

But word of the maiden's arrival had soon spread to other villages and many came from far away to see her. Though she was a novelty, the people of his village soon grew used to her presence. His step mother and his birth father had made her a sturdy outfit of skins and cloth, for her supple white dress did not match the standards of modesty or indeed, the wisdom of the climate.

He smiled at the memory of her naming. At first they were all guessing from her gestures; was it water? Air? Clean? In the end Rayn decided it was "Pure", and since that was what he called her, that was what her name became.

But in time, Rayn had come to notice a gentle sorrow in Pure that never quite seemed to leave. She was friendly to all but never really close to anyone. And sometimes she would just cry when left alone, or in the shadows. He didn't know what had happened to her and she didn't bother explaining. But she didn't let anyone close to her, physically or socially.

Yet in time the village came to take her presence for granted. She learnt quickly and though a stranger by birth, almost seemed to belong. Perhaps she would be a great candle maker, or seamstress? She seemed to prefer writing, which was a very unwomanly pursuit. But all took care of her as best they could, for that was what was right to do.

His eyes shifted to meet Jayd's. She had seen him watching and to his annoyance, winked. But he did not stay angry long. She was sitting at a table with all his best friends, keeping the boys well entertained with stories of her own. They laughed a hearty laugh, sipping the weakened mead that was their lot as youth. Thankfully he was not a summer from becoming a man, and he looked forward to the weeklong ritual of fasting that ended with a fox hunt with great anticipation.

His eyes fell on Rhoc, his silent friend. He was laughing along with the others though he couldn't hear a thing. At his side his little axe lay, a tool for pruning and polishing wood as much for felling wild beasts and self-defense. Rhoc meant 'stone', or more specifically, the stone that was used to sharpen the axe, and Rhoc loved axes. He was wise, but only Rayn knew that, as none others gave him heed. Perhaps even wiser than the apprentice to the village wiseman? Perhaps.

Rayn looked out at the group and felt that his life was complete.

The peace of the night was shattered by a woman's scream from outside. Rayn was nearly pushed to his death as the men ran out to confront the darkness. He saw a concerned look in Jayd's eyes, then remembered he too was almost a man and so ran outside as well.

There, running from the darkness, was the trapper, Hak, and at his heels a score of wolves. They tore at his clothes and tried to bring the great man down into the dust, where they could no doubt gorge him to death. But the mighty man kept running as though the fear had given him inhuman strength.

"Watch yourself," he roared. "Stay indoors! The wiseman's light will chase them off!" He seemed wounded by many deep cuts and gashes.

The women and children piled back indoors and the men took up arms. The wild beasts chased Hak right into the center of the largest street, lit with the most lamps. But the light did not drive them away.

"Away!" A powerful, commanding voice sounded from over Rayn's shoulder. It was the wiseman. "Be gone. Return to your place. It is not given you to hunt here. Return to the forest!"

It was a powerful command, Rayn himself stumbled under the authority of that man's faith and power.

For a second the wolves stood their ground, then returned a dark, baleful howl. It was unnatural. Rayn had never heard anything of its kind in his life. Several men fell to their knees, their sharp blades clattering forgotten to the ground.

"Stay back!" Hak ordered. "There is some devilry here. The wiseman's faith has failed!"

Several men gasped, but Rayn did not.

He was offended. How *dare* the trapper speak so disrespectfully of the Divine, even though his life be threatened by wolves! Better to die honest than live with a curse upon your tongue towards the village wiseman.

"NO!" Rayn roared, the strength of his own voice startling him. He tore his little knife from his belt. Without stopping to think, consumed by righteous indignation for the slight against the Divine and its servants, Rayn rushed into center of the village square to stand back to back against the trapper. "Divinity will NOT fail us!"

"Boy, get back-" Hak began, but gasped as he saw something.

Rayn turned, and gasped in disbelief. He was not alone, for two others had drawn their weapons and joined him in the ring against the horde: Jayd, pulling not one but two sharp blades from her belt and boot, and Rhoc with his axes, of course.

"Jayd, what are you doing?" Rayn shouted, fending off jagged teeth with his knife and the long rod that was used to light the lanterns. He'd almost forgotten he was still holding it.

"Saving your behind, again," she said, keeping any wolves from attacking him side on.

"Children, this is madness," Hak said, his back to them all.

Rhoc was looking this way and that, not having any sense of hearing to help protect him. The four pressed up back to back, presenting a wall of sharp blades against the bare fangs. The other men in the village scrambled for weapons but few seemed to know what to do, and thankfully the wolves seemed to be ignoring them.

Rayn poked the lantern pole at one, and in an instant it had snapped the end off. Their strength and speed was terrifying.

Hak stepped forward and took a mighty swing at a wolf that had come too close.

"Ye needn't spend your own lives for an old trapper like myself," he shouted.

Rayn couldn't reply, for in that very moment the wolves attacked, springing as one with supernatural co-ordination. Each was stuck with steel but another was on the weapon bearer's arm or leg in a heartbeat. Rayn heard Jayd squeal as a wolf tore at her leg and she fell to the ground. Rhoc bellowed as one took the axe from his hand. Rayn had only just struck one wolf along the face when a second one clamped its jaws right on his sword arm, biting down hard. But before the beast could do any further damage, he dropped his knife into his left hand and stabbed the beast in the neck. He heard it whimper and felt it loosen its grip as warm, dark liquid poured over his hand. Then he felt a mighty push on his back as a wolf leapt on him. He heard Jayd scream as he fell face first into the dirt. He'd seen wolves attack this way before. He knew the tactic that followed and fully expected the powerful jaws to clamp down on his neck in his next fevered heartbeat.

But it never happened. Suddenly the area was filled with wild, flickering light, as if from a wildfire. The wolves were crying out in fear and pain. Rayn scurried to his feet and didn't have time to grab his little knife before he saw the source of the light.

Pure, the white maiden – her hands were covered in strange orange fire, yet she seemed unharmed. It burnt high into the night, distracting the fevered animals. She reached out her hands and muttered words he could not hear. The fire blasted a pair of wolves, one off Jayd and another from beside him. The wolves, as one, began to pull back.

Rayn heard Jayd whimper and turned to help her. The wolves had held her by the neck and she was bleeding from several wounds, but it did not seem too serious. He helped her up and she gasped at the fire around Pure.

4 Pure, the maid of fire

Pure ran up and, muttering strange poetry of power, drew a circle in the air. The fire completely surrounded the five of them, hedging the wolves out. The circle continued to grow even as she continued to hurl fire at the wolves. Everyone stood speechless, but Rayn took the opportunity to act. He began to hurl whatever he could at the stupefied beasts. Terrified of fire and confused at the stinging projectiles, they turned and fled with their tails between their legs.

The town fell silent. The fire began to die in the maiden's hands.

"She saved us…" Jayd whispered, loud enough for all to hear.

Rhoc fell on his hands and knees, thanking her. Other citizens began to follow suit when suddenly, and completely unexpectedly, Hak grabbed Pure by the hair and forced her to the ground.

"Demonry!" He shouted. "See, now you have *all* seen it!"

"Hak, unhand that maiden," the wiseman demanded.

"Oh no," he said, his voice dark and victorious, "you have all seen it now. You cannot deny it. To command fire as the Divine, without invoking their blessing? This is only the work of a *demon*. She has brought a curse on this village, know I not that it was *her* that summoned these creatures to slay me? I who alone can see her for what she is? And even *if* she failed, she would deceive you further into her trust."

Rayn was speechless. He couldn't believe this was happening. After she'd just saved them? Yet could it be true? Hak's words seemed so convincing and carried such conviction.

Pure just knelt there, a look of fear and pain on her face, waiting quietly. She did not struggle, and in her eyes there was only… innocence.

"No," Rayn said.

"Be quiet-" Hak began.

"Trapper!" The wiseman shouted, loud enough to dissipate the confusion, enough even to frighten the staunchest warriors. "Stop this madness! She is innocent. She just saved your life! Has that no meaning to you?"

Dr Joseph Ireland

Hak spat on the ground and flung her away. Rayn and his three closest friends gathered at the edge of the light, and the wiseman moved up to stand in front of them.

"My life has no meaning while you all slumber under the enchantments of this demoness," Hak shouted.

"Enough!" The wiseman shouted with all his authority. In the light, the etched runes in his staff began to glow, as they ought when the light of justice speaks. "She is *innocent*."

"Then how do you explain all this fire?"

The wiseman paused. "I do not know how she is able to do this, but I do know it was not for evil."

"Then the stone," he said, pointing to the still glowing diamond at her brow. "Is this not a demoner's stone!"

The wiseman was silent for a moment. Then he spoke. "Enough, Hak. You have made your mind clear in this matter. But tonight she saved your life and many others. I will not spurn this revelation of the power of the Divine but rather give thanks. Yet you would cut her down?"

For a moment there was only silence.

"Banishment," Hak called. "Banishment, I say!" He turned to the assembled village. "You have seen the fire! Divinity has revealed to you that she is a demoness! She is twisting your hearts and poisoning your faith! Banished, banished! Who is with me?" He roared.

Townsfolk looked about at each other, silence in their questioning faces. But none spoke for him.

Hak looked confused. He hung his head and pressed his hand to his brow. Only Rayn and the others were close enough to hear his words, though they made no sense. "But... he promised. The man in the red cloack promised..." Then he laughed, a cold and insane laugh.

Pure moved away from him, into Rayn's arms.

Then the trapper grew extremely angry. "I have suffered your vile wickedness long enough!" He roared and leaping forward, went to grab Pure's ankle.

She screamed and dodged aside. Rayn went to grab his knife but found no strength in his injured arm and instead found himself thrown to the ground by Pure's fevered attempt to escape the mad tracker. But the wiseman was faster than all of them.

He took a single step, his face and head lit up with a brilliant white light, a violet nimbus forming around the edge of his staff. As the staff struck the ground, the stone cracked as though struck with a mighty hammer. The nimbus crashed into the soil and Hak was thrown several paces away and onto the ground. Everyone else within that light was completely unharmed.

"Enough," the wiseman, wreathed in power, whispered. "You are hereby banished for two brightnights to think about your rudeness. Go cool your head in the brook of Mindron 'ere you return!"

Pure looked up in surprise at the wiseman.

Hak stood up painfully. Then his insane, inhuman laughter filled the night air once more. "You think I fear your words any more, old man?"

Then the wiseman uttered his final curse. "I perceive you will serve the darkness and it will consume you. And should you ever raise your hand against the white maiden's cause, her family, or her form, your sin will only be purged by fire that sets on stone..."

The townsfolk gasped. It was the most powerful threat the wiseman could level at a foe. It was like drawing a line, and if any crossed it, well, none had for the stories were too evil to mention.

Hak roared in defiance, and then, without a hint of regret, bent down and grabbed Rayn's lantern pole. Without pause he threw the broken pole at the old wiseman with such strength and speed there were none who could stop it in flight, and the wiseman had no time for his defenses. The rod struck him in the chest and almost went clean through. The old wiseman stumbled backwards and fell, blood spreading rapidly through his blue cloak. Hak grinned, eyes filled with an insane bloodlust that he had never seen before.

Rayn roared and leapt up. Hak parried his clumsy blow and punched him in the chest, knocking him to the ground. Then he grinned down at Rayn with callous indifference. Clearly he did not consider him any kind of threat to him tonight, and with his injured hand, Rayn knew there was little a boy apprentice could do.

Hak laughed again, and other citizens drew steel at an offence which had earned him death. But he ran with inhuman speed, leaping to great heights, mocking them all with his bestial laughter, and fled after the baying wolves into the dark night.

Clearly, it was he, and not Pure, that had been talking with demons this night.

"Rayn," Pure called out, indicating towards the wiseman.

Rayn was by his mentor's side in a moment, kneeling beside the old man's wife and two young children. The old man was bleeding from his mouth, his eyes unfocused, his breathing coarse like a child with the rattling. Death was a common companion on the Celtwyld; half the pregnancies failed, and of the successful births half died before their second birthday. To lose a full grown man was a tragedy, yet none but his immediate family were allowed to mourn him. They ran to assist him now.

But this was more than a man to Rayn. He was like a father to him, as a father to the entire town. This was the village wiseman.

Pure stood aside to allow him to clasp his master's hand. Rayn's eyes suddenly filled with unbidden tears.

"Rayn," the dying wiseman whispered and pushed his staff into his trembling hand.

"No, wise one, not yet! I'm only a boy."

The old man chuckled, new blood appearing at his lips. "And tonight, you become a man."

"No," Rayn said, pushing away his tears. "You'll live for many years yet. We are not ready for you to leave yet, and I am far from ready for the staff!"

The old wiseman smiled. "I have known my last day was soon for some time. And I have known that you were destined for greater things. Take this staff, and with it begin life as a man. You already know all that I can teach you. My spirit will not leave you," he whispered.

"No, not..." Rayn began. But this was worse, a hundred times worse, than fasting for a week, a thousand times worse than braving a forbidden cavern at the dare of his sister to prove his manhood. All he wanted was the evening again, to sit by the fire and hear his friends laughing.

He looked up and saw his three best friends surrounded by the entire townsfolk. Good people. Good people who had watched their gentle wiseman die tonight defending what was right. Good people that needed a strong wiseman to serve them.

Rayn looked over at the chieftain, and to his dismay the old warrior nodded his support of the wiseman's words.

Indeed, it was tonight.

He took the staff.

"Your name goes here," the wiseman muttered, pointing to a spot low on the staff, underneath the dozens of carved names that had served this town over the centuries.

"But I'm not ready..."

"By what did Saint Thalos walk the waves of Tengrin Sea? By what did the Lady of Willith calm the beasts? By whose power did the child, Ourk, heal his mother from the curse?"

Rayn knew the words but his lips trembled. The wiseman was more than a father to him, how could he say goodbye? But he knew in his heart it was time.

"By faith."

"And by faith you now will work too. All works are done by faith. I perceive you will rise above the mountains and heal lands beyond naming. You are good, young wiseman Rayn. It has been an honor for me to know you all the days of your life and it is an honor for me now to pass this staff along to you. You may not feel ready, but would Divinity have allowed it if you weren't? No. The lights know you are capable of *far more* than you'll ever know untested..."

Rayn took the staff in trembling hands, and as if to validate the words of the old man, Rayn's personal rune, the symbol for the rich spring rains that bring new life to the world, wrote itself with bright blue light in the staff. The townsfolk gasped, for there was no greater witness of the transfer of authority.

The old man struggled for breath, as if to say more. But smiling, he fell silent and with a look of profound peace of a man at rest with his creators, he died.

Vengeance

"Vengeance!" The people called.

The new wiseman of the village stood. Rayn looked out at them. Their faces a visage of anger and malice in the flickering lamplights. They wanted the trapper caught and called to justice for his crime of murdering a holy wiseman. There were none in the village with the authority to make that claim, not even the chieftain. Only the wiseman could make that call. And as of right now, the wiseman was him.

Rayn looked down at the staff in his hand, the symbol of his authority. It thrummed with power he'd never understood before. For all his years growing up, no child dared touch the wisemen's staff for fear of burning their hands. Now it yielded to his touch as though he had owned it his whole life.

He looked down at his dead mentor and grieving family. The village wiseman, cruelly slain by a man driven mad for no other reason than that he would not let a woman go without proof of her evil. There was evil in this town, and it was in the trapper Hak. A trapper whose life needed only his word, and the dark light which had slain the wiseman would be put out of this world, his body buried in the earth, his soul chained in the darkness without saving ritual. Rayn would avenge the death of his friend, and Hak would be tormented forever.

"Vengeance…" he muttered.

The villagers nodded.

"Vengeance!" He shouted. Then he cried out as the staff shook him. It shocked him as with lightning, though none could see it.

Rayn watched the staff as the others fell silent. Its runes glowed dimly now, not bright as when the wiseman had wielded it. He knew what this meant; he was falling from the path of Divinity. He had not considered wisely his path.

The citizens waited for his command to bring back the murderer, but Rayn knew they had to wait. There was something more to this. Perhaps, in some way, Hak was not entirely responsible for the wiseman's murder? But how could it be?

Rayn pressed his fist to his temple and turned his back on the expectant crowd. He suffered their murmurs. He was a young wiseman, too young to make that decision, too young to declare a murderer should die. Perhaps, he was too afraid?

Rayn breathed in deeply. He had to do what was right, not popular.

Yet there were so many voices. What was he to do? Hunting a murderer was the only right thing to do, yet... in his heart... there were other voices. Carefully, he picked up the staff again.

"Jayd!" He called into the darkness. The town fell silent as she ran to his side. Without even thinking she bowed at the staff and it made Rayn smile at the irony of it, but secretly grateful she reminded him of who he was in showing the respect a youth should have of a wiseman.

"Yes, wiseman?" Her voice soft, the first time he'd ever heard her like that, to him. That was going too far. He didn't need a child tonight.

She was always the first and the most honest opinion he'd ever heard. He needed Jayd tonight.

"Don't, just, speak freely," he said. "I… I just don't know what to do."

She waited.

"The wiseman is dead, I am his heir, twenty years too soon. The townsfolk are calling for vengeance and I want it too, I want it so badly! Yet the staff, this staff, would seem to disagree."

Jayd was silent a moment. "I noticed… how Hak fought. His strength was inhuman. You were caught up with the wolves. But you don't suppose, perhaps, *the curse* may be at work here?"

Rayn was stunned. *The curse? Yes, that would explain it.* The curse resurfaced every few years or so. Sometimes as a great plague killing thousands, usually as a single illness which inevitably disfigured an individual's body and mind, granting them bestial strength and stamina. Saint Etmo, a wiseman of extraordinary devotion and faith, bore the illness in his body thirty two years, working great miracles of faith and power until eventually it overwhelmed his mind. It took twenty men to slay him, and they all died that day or later from their injuries. In the end another wiseman commanded him to lay down his weapons and he was slain by arrows from the chieftain's sons. That the curse could strike at random and turn a good man to evil was well documented.

But he needed to know. With the town watching on, he lay the staff across the dead wiseman's form. The old man had taught him from his youngest days that Divinity can reveal any truth and will answer every need, provided the right question was asked.

*Is this caused by **the** curse?* Rayn asked. Immediately the lights brightened on his staff, so much so he nearly dropped it, and the answer formed itself in his tired mind; a definite, certain - YES.

He gasped a sigh of relief, then his voice caught in his throat. The wolves...

Were the wolves also taken by the curse?

Yes.

Then... he didn't dare ask. *Will any others here in the village, including myself, receive the curse from the battle tonight?*

Divinity seemed to take its time before answering.

No.

He gasped out a desperate sign of relief, and held up his hands for everyone's attention.

"Silence, the new wiseman speaks!" The chieftain roared.

They fell silent immediately.

"It is the curse," Rayn said flatly. Immediately citizens clapped their hands and stroked their forearms, in an ancient evil warding sign. Everyone stood back from the old wiseman.

"The curse will claim the bodies of the dead," Rayn explained from what they all knew, "returning them to life and murder. We must... burn the body tonight."

The chief nodded and gave the orders. Everything the trapper or the wiseman had touched was to be burnt; only the staff was immune to the curse.

The chief walked up to Rayn. "As for Hak, you know he must still be hunted but not for vengeance- for pity, that his murders do not spread. Will you, good wiseman, lead this hunt?"

Rayn was silent. He was young but better to lead a hunt than to sit, confused and young, among a town long served by a man three times his age.

Rayn nodded.

Then his eyes fell on Pure. She was sitting by the good wiseman's body. No one stood near her; they'd just seen what she could do with fire.

He walked up to her. "Nothing can be done now," he tried to console her.

But when she looked up her eyes held not sadness, nor fear, but confusion. "This, I do not understand," she said one of her favorite phrases in her strange accent. "What is this 'the curse'?"

Rayn knelt down beside her. "An ancient evil. It strikes at minds and hearts, causing deformities and madness."

"It sounds like a disease."

"I do not know what that word means," Rayn said.

"Animals; except ones so small that you cannot see them. They can live in your blood."

Rayn laughed. It sounded ridiculous. How could there be animals small enough to live inside blood? Did she not know that illness was caused by an imbalance in the natural order, brought about by curses or the seasons or disobedience?

She looked at him, her head lolling to the side as it did when she was growing tired of trying to help others understand her. "No; disease. It's not a curse. How often does it strike?"

"Every few years, though a great curse occurs every hundred years or so when people are not faithful to the rituals enough."

"Yes, I see that, but nevertheless, it is a disease. And there are cures. What are the other signs of this 'curse'?"

"It also causes great strength, and-"

"No," she said in a husky voice, "it can't be."

Rayn wondered what she meant.

"Deformities, madness, strength? It cannot be. I have been asleep for so long, how could the Perish still survive?"

"Perish?" Rayn wondered.

"An illness which takes control of a person's mind and body, using them to spread the infection."

"It sounds like the curse."

"It's not a curse! It's a disease."

"Animals that live inside blood?" Rayn asked, skeptical.

"Rayn, trust me. That sick man wanted me. He wanted me! That is something I did not know the Perish were capable of: forethought, planning, cunning. I have been asleep for a very long time but if this disease has reawakened, Rayn, you can expect a plague unlike any you have ever known in your history."

Her seriousness chilled him, even if her knowledge of the natural order of things was all wrong. Besides, the curse had always shown a kind of cunning. "Then we must look to the Divine for answers. I will order the town to renew the rituals, and send messengers-"

"Yes, do that," she interrupted him, which was a little offensive for he was now an adult, "but have them stand afar off. The disease can transmit through touch so they must not touch those to whom they bring the message."

Rayn did not see the wisdom of her instruction, and he showed it.

"Please, for my sake, tell the messengers. And we must all wash our wounds before we leave to find that man. I must go with you for I have questions too."

Rayn stood up. He did not like this. She was just a maiden, and he a man. True, he'd only been a man for about a hundred breaths now, but he was still the only grownup of their group of friends. She should stay in the town where they could keep her safe, not hunting murderers.

Then she stood up, her stone glistening with light in the darkness. She stood up to him face to face, standing beautifully and confident in the lamp light. And in that brilliant moment his resolve forever melted and he knew he would never deny this person anything she wanted. If she wanted to come, there was nothing he could do to stop her.

Besides, if she was a demoness, who better to redeem her than himself? Rather than having her running amok in an undefended town. And if she was not a demoness, well, after seeing what she could do with fire he knew that skill would come in very useful.

He relayed her instruction to the chieftain, who hated it even more than Rayn, but obeyed the word of his young wiseman anyway. They also burnt every weapon or tool that had touched the cursed tracker Hak, just in case. Pure assured them it would kill the invisible animals, but Rayn knew better.

***

That night he barely slept, spending what seemed like the entire night in prayer, or thinking about praying. It was all happening too fast. Boy one morning, wiseman in charge of hunting a murderer that night. He did not sleep well.

But he must have slept, for some time near dawn he heard his step mother calling and it was a little effort to get up. He entered the common room from the sleeping hall and was surprised to find his step mother and a dozen other women, who clearly had not slept at all that night, holding up new wiseman's robes.

"We started years ago," she began, "these were completed in haste. We did not have the fine fabric the last wiseman held."

"And, as you know, he took those with him," another woman said with bitterness, though others hushed her to silence even in her honesty.

"And," his step mother continued, "perhaps it was the will of the Divine, because we used good, solid fabric; better for travelling, yet still holding every token of office and prayer of our people's heart for your protection. The people's and my own," she said with tears.

He didn't know what to say. He had never been close to his step mother, though he never doubted her love and care for him. Now it shone so much it might have blinded him.

These women looked pleased with their work but still did not meet his gaze. He wanted to hug them all, like he might have freely done yesterday. But he was an unwed man, and there were rules about that sort of thing.

So he took the robes in speechless gratitude. They fit perfectly. Light enough for travel even in the heat, yet thick and strong that it might be a blanket at night or shelter from the rain of the sky. Following tradition it was dyed dark blue, likely that very evening, dried and embroidered in great haste.

One hour later they left: Rayn, Pure, and eight of the strongest warriors in the village including the chieftain. Rayn took a moment to savor what could be the last look of his home town, searching for words to speak. The sun was hardly up yet he'd already been called on to heal a bruised wrist, bless a pair of new swords, and name a child three days early in their haste. But he was leaving and they did not know when he would return.

Yet he was not blind; many were glad to see Pure go.

He held aloft his glowing staff, willing a great blessing on the entire town. Divinity must have smiled on his deed, for the runes of blessing above each and every door began to glow in sympathy. In their glow, Rayn knew that he'd see them all again, and that each and every home would be protected until he returned.

There was work to be done.

Traitor

The chieftain stood, conferring with his best hunter.

"I am sure of it, he went this way," the man said.

Rayn watched them in patient silence. He felt he had matured a lot in a single day, yet he still was no better a hunter than before. That skill was left to others. But one skill he did have comforted them all: his faith, and the staff he held - because the path the murderer took was leading right to the howling ruin, and they feared that place mightily.

He saw the chief cast a worried glance in his direction but Rayn only nodded. This was not the time to show fear.

He glanced over at Pure. Her brow was furrowed in concern yet she said nothing. Her look told him that she would see this through, no matter where it led.

He wished inside that they had brought Jayd. He did not know why. Then again, she'd always been amazingly good at finding things. She'd be good to have around.

They walked the next hour, weapons drawn, wiseman and maid in the middle of all the warriors, surrounding them on all sides.

When they reached the cave, Pure screamed involuntarily at what lay at the opening. There the remains of a man lay across the mouth of the cave, strung up on all fours like a butchered pig. Flies had already made good use of the carcass though it could not have been more than a day old.

The hunter alone had the courage to face the slain man.

"What dark times are these?" A warrior muttered.

The hunter did not touch the corpse but indicated to Rayn. Stealing all his courage he approached. Using the staff, immune to the curse, Rayn lifted the man's head. It was Furrow.

"Hak's brother. This is a demoner's bargain, no doubt," Rayn explained.

Many made the ward evil sign.

"Cut that innocent man down and burn him." The chieftain signaled.

"I will do this," the maiden said.

"No!" A warrior insisted, the cousin of Furrow and Hak. It was brave of him to be on this quest, or was it mercy that drove him to hunt his cousin? "*I* still don't know your powers aren't demonry," he breathed.

Pure stood back in surprise at his vehemence. She looked over at Rayn, who kept his silence. To be true, he did not know where her powers came from either, though she had only used them to serve others so far. So he said nothing.

She looked offended and the warrior turned his face away from the wiseman. But nothing more came of it.

Pure stalked over to him. "I can do it. There'd be no need to harm the trees."

Rayn shook his head, acknowledging his people's fear in a time like this. "We will use wood. But thank you," he said, offering her his hand to show he did not fear to touch her.

She huffed and walked off. The warriors watched her warily, afraid she may work her powers again but Rayn could tell she was simply displeased.

The fire lit the sky in the fading light. No one said anything but Rayn knew what they were all wondering. Would they camp here? Or risk the cave?

"I'd rather not wait to see what night holds, but be long from this place," the Chieftain muttered in his ear.

Rayn had to agree. Bearing his glowing staff aloft he spoke, "Let the shadows know to fear the light we bring! Come, bold warriors, know no fear!"

They shouted loudly at his call to arms, drawing weapons and lighting torches.

"You know, good wiseman, this may be a trap," the Chieftain muttered.

"Let us hunt the murderer from his den," Rayn replied.

"We could try smoking him out?" The chief suggested.

"You forget, I've been down this cave before. It's too long. I will go down first, keep the maiden at the rear. I will draw the madman's attention. You and your men must fill him with arrows. Then the maiden can use her flames, if the warriors aren't the first to it," he smiled.

The chief chuckled. "Well said, Rayn," using a name he was not supposed to on such formal occasions, but Rayn and his great uncle had never been much for formalities. "Let us take him as the stories tell of the curse. Well said."

They clasped hands and faced the darkness together.

It was clear from the noise that someone, likely the murderer, was down here already. Rayn had expected to find him near the middle, that he might have somewhere to retreat.

Instead, he was right at the end, sitting atop the maiden's coffin. The warriors stopped in wonder, pressing each other aside to see the strange scene.

"You're late," he said, his voice confident, almost casual.

The chieftain pushed Rayn forward, nocking an arrow.

Rayn cleared his throat, but the damp night air must have affected his voice for it came out weak. "Hak, you, ahem, you are possessed of the curse. Submit to the purge or… die."

The condemned trapper laughed. "You sound so afraid. Is it what I have become?"

Rayn took another step closer, the men following a pace behind. This time his voice was more confident. "Kneel."

Hak paused, as though wresting within himself. "You should join me, you know. He offers such power!"

"Whom?" The chieftain asked.

"Why, *the* curse himself!" Hak grinned in triumph. "Leader and high wiseman of a new humanity. My master; he has shown me the way, he will show us all the way! The *true* way. And all he asks, is her," he said, pointing at Pure.

She said nothing.

"All?" The chieftain asked. "Or did he also claim your brother?"

Hak said nothing, for a moment. "You know nothing of right, or power, or obedience. I did what I *had* to do. What had to be done. And now you too will understand. Join me!"

He leapt off the coffin with incredible power, but Rayn foresaw it. Finding his courage at last, he stepped towards the danger holding out the staff, his confidence filling it with a blinding light blue light.

"Stop!" He ordered, and Hak fell back mid-flight, cringing on the floor like a frightened animal, staring at the glowing staff. Rayn's heart beat thundered in his ears, his voice rung through the cavern. "You are ill! Stop."

Hak laughed, but did not move his eyes from the staff. "No. No, no, no, no, no! I am beyond your reach!" And he howled. It was the same noise the wolves had made before and weapons fell from the men's grasp at the inhuman noise the trapper made.

"Now! Now!" Rayn ordered the warriors.

But only the chieftain still held his bow. He let fly an arrow and it buried itself right into Hak's chest.

Hak laughed a husky laugh. "Beyond," he cried.

The chieftain frantically tried to reload.

Suddenly the noise of wolves could be heard entering the cave. Dozens of wolves.

Hak was in command; the curse was more powerful than ever before. In that fleeting moment, Rayn had a horrible vision. He foresaw the downfall of his people, towns left desolate and the cursed wandering a broken land, gnawing the bones of the fallen.

And in that fleeting thought, the light dimmed. Not much, but just enough for Hak to break the tenuous hold Rayn had over him. He leapt forward and with a single blow, crushed the chieftain's chest. The man died without a groan. Yet swinging about Hak met with the raised blade of the hunter, severing his hand. Hak fell back, grabbing up the chieftain's blade in his other hand.

For a moment Rayn couldn't move. The unbridled ferocity, the bestial power of the curse. It was greater than ever before. He felt his faith wavering as he saw his great uncle die, but he could cry no tears lest he dishonor his name.

"Pull back!" The hunter yelled. "There isn't enough room to swing a blade in here! Maiden, use your fire!"

The tunnel lit up behind Rayn but he could not see what she was doing. The light and heat seemed to snap Rayn out of his despair. He realized that just as the sun rose each morning on a world full of turmoil and despair, they would find a way to prevail. Somehow, they would survive. But he also realized with startling clarity that they were going to need help above and beyond any they had ever called on before. How the Divine would provide that help, and if he would live to see it, was unknown. And to be fair, it didn't matter. There would be a way, even if he did not live to be a part of it.

Leaving the fallen chieftain where he lay, Rayn backed up with the rest of the group, holding out the glowing staff since it seemed the murderer was loath to enter its immediate light. The tunnel flared again, and the noise of hunting wolves crying out in pain filled the cave.

The cavern roared with fire. Another painful hundred breaths of retreat awaited before they met the cloud lit sky again. In a moment they were surrounded by the maiden's fire, wolves and Hak prowling outside.

"This is your last chance!" Hak called. "You see, I am more powerful than all your wisemen! The beasts fulfil my every command. Strike hands with me and -"

"Never!" Hak's cousin shouted. Risking death, he leapt across the fire, and Pure dismissed it immediately. Racing to face Hak alone, the wolves charged the rest of them.

5 A plague cursed wolf

The battle was desperate and swift. At least a dozen wolves died in the first few seconds, as well as three or four of the warriors. At this rate, they would not live to see the morning, their corpses rising to inflict horror and plague on their town. Rayn stood in the center, holding his

Dr Joseph Ireland

staff high, bolstering the courage of the fighting and sending on the souls of the fallen. He tried to have faith, but the wolves were so many.

A moment later Hak sundered his cousin's blade and split his skull with his bare hand. The wolves stood back, and the maiden reignited her flame circle, though it burnt lower this time.

Hak laughed.

"You see-" he began, but never finished. Suddenly he cried out as he was cut down from behind. He fell forward, great gashes along the back of his knees, an axe buried deep in his spine.

And behind him, in the shadows, stood Jayd and Rhoc.

The two groups cried out and rushed to be joined, the wolves racing to stop them. But before they could finish off Hak, two wolves had grabbed a leg each and begun to drag him away at his bidding. Two warriors tried to pursue but were cut down as wolves, hiding in the trees, leapt upon them.

Several breaths later it was over and the remaining wolves fled. For a moment no one spoke, as Pure wept over the dead. Rayn bent down and closed a warrior's eyes. There were only five warriors left standing of those that had headed out today, two uninvited: the hunter, Rayn, Jayd, Rhoc his best friend, and Pure.

Rayn couldn't help it, he hugged his sister right away. Then held her at arm's length.

"What madness-" he began to chide her.

"Shut up, Rayn," she replied with inexhaustible courage. "We just saved your life! You knew you should have taken us with you. It started with us four. It must end that way."

"I…" he stuttered, but could say no more. "Are you injured?"

"Not a scratch," she forced a smile.

"Rhoc?" He asked.

Rhoc nodded that everything was fine.

"I'm fine too; they didn't want to touch me," Pure said.

Rayn sighed with relief, and as the wiseman, he was the last the warriors would allow to be harmed.

But the hunter was silent.

Rayn looked at him and could see he was concealing a wide gash along his arm. "Let me heal it."

The hunter slowly consented. Rayn summoned all his faith, seeing the wound mend perfectly in his mind, seeing the man enjoying his family for many years. Yet the vision would not come. Something was very wrong.

Rayn looked down and found the wound was sealed with soft mucus, not pure and restored skin as it should be. And in the flickering light of the torches it was clear to see the wound was still red and sore.

"St Etmo's curse," the hunter said, regret in his voice. "As I knew it would be. You do not have the prayer to heal me, young wiseman, none do, though I am sure your faith is sufficient. Do not fear for me. Stay here, burn the bodies, see your quest out. I will return and report our failure to the village and warn the others."

"This plague will spread, nonetheless," Pure said, her voice sad. "I've never seen it like this."

"What do you mean?" Jayd asked.

"When I was a child a similar 'curse' destroyed my people. I believe I am all that is left. I do not know how much time has been since I was secreted by my mother inside the... bed... that lies at the end of this cave. All I know is that it has been many thousands of years. That I was not awakened sooner can only mean that they, and all their knowledge, were destroyed."

"Your people have fought the curse too?" The hunter asked with hope.

"Yes, and clearly it destroyed them," Jayd said bleakly.

"Worse, I never knew it to act intelligently. This Hak, he was still in control of his thoughts, his memories. He could tell one of us from the other. The Perish I knew could never do that. They must have... grown somehow."

The night echoed their silence.

The maiden sighed. "I only wish there was some way to get more knowledge! My headband indicates the net that spread across the stars is long broken. All I can hope is that somewhere on your world there is a... what would you call it? A teacher? Perhaps, or a book made of stone, seeming wise with eyes of light?"

"What do you mean?" Rayn asked.

"Aarg! They were invented by us with the dragons, great beasts that rode..."

"Dragons?" Rayn asked.

"Yes, dragons, great beasts, as wolves without fur, armed with steel, wings as a bat, teeth, umm, and very wise, speaking-"

"Dragon," Jayd echoed, "yes, we know the dragons."

The wounded hunter laughed. "You speak of fables, child," he said, speaking down to Jayd. "No such beast has been seen in a hundred years, all were slain or died of hunger, driven from their thieving in human lands."

"A dragon would never steal!" Pure protested.

"Then you know not the heart of dragons. I have heard only that they are fierce beasts, claws like blades, breath of flame, eyes that freeze you to the ground while they draw the very life from you to fuel their insatiable hunger. They are beasts of fear and darkness and shadow, and none live that have met them."

His words were true, in all the legends that Rayn knew of, none spoke well of dragons.

"Those are not the dragons I know. My brother rode with one-"

"Rode?!" the hunter scoffed. "I have seen strange things these days, not least of all yourself. But never heard such nonsense!" He coughed against the night's cold.

The curse was slowly claiming him.

"But there are dragons here?" she asked.

"Yes, one lives right up at Nelwyn peak," Jayd proclaimed.

Everyone looked at her in surprise.

"Haven't you heard?" she asked, "I recall a journeyman claiming that is why the elk avoid the place, and a few years ago some hunters entered the region. I'm sure they sought dragon scales."

Truly Jayd really was amazingly good at finding things: miraculous. Their mother had called her 'find-it-girl', but even she would find it hard to believe Jayd could simply know where a dragon lived.

"How…" Rayn began, but let it drop. Right now, it was as good a beginning as any.

"Then we will have some answers," Pure said. "The dragons will speak to me. I am sure of it."

"If we live to tell the tale," Jayd admitted, her hands fidgeting the way they did when she was nervous. "And we've a mad man and pack of wolves on our tail."

"How did he live through the axe in his back?" Rayn asked.

"The Perish, I mean the curse, it grants great stamina," Pure explained.

"Enough talk. Just burn the bodies," the hunter ordered again, clutching his chest. "Make sure you claim the chieftain as well- leave only ash or they will rise to torment us all."

"What of you?" Rayn asked.

"I will return to the town and report our failure. I will tell your mothers that you yet live, and embark on the fool's quest to seek the aid of the 'dragons'. But I will be long dead before you are slain to feed their young. The first thing I will do is build my own bier."

"What?" Pure asked.

But Rayn had heard enough. "Burn the bodies, Pure. Use your fire, if you have any left in you."

She didn't question him, though her face was full of dissatisfaction at his answers. The hunter ran into the darkness, so after a moment Rayn took the liberty of explaining further to her. "He will return our news, then build his own bier of wood. He will bid his loved ones goodbye and his last act will be to fall on his own sword."

"What? But he can't-" Pure protested.

"Either that or fall to the curse. There is no wiseman in the town to sustain him and this curse is new and untested. He will not risk spreading the curse to his own children."

"But…" Pure protested, her voice strained with sorrow. But she said no more, for there was nothing more to be said.

Race

Pure ran back into the howling ruin, mighty fires lighting the night for leagues. Rayn followed along behind her.

"There are some things I need to take," she muttered, almost to herself. When she got there she woke her coffin up with a wave of her hand. "Look, Rayn."

He saw a floating collection of about a hundred lights.

"This is the local group of worlds," she explained, "each of these dots is a sun and around each sun there are worlds. Most have no life, except these seven."

"Wait, what? There are other suns in the sky?"

"Not in the sky, above the sky."

"Then why do we not see them?" He asked.

"They are hidden by the clouds of this world. It's always covered in clouds, always has been. And that is why it is called 'Pearl', seeming like a gem from the space above this world."

"Space? The other worlds above ours are inhabited by the spirits of the departed, right?"

"No, people. Just like you and me."

"No wonder you never told us this, my people would think you mad. There is nothing above the clouds, the throne of Divinity which brings us warmth and light each day."

"Actually," she smiled, "this world is only an average sized one, and only one of countless other worlds in the entire… space."

Rayn pondered this, but knew better than to share her strange beliefs with others.

"See," she continued, "all these seven worlds that held life were joined together. When the Perish, that is, the 'curse', first attacked us we thought little of it. But it changed so quickly and could infect any living organism, but more especially those with blood. We were about to be overrun. I scarcely remember my life before I came to be in this escape capsule that you call my bed, for my memories are hidden from me. But I do know that if the other worlds still stood they would register on this map. There is only one thing I can assume – we are alone. The other worlds did not survive the original attack by the Perish either."

"Then why did we survive?" Rayn asked her.

"That is why we are going to see the dragons," she explained, "for I do not know how we could have possibly survived if the other worlds did not. Also, I need to know what happened to the friendship between dragons and humans, for that is what had always protected us in the past."

"How long do you think you were in the escape bed?" Rayn asked.

"Thousands of years, it is difficult to tell. But Rayn, you must realize, I was only four years old when I was placed in here. You… you can't understand what it's like to wake up one day and find yourself fully grown into a teenager."

"Actually, I kind of do," Rayn muttered, but he knew what she meant. One day she was four and the next morning she was sixteen or something, her family and people gone, and she found herself surrounded by complete strangers. One of whom stood over her with a sword.

That could not have been a very good day.

She took an object from the bottom of her 'pod'. It was a silver armband, strong and well made. "This bracelet emits, oh, you people have so few words! An invisible light that was used to keep the air around a person and their dragon so that they could survive the nothing of space. You can use it to control the wind around your body but it will send out a… sound… that the Perish might be able to hear. So we need to be careful how we use it."

Then she took out five little silver bracelets. "Here, these charms are most important. They strengthen the body to make it more resistant to the disease, I mean, the 'curse'. We should all have one."

She handed him every charm she had, five in all, and they were all inscribed with an old symbol from the ancestors, one that was found long ago not to be terribly effective against the curse. But he kept them anyway, one for each other them, and a spare.

Then she pulled a bottle from her boat. "This liquid here helps the body heal quickly from any condition or illness. I don't think we'll need it as long as you hold your staff, but it might come in handy."

"There isn't any demonry, is there?" He had to ask.

She looked taken aback. "How can you say that? I don't even know what you mean by demonry. But it can't be, just knowledge. My people knew much, much more than yours. If you are our descendants, then you have lost almost everything we once knew: how to travel between the worlds, or to lift objects by thought. I was never any good at that, but I knew fire. It's not demonry, it's just knowledge your people no longer have."

"So any of us can learn it?" He said with a subtle grin.

"Of course, but it takes many years. We used the teachers to improve our minds. I was many years from a full understanding, so my knowledge is very incomplete. I know it must seem like the supernatural to your eyes but it's just understanding. I only wish you still had a teacher here that we could use it to finish my training, and begin yours." She smiled.

Rayn was not convinced. He did not believe in his heart that she could be evil. But there was no power that could command fire, except the Divine. And the Divine was to be used only through the sash, the robe, or the staff.

She seemed to guess his thoughts. "Your staff is a device as well. My people used to make them all the time. They focus a person's power to create events."

Now Rayn was just confused. Her words seemed blasphemy, but he held his peace. Perhaps there was something in what she taught? Besides, they'd need her help to stay the coming plague. "We were always taught that the staves were created by the Divine at the beginning of time and respond to the faith of the wiseman to work the will of the Divine. And as one develops more faith, greater power is manifested. Sometimes key words or phrases were given to the wiseman to heal certain wounds or turn aside the wrath of nature or hold the mouths of beasts. Mother Wynter once found a prayer that stayed the curse four hundred years ago, but it has resurfaced in new forms since then."

"Yes, that's exactly what the staff was designed to do. It acts as a, um, tunnel for knowledge and power from, um, oh. Grrr. At least this means you must still have a working obelisk on your world or the staves would fall silent."

Rayn said nothing, pondering inside her suggestion that the staff might be some kind of machine and not a conduit for the Divine. But he *knew* it would work as long as the higher lights shone, which would be forever. "Be that as it may, I am sure we agree that it is by faith that it operates."

"Of course, faith is, but wait a breath. It doesn't work by faith in the Divine. It uses faith as a power in itself."

"So it *is* powered by faith."

"No it's, oh, you're just never going to get it!" She returned to rummaging in her 'pod', which still looked like anything but a seed casing.

When she was done she stood up and, with a wave of her hand, it disappeared.

"How?"

"I, well, I pushed it, um. Oh, I don't suppose you have a word for 'set it out of phase'," she said in her native language, and to his surprise, Rayn found he knew exactly what she meant.

"Yes, you pushed it sideways without moving it," he said.

Now she looked surprised. "Yes, that's what I did. More or less. How did you get that? You don't even speak my language, let alone understand the knowledge of my people."

Rayn shrugged. The authorities of the wisemen were many. Perhaps if Divinity had a need to protect her, then it would give him understanding of her language at times.

"Let us leave this place," he said instead.

They went out to find the bier, with all the bodies, burning low. Rhoc and Jayd had gathered together a small collection of gear.

"I got two tents, and we'll all need a bedroll," Jayd explained, making plans. "Rhoc can carry the water and tents, since he's the strongest, but we'll all need to take our own food."

Rayn looked at it all and was impressed. Jayd had done a great job even without help. She was always the sensible one, grounded. Doing what was needed, not always doing what was right – like sneaking after a hunting party and helping to save their lives.

Rebellious Jayd! He thought with a smile.

Rayn hoisted his pack. "If we're off to see the dragons, we'd better leave soon," he said.

Sequestered

They were running.

His mouth was dry, his tongue clung to the roof of his mouth. The last two days had been exhausting. They'd slept briefly, only every few hours, always staying just ahead of the baying wolves. But they'd grown increasingly tired as the beasts pursued them relentlessly. Even with the strength of his faith, their physical power was failing. Every muscle ached and his shoulders burnt with the pain of his burden.

"If only we could lose them!" Jayd repeated.

The baying of wolves in the distance spurned them on; they were not an hour away, by Rayn's estimate. If they'd caught their scent, they'd surely speed on and catch them soon.

Suddenly Rhoc stopped. He grunted and pointed his fist at the ground.

"Yes," Rayn agreed, "we need to make a stand. We cannot go on."

"Why are they pursuing us?" Jayd asked. "Didn't we kill the trapper who controls them?"

"I don't know," Pure breathed, lowering her pack to the ground. She was slight of build and while she did not complain, Rayn knew she bore the burdens worst of all. "He may still live, but I doubt he went with them. The Perish, I mean, the curse never had the power to heal, but they knew each other's presence even across the stars. He may still seek my life and revenge for his wounding."

"What on Pearl is a star?" Jayd asked, but none answered.

Rayn looked about. "We cannot make our stand here," he assessed. "We need somewhere that they can't surround us. We have not done well with that tactic before."

Pure held up her hand, the other one clutching her side, trying to speak. She swayed on her feet and Rhoc dashed to help her. "We have another option, one that proved successful against the foes of my people in the past: Sanctuary," she said, indicating towards Rayn.

"What?" he asked, time was running out.

"Aarrh!" She cried and fell to the ground clutching her side.

They ran to her. Rayn touched her side and for the first time felt he could "see" inside another person's body. It was the sight, the gift of the wisemen to heal. He saw the great muscles of her side cramping up, feeling them twist with guilt and fear. He held the staff over her and the fear left immediately.

Pure looked surprised. "You're very good at that," she said.

Rayn was stern. "Not I, but the Divine through me."

"Whatever," she disagreed and stood up. "Thank you."

"Don't thank me, thank-" he began.

She cut him off, a rudeness punishable by fasting in the village. But then again, they were not in the village. They were running for their lives and they were running low on time. As if to answer his thoughts, the wolves bayed in the distance. They were catching up fast, and would be there in a hundred breaths, at most.

"Sanctuary," Pure explained, "is a power of the wisemen over the minds of others. You must *see* yourself as hidden. What is the word you use? Unseeable. Unsmellable. Hidden, 'sequestered', if you can guess the meaning of that word."

"I think I can," Rayn said.

"Good, then perhaps we can make our stand here."

Rhoc drew his axes with enthusiasm.

Rayn looked around. The forest was thin here, and the grass long...

"Water," he announced. "I need running water. You, maiden, might need fire. But I have always found strength in running waters."

"Water? Really? That's very curious, though I'm not surprised. The lights move with running waters and there are cleaning processes that the water... I guess now is not the time to share my knowledge."

"You're quite right," Jayd said.

"Where is the water?" Rayn asked Divinity to manifest in the staff.

"Over there," Jayd replied.

"What?" Rayn asked. She was interrupting his concentration.

"Over there!" She insisted, grabbing his arm, breaking his thoughts. "Look, the mountain stands over that valley. It's obvious that the waters would run down through this valley here. Come, now, it'll only take twenty breaths."

Rhoc nodded.

"That does make sound sense," Pure said.

Rayn waited. He was in charge. He was the wiseman. Desperately he tried to push aside his pride to find wisdom. He needed running water. He knew it.

But when he thought of using the staff and his power, he grew angry that others were so quick to push him aside.

When he thought of running off in search of Jayd's water, he felt enthusiastic. He felt like running.

The old wiseman had always said 'Peace and freedom are the children of truth.' Perhaps the Divine was answering his question already?

So they ran.

It was much easier this time; soon they found a downhill slope.

"There!" Jayd called. She pointed through the trees to a thick, fast flowing river.

They picked up speed when suddenly they heard a screeching in the sky.

Rayn stopped and looked up, holding out his staff against the evil.

It was a pair of mountain falcons, their forms distorted, their eyes white. The curse had found them.

They ran.

But the cursed falcons were still much faster. They were about to reach them when Rayn swung around and held out his staff. "Back, back! Back, I say, demons of the curse!" He roared, trying to drive them away.

But with a cry of denial, they dove on and in a less than a blink, they were on them. He held up his arms to fend off the attacking falcons, knowing it was foolishness since any wound could mean his death…

… and the birds suddenly were split in two, Rhoc sundering them with thrown axes before Rayn even had the chance to contemplate the failure of his faith to hold them at bay.

"Get 'em. Get 'em Rhoc!" Jayd cheered.

"They… have grown stronger this time," Rayn apologized.

Pure frowned. "Then why do they only infect a few? Is this the wisdom of the tracker cursing but a few? Or is the curse in fact much weaker? I do not know. Why only two birds and not a horde?"

"Yeah, and quit jabbering, run!" Jayd shouted.

Far among the trees, the grey shadows of the wolves could be seen.

They had barely reached the water's edge by the time the first wolves caught up to them. The maiden held them away with her flames while they waded into the rushing waters, knee deep at its deepest point. But it was enough.

We are silence. Rayn told himself. *We have no scent. We are not seen. We are… sequestered.*

At first, it seemed the wolves were not fooled but soon some began to prowl along the edges of the stream. Their eyes were milky in the twilight with undeath, their forms twisted and bloated with the stolen powers of the curse.

"Look, their wounds…" Pure whispered.

Rayn opened up one eye and his heart skipped a beat. Instead of running bodily fluid constantly, as was told in the past, they had developed bloated pustules that protected them.

They were healing. Maybe not like living creatures could, but they were healing…

This was worse than before.

Rayn struggled to master his concentration once more. He said nothing but kept intoning his silent chant. He felt his blood burning with the conviction and, in a second, found his mind in a state of absolute peace. They had no scent. They made no sound. The water rippling around their knees lost all turbulence, as though they had no presence either. Yet they were clear and present to each other's eyes, almost standing out against the background. Slowly, seeming confused, the wolves carried on downstream, their frantic cries disappearing in moments.

Pure put her gentle hand on his shoulder. "Well done, wiseman."

Jayd nodded.

They waited at least an hour more and by that time Rayn was quite exhausted. They waded upstream as far as their strength would carry them and then, finding a grotto by the river where the thick vegetation would prevent wolves from finding them, they collapsed. Without setting up their tents, he fell into a deep and undisturbed sleep.

The dragon

When Rayn woke up, it was with a start. He looked around in alarm, knowing something was amiss. Rhoc slept fitfully in the morning twilight, resting against the packs they carried. The maiden was stretched out at the water's edge, gathering dampness as her legs dragged in the water. Wasting no time in self-chagrin for his failure to care for her, Rayn noticed immediately his concern; Jayd was gone.

He roused the others and they pushed the sleep frantically from their eyes. Pure rose up painfully.

"Where is Jayd?" He whispered.

No one answered.

He scowled openly, yet hid well his fears. If the curse had somehow taken her, she might have wandered off in the night.

He drew his staff up and it lit up with a gentle blue light just as it should. It had always been a gentle purple to his mentor. It was interesting that the staff manifested pale blue when Rayn held it, but he didn't have time to ponder on the significance of it.

Splodging again through the mud at the river's edge, they left the security of their hiding place, not waiting for Rhoc with the gear to catch up.

Rayn reached inside for Divinity's guidance. *Is Jayd in any danger?*

Just a little.

He was not surprised, she had a way of getting into trouble. It seemed to be what she was best at finding.

Has the plague taken her?

No.

Where is she?

No answer.

That was not surprising. The staff really only handled yes or no answers, and it took much more preparation and skill at asking questions to learn more.

Holding out the staff, he allowed it to float gently in his hand. He held nothing in his mind but the thought that he already knew where Jayd was and that they were talking again, knowing this act of faith would reveal to him the direction in order to bring about this belief.

West.

They hurried along, Pure seemed alert now, Rhoc still struggling under the baggage and his sleep.

They wandered at least a hundred paces when the staff indicated it was time to stop. They had arrived.

Yet she was nowhere to be seen.

They looked around. Rayn first felt angry, then annoyed, then afraid.

"Maybe she's shifted…" Pure suggested.

"I don't think-" he began.

"Uurggh!" Rhoc said, bending over to catch his breath but pointing up into the trees.

"Oh, hey!" Jayd's voice chimed from high among the branches, twenty lengths or so up.

"Jayd!" Rayn called, more relieved than annoyed, though his voice sounded more angry than he intended to.

Pure raised an eyebrow at him.

"Whaaat?" Jayd protested. "I'm getting some breakfast, is there a problem with that?"

"What, I, no…" Rayn stuttered. He didn't know what to say, and her disrespect was unsettling. Her respect had been short lived, or was that just in front of their townsfolk? Would she ever see him as more than a brother? Maybe that was because that was all he was. But no, wisemen needed faith, and the people could build a wiseman's reputation. But faith could not be commanded, only earned.

So in the end he didn't really say anything, his thoughts just not turning into any useful words, or even into thoughts that he could really pin down. He just looked angry.

"Ok, don't burn me," she teased. "Look, I got eggs."

"I hope you left one for the dame!" He shouted. It was tradition to leave at least one healthy looking egg for a mother bird to raise.

She sounded annoyed. "I left one for the dame to raise. What, you think I like getting in trouble with my village wiseman?! Even if you *are* my brother."

Now she was deliberately being annoying.

"Just, oh!" he said, getting frustrated.

Pure put her hand on his wrist and his staff turned blue again. He hadn't even noticed the strange green streaks of light that it was emitting. He calmed down immediately; wisemen had a higher law to live.

"What kinds of eggs do you have?" Pure asked her.

"I don't know. Look, they're purple!"

Jayd finally could be seen clearly in the branches. She was walking along one instead of crawling carefully, two large eggs in her hands.

"Jayd, be careful!" he said, like a brother.

Rhoc did something like a laugh, looking at her.

Jayd smiled down at them.

"Whatever…" Rayn smiled with a dismissive wave of his hand, unable to truly contain his envy at her confidence and cheer in such a dangerous situation.

Suddenly she squealed and slipped, just clutching onto the branch at the last moment as the eggs fell from her hands.

"Rayn, did you do that?" Pure shouted at him.

"What, I… no," he said, and the staff shocked him.

"Who pushed me?" Jayd shouted.

"Jayd, hang on, we're coming," he replied.

"Rayn, oh Rayn, help me, I'm slipping!" She screamed, her voice echoing in the trees.

Rhoc dropped his gear and ran underneath her.

Then she fell, ten lengths. Time seemed to slow down.

Pure held out her hands, trying to use her understanding to slow the fall. But he could tell from the look on her face that it would have no useful effect.

Rayn planted the staff in the ground, holding out his hand against her fall. He imagined her slowing down, landing softly on the ground. Smiling. Suddenly his heart ached, it was what he wanted more than anything else in the world. With that feeling came a deep sorrow and regret that he had allowed himself to become angry at her. Angry enough to want to hurt her. He owned that feeling, and it hurt.

Rayn opened his eyes, just in time to see Jayd floating the right way up, gently onto the grass, a look of wonder in her eyes. Rhoc stood back, not daring to touch her. Jayd stood on the ground and as the diffused light of the clouded sun shone in the trees, she smiled.

Simultaneously, they ran to embrace.

"Thank you, Rayn," she said, not bowing.

Not needing to.

"I'm so, so sorry Jayd. I will never let my anger get the better of me again!" He promised.

She looked a little confused; clearly she had not blamed him at all. But he knew he had misused his authority, and only the grace of the Divine had given him power and forgiveness to save her. It was a mistake he vowed to never repeat again. She gave him another hug.

"I'm sorry, I think I dropped the eggs," she said sadly.

"Here," Pure said. "Oh, look, one had a little bird inside."

"What?!" Jayd said in protest, "Oh! That was not a breakfast. What do we do now?"

Rayn sighed. It was a simple enough mistake to one who did not know the signs, or was too hungry to care. "We can bury it. Mistakes happen."

"Bury it? No, we can still eat it. It would be such a shame…" Jayd started to say.

Suddenly she fell silent. A solemn feeling had descended on the forest. All the birds were silent, the insects too. Rhoc was kneeling, trembling in fear, looking away into the forest.

Then Rayn felt it. A powerful presence had been sneaking up on them. It did not feel like a man. It felt larger and much more powerful, and angry.

And it was - right - behind - him.

Rayn turned around and all breath left him. He was too terrified to scream. Or even move, for it had him already, it had them all in its great green eyes.

The dragon regarded them with disdain and loathing.

***

Pure went to stand up but he and Jayd pulled her down, their palms on the ground, their heads bowed, their eyes averted. Just like in the legends.

"But…" she protested.

The dragon snorted, a breath of sulphur and ash choking them. They waited there in silence.

Dr Joseph Ireland

The dragon said something, muttering in a language he did not know, but it sounded like it said: "Come."

He looked up and saw the shattered egg and little chick floating in the air. Floating as effortlessly as he had just saved Jayd. The dragon eyed the little chick floating in the air in front of it, just in front of them.

It would be less than a morsel to the massive beast, less than a wafer. But it studied the dead chick with great intensity. Rayn pondered if this was the time to run but one glance from the dragon informed him that it was not an option.

Then the dragon sighed, or hissed, it was hard to tell. Rayn could hear words coming from the beast, thousands tumbling from its mind like a great scroll being read in an instant. Then it gently breathed on the little bird.

And then, before their eyes, the chick twitched, then peeped. Then in a wonder beyond a miracle, it lived.

Within seconds it had grown a full crop of down, as a day old hatchling. In a second it fluttered its downy wings. But it was the will of the dragon that saw it float towards the nest and re-join the intact egg there.

The dragon then raised its head and spoke a thought clear and loud, *Mother, return to your nest!* The noise was so loud it made Rayn wince but the others didn't seem to notice.

Then it turned to them.

Rayn gulped. He heard Jayd crying.

They had found the dragon, and as the hunter had said, it might well be their last act. They had come so far and braved so many dangers! Yet...

The monster hissed as if to say, *Humans, this is just like you: destroyers, spoilers of nature, tyrants to the Divine balance! Be gone fools, this is not your place!*

Pure gasped.

Then without another word the dragon beat its mighty wings, throwing them to the ground. Leaping into the air, the dragon navigated its way between the trees and was gone in a matter of heartbeats.

Pure was weeping.

"There *is* something wrong," she cried. "What has happened? The dragons were never like this. She was - angry. At us. At us for being *human*. What happened to them? What happened?!" She screamed.

No one had any answers.

"I guess the dragons aren't going to help us," Rayn said.

Pure turned her tear streaked face to him. "Then we will surely die!"

They were silent.

"She is right," Jayd said. "We cannot hope to defeat this curse on our own. We will have to wait it out, just as the stories tell, and wait till the survivors return life to the land."

This time Pure turned on Jayd. "Don't you *get* it? There aren't going to *be* any survivors! Not this time. The plague has learnt new tricks. They are healing. It is aware now. It will hunt the survivors until they are all extinct. There will be *no survivors!*"

Dr Joseph Ireland

They were silent.

Rhoc came up and gestured towards the direction of the dragon with excitement. Rayn held down his arms, he was clearly having trouble understanding what had just happened.

Pure walked on a few paces, looking out into the forest.

"We have to find her," she said. "We have to risk it all."

So they were thinking of following the dragon. Rayn knew it was foolishness. "Pure, we can't. We'll have to return to the village. They need us, they need me. And we can't tell if we've taken the curse as well. We're just lucky we survived-"

"Dragons don't harm people!" Pure screamed in defiance.

It set Rayn on edge. He was tired of everyone ignoring his counsel. He was young, yes, but he was still a wiseman.

"Enough, maiden! You are still under *my* care and *I* say we turn back. The hunter was right; this is a fool's errand."

"Do so, if you will. *I* will hunt this dragon across the whole world if need be!"

"And who knows but that you spread the curse yourself wherever you go? Leave it be, it does not want to be approached by humans now or ever! And I forbid-"

Suddenly Rhoc grabbed the staff.

At first Rayn was just angry that someone had touched his symbol of authority; something that meant so much to him personally. Then he was suddenly smitten by the idea that Rhoc was not shocked at the staff's touch. It made no sense.

Rayn tried to pull the staff from his grip, gently, then once again with all his strength. But Rhoc held on without expression, calm as a winter day, barely moving.

By the Divine, that boy is strong, Rayn thought.

"Rayn," Jayd said, still visibly shaken by everything that had just happened. "I think Rhoc is trying to tell you something."

"What!" Rayn asked in frustration.

"You need to ask what the will of the Divine is for us," she replied.

Rayn stopped struggling. She was right. Rhoc was right. And Pure was probably right as well. He needed to stop asking what his duty was, what the law said was the right thing to do, and ask what was the will for the Divine for them.

He nodded, and Rhoc let go.

Sometimes, Rayn had to wonder, Rhoc seemed so wise. It was a wonder how he thought sometimes.

Rayn held out the staff. "Should we pursue the dragon?"

At first, there was nothing. Almost a nothing, a kind of silent expectation. Rayn felt his heart grew heavy, and knew he had to apologize. "Guys, I'm… sorry."

"That's all right," Pure said without pause.

Jayd just looked at him, and let him speak.

"No, no, it's not. Not really. It's just," he sighed, trying to keep the trembling out his voice, and tears that rose unbidden to his eyes. "We nearly died. You all nearly died, and I couldn't help that."

Pure was going to speak to Jayd put a hand on her arm.

Rayn didn't know what he wanted to say, "I'm sorry. I'm... trying guys. That's all. This is a lot to... I'm not sure what to do and I'm too young to be doing it. I wake up one day and suddenly find I have all this power and all this responsibility, and all your lives depend on me... I know I can be commanding sometimes but I think, sometimes, I guess, I am afraid."

They were silent for a moment, till Jayd told him flat out, "We can tell."

He smiled at her, and she nodded at him. It was nice to have someone who stopped to listen to what he was trying to say. Pure said nothing, looking a little confused. Rhoc grunted, and shook his shoulder with one enormous hand. Rayn then felt that they knew he could do it, or that he'd get it eventually. And they weren't going to leave, they were here for the journey. He was glad they were here, and began to feel that things were going to be all right.

Suddenly the staff rose up high from the ground, sending out a brilliant blue light. An aura of profound peace and contentment filled his heart, and right along the staff every rune of every wiseman who had ever held it glowed in a brilliant hue of silver.

"That," said Jayd, her voice muted in reverence, "is the biggest yes I've ever seen."

Rayn didn't even mind the obvious disrespect of her interpreting a Divine sign, he was too overcome by the spirit of the staff. And it seemed that the Divine was teaching him, again and again, to be humble. To allow others to teach him. To allow others the light of the Divine, not just the wiseman.

"I agree," he whispered as his staff floated down and into his hand. In that very moment he felt so very, very small compared to the enormity of the task they were going to undertake.

Then Pure reached out and hugged him, and he found himself lost in her soft embrace. Then Rhoc joined them, though it made him laugh. Then Jayd.

"All right, we do this together then! We hunt the dragon from Nelwyn peak!"

They all agreed, even Rhoc, and the light of the glowing staff joined their hearts in an oath of promise.

"To see it through, right to the end. Come what may," Jayd offered.

"Come what may," Pure agreed.

They looked at Rhoc. He threw his head back and roared. If ever there was a noise for dragons or the cursed to fear, it was that.

They were going to find the dragon, come what may.

The swamp

"Are we there yet?" Pure begged, a frustrated whine breaking through her usually gentle voice.

They had been walking for five days. The ground under their feet was becoming increasingly boggy. The air, moist. The trees, thick with vines and covered with broad leaves, gave the area a dark mood. Rayn found his usual patience was wearing thin.

"Are you sure this is the best way?" he asked Jayd.

"Yes, I'm sure!" Jayd replied. "Look, Nelwyn Peak is right up there. This valley passes right to it. We'll come to a river soon, you'll see. We can walk the bank with ease 'till it leads right up there."

"I can see the mountain," Rayn replied, "and you've guided us right so far. But still, all these plants, they just keep getting in the way!" He kept trying to push through them with his staff.

Jayd sighed. She was probably thinking the same thing, and it was just getting harder and harder. Was she sure the river would have a clear bank, or did the clutching trees come right up to the bank as they did here?

It was almost as if the forest was fighting them.

"You did seek the best way to get us there, didn't you, Jayd?"

She didn't answer.

"Jayd?"

When she turned he saw it written on her face that she hadn't.

"What did you seek, Jayd?" He asked, voice fading with concern.

"I sought the fastest way, not … the best …"

"I think-" Pure began. She sounded like she was about to say 'get out of here'.

But it was already too late.

Wild men, arrows nocked, emerged from the trees. Rhoc moved to attack them but Rayn held his arm down.

Then a dark feeling crossed his mind, a memory of fear that did not seem to be his own. A man emerged, covered in tattoos, bone piercings and the skin of beasts.

A demoner.

Rayn held out his staff, and at first it burnt out brightly but as if clutched, the light faded into nothingness.

"Deliver your weapons," the demoner told them.

"What did he say?" Jayd asked, and Rayn translated.

"I think I'd rather go down fighting," she said.

Rayn nodded, yet they were outnumbered and outclassed. He sought desperately for some sign or vision but there was none. Just some hope in his heart that what these people truly sought was life and peace.

It would have to do.

He lowered his staff and the others followed his example. In moments they were bound and blindfolded, and marched towards an unknown destination.

It was precious time they could not waste, if they survived. But the stories of the demoners were all too horrible to mention, so none spoke.

After what seemed like an hour they must have arrived at the demoner's village. There were other voices, yet they were unlike the savage and cruel voices of the demoner's men, these were normal people, terribly afraid. They were talking about the omens; they were speaking in whispered tones.

They were begging for his life, and the life of his friends.

He heard Pure squeal and suddenly Rayn felt a mighty push on his back. Without warning, he fell headfirst into a pool of salty water, uncomfortably warm. He struggled against his bonds, only just barely breaking the surface to take some ragged, desperate breaths.

Then someone removed his blindfold.

They were in a town of some sort, though very much in disrepair. All except one ornate and well-appointed building that could only have been the housing of the demoner. He sat on a throne of polished wood, very finely crafted. Two women sat at his feet. All over the town square, frightened citizens watched while the debauched soldiers of the demoner grinned malevolently.

And underneath him, surrounding the water filled pot into which he had been thrust, was a blazing fire.

Rayn shouted and Jayd struggled against her bonds. The ropes that held Rhoc creaked against his straining muscles.

The demoner waved a hand and the hair on Rayn's neck stood up as the infernal wave of demonry slashed past him and into Rhoc. The boy never stood a chance, and fell unconscious in an instant.

This demoner's faith was strong.

Then Rayn felt fear.

"Tell me, wiseman," the demoner said, brushing down a woman's hair with a casual hand while she winced, "since you are so well versed in understanding the hearts of men and in interpreting the signs in the world. What was my price? What did he pay me to see you trapped this day?"

Rayn was silent, unsure of what the man meant.

The demoner shouted, raging and running up to him with demonic fury. "I know you can understand me, wiseman!" He swore and struck Rayn on the face. Then he stood back, composed, completely enjoying this sport.

Rayn would have rubbed his jaw but his hands were tied.

To be truthful, Rayn didn't care what this man's price was.

The demoner smiled, as though knowing his thoughts. "Ignorance? You prefer ignorance? Then ignorance it is! Look to me, my people!" He called, opening his arms to the assembled village and its frightened residents. "So you see it again, again this evening! A wiseman prefers to remain *ignorant!* Then you know what we must do, don't you?"

A child gasped.

"We must teach him, mustn't we!"

His men laughed cruelly, the people shifted uncomfortably.

Rayn began to wonder if this people were the same as the demoner's. They had similar dress and similar accent. Perhaps he had fallen from their grace long ago and been cast out, and now he returned to claim their lives one and all.

Rayn recited the prayers of forgiveness and protection for all of them and for himself. He was not afraid. He was not allowed to be afraid.

Dr Joseph Ireland

All the stories told of the terrible judgments that were passed by the Divine against those that wielded its powers for evil, such as the demoners. And that fate was so horrible as to invoke pity in the hardiest of souls. None escaped that judgment. Ever.

But what became of him while Divinity waited for the correct moment to pass that judgment might be a truly horrible fate indeed.

But judgment *would* come.

Eventually.

The demoner stared at him, as if daring him to pray further. "Yes. Lessons must be taught. Is it getting hot in there for you, Rayn of the Celtwyld?"

The demoner laughed, as though knowing his name was a great secret. But Rayn was not surprised. He'd heard what demoners could do.

Even so, it was warm in the pot, but not hot.

Not yet.

The demoner walked up to him. "Yes, a price, such a price for the new wiseman's life! But was it worth it, to eat the soul of a young wiseman? No. That was not the price."

He walked up to Jayd. "Perhaps another pretty wife to keep me warm at night?"

Jayd was fast. She leapt forward and bit his finger before he had time to pull away. Had she an instant more she might have bitten right to the bone, but his men pulled her back. Roaring, the demoner raised his fist as if to strike her.

Then stopped and simply grinned in victory.

"Or maybe this, this bag of meat," he said, kicking Rhoc. "Exercise for my men? Perhaps food for this starving village which seems almost *incapable* of taking care of itself."

A woman cried.

"No, that was not the price. Not at all. It was - all of them. All of this pathetic, tiny hovel. All their lives, ALL OF THEM," he roared, and women wept. "The curse returns! I have seen him, the man cloaked in *blood*. He has spoken to me! Soon he will turn this land with dust for the last time. All - except this town. So you see, I am now its god. I am its savior. Because of me, all these shall live. I have been promised. And all I need... is to give him... this!"

He turned and with a kind smile, gestured towards Pure.

She was about to say something when he suddenly reached up and tore the headband from her brow.

Instantly Rayn felt the heat began to increase underneath his feet.

"Stoke the fires!" The demoner shouted, folding his arms.

Pure screamed.

Jayd struggled.

Standing as best he could against the warming metal, Rayn shouted. "Why do you wait, good people? The demoner is right. The curse is coming. I have seen it! But you are wrong, demoner, if you think it will preserve this land for you. For when all is dust, what will you eat?"

No one spoke, but people sat trembling.

The demoner stood forward and whispered with a malicious grin, "We will gnaw the bones of the dead."

Dr Joseph Ireland

"And when even they are spent?" Rayn asked.

The demoner spat. "Countless dead will feed us for eternity!"

"You are being deceived!" Rayn shouted, trying to drown out the demoner's exultant cries. "You are dead either way! Set us free, set us free if you have any desire to live!"

The demoner fell silent and turned around, smiling maliciously. "What, so you can go and speak to a *dragon*? You're wasting your time. No dragon will speak to you, they *hate* us."

There was truth, even in those words. Rayn felt his heart failing in the rapidly growing heat. The demoner laughed.

A laugh not unlike the one Hak had given at the howling ruin. The laugh of those that sought only to destroy.

Rayn looked around. He did not know what demonry held these good people in such fear. Had they seen their own wiseman meet a similar fate? Was his faith not enough to save them from living in horror?

Or perhaps he wasn't trying to save the entire world.

Suddenly his prayer was interrupted by the demoner's fist. He pounded on his face and skull and then, as though to add insult to injury, he shoved his head under the rapidly warming waters.

Rayn struggled, wishing only for a chance to bite the man as Jayd had. He could only imagine her and Pure struggling. He couldn't imagine what terror they faced at the hands of this murderous demoner.

Then, suddenly, his soul was filled with a terrible silence. It was as if death had come to claim him already.

Peace, its seductive voice whispered. *If your Divine is so powerful, surely it will not allow the young maids to fail in their life's purpose, whatever that may be. Your time, however, is come. Rest now, young man. Rest, and take upon you no further burdens of this life.*

It was tempting, tempting beyond anything he had ever before imagined.

Suddenly, in the midst of his obliviousness and through the suffocating waters, he heard Jayd scream.

He thought of her. He thought of Rhoc. He thought of all the frightened and tired people of this town, and how they reminded him of the village he had left behind. A village without a wiseman. Without someone who could bless the children and the weapons or read the omens. Or even heal a sick goat.

To die, today, would be the easy way out, he realized, thinking to the power that held him. *Had you asked me this time last week I might have agreed, because last week I was only a boy. But giving up because life is hard work is a boy's thinking. Leaving important responsibilities to others is a child's right. But I am no longer a boy. I am a man. And there is work to be done!*

Wreathing himself in faith, Rayn knew it was time to fight. He had offered this demoner a chance to flee. His first duty to offer mercy was fulfilled. Now it was time to save this village.

He filled his heart with prayer and faith.

He felt his soul fill with the prayers of his people. He saw his father's face and the light he had always known as his mother. He heard a heartbeat and felt an enormous power nearby and all throughout him.

It was the power of the world.

He didn't hear the pot shatter into a hundred pieces, dousing the fire in a shroud of blistering steam. The demoner was thrown several paces away and onto his back. The entire village was silent.

Rayn's bonds loosened and he stood in the enormous puddle that now filled the fire pit.

The people cheered and the demoner's men looked around nervously.

Then the scarred and tattooed man began to pull a small stone from his shirt.

A demoner's stone.

Rayn suddenly remembered the prayer he'd used to save Jayd. Reaching out, he called his staff to him. For a moment nothing happened. Then it twitched.

Then it leapt right into his hand.

But the evil man stood quickly, taking a few steps towards the bound Pure. He clicked his fingers in front of her face and for a moment she seemed to be able to stare at nothing but them. He whispered cruel enchantments in her ear, waving his stone at her soul. Slowly her eyes fell back as though she became asleep with her eyelids open.

Jayd screamed.

The demoner handed Pure her headband back and Rayn knew just what he was planning. He was planning to make her incinerate him alive, releasing her only a moment later so that she could witness her own horror. But this was an old tactic. Rayn waited until the headband went on and with a prayer of purity, cast out the demoner's soul from Pure.

Pure blinked, her visage returning to normal in an instant, but the demoner roared as though struck with pain.

He commanded the girls be thrown to the ground and made his men start chanting. Their voices rose in dire unison. Rayn had never heard the words before but they were clearly an oath of the purest evil. But he did not fear, nor move from his place. A pale blue cloud of light began to settle around his face and arms.

But the demoner only smiled. As his cacophony of evil rose to a crescendo, he pointed his stone at the sky above Rayn. It cracked with dire purple electricity. Rayn looked up and saw a strange sight. It was as if the demoner was opening a door. It led to a terrible place, so very far away from the normal world. It must have cost the man greatly to peer into this place.

And then the dark purple fire erupted from the door and into the air, exploding around Rayn.

But he felt no fear or pain. Reaching deep within, he drew up life forces from the world of Pearl. With all his power, he pressed away the flames so that none could touch his skin, though his coat edge was badly singed.

But as the flames receded, Rayn heard a blood curdling roar. Looking up only just in time, he saw the demoner had leapt impossibly high into the air. He had drawn a wicked, serrated blade. In less than a blink, he would surely plunge it into Rayn's heart.

Rayn knew what to do in the moment it all happened. He told the water around him that it needed to be steam. There seemed to be plenty of heat lying around, the drenched embers still glowing in places.

The steam exploded up around the demoner in a thunderous eruption. The man screamed, roaring in pain again and again while Rayn stood unharmed. He drew strength from the staff and it would not let him stop until several breaths had passed.

A moment later the steam subsided and the people gasped. There the demoner knelt, his skin half burnt away. His hair burnt off completely, the muscles underneath raw and red.

He should have died, but the demoner held many powers.

Even so, it must have prolonged his pain terribly.

The demoner trembled in his pain, too full of agony to move as Rayn walked up to him without fear. He stood before the man and, in a slow and deliberate gesture, pressed the end of his staff into the center of the fallen stone.

It shattered and with it, the demoner's powers.

Rayn spoke so that all would hear. "Your power is broken. You are going to die in this place. Perhaps they will care for you? It is more kindness than you have earned."

"If you have any mercy, end me," the demoner demanded.

But Rayn knew it was just another deception. "It is not my place to so do," he told the injured man. "But we are leaving. These people are free. And you, you will be preparing for death now."

With a pathetic cry, the demoner shouted and scrambled for his sharpened knife. He tried to cut his own throat but his fingers were so badly damaged they would not obey him. For a moment, for just an instant, a look of realization crossed his face, as though a part of him would accept the judgment of the Divine. But then with a cry, he threw himself down into the dirt and thrashing about, moaned piteously.

The people cheered. The demoner's men fled or surrendered immediately, their power having deserted them. The people cut Jayd and Pure's bonds and nursed Rhoc back to consciousness immediately.

But Rayn and his companions did not stay to celebrate, but left as soon as they were able. The villages put them on sturdy rafts that sped their journey immensely.

Pure looked back at the waving villagers. "I wonder if that detour was truly necessary."

No one answered. They were all desperate to put as much distance between them and the broken village as possible.

Snow

It took two more days. Nelwyn Peak was always covered in snow; it knew no other climate. Many had suggested it was a curse laid on the mountain long ago, others said it was just a result of local weather conditions. Now, with Jayd leading them on in all the best paths, they had a new explanation: It was what a dragon wanted.

They passed through a strange little town at the foot of the valley next to the mountain, where people with strange accents looked out at them in distrust. Rayn realized that they must have looked a sight, perhaps still as children to their eyes. Two girls, a boy warrior, and a strangely young wiseman. None asked their business, and they did not stay the night.

The journey up looked like it was going to be cold. They managed to purchase a coat each, with some cold weather boots and gloves, and a hood for the maiden since she was so very thin. They used some coins that Jayd appeared to have, but Rayn didn't want to know where she'd got them from; perhaps they'd once belonged to the warriors? He didn't ask.

They were heading up the mountain when Jayd slowed down to level with him.

"You know, brother wiseman, that we are being followed?" Jayd said, and his staff immediately confirmed it.

I wish you'd tell me that kind of thing before it's an emergency, he said to it, grateful that Jayd had spotted the follower's shadow.

Now that he knew, it took only a moment for Rayn to spot them as well. Whoever it was, they were certainly inexperienced. The four of them turned a bend in the path and waited, and the shadow almost walked right into them in her haste to catch up.

It was a youth from the village, barely fourteen, with the same dark hair and eyes of all her clan.

For a moment they stared at each other. Then she turned to run.

"Stop!" Rayn commanded. Whether it was his voice or his authority, he did not know. But she did stop.

"For the light of Divinity, I compel you to tell us why you followed us."

She looked at him darkly but bowed at the staff anyway. "I wanted to see you. I know what you are doing. You are hunting our dragon."

The four exchanged glances.

"So there really is a dragon in this peak?" Pure smiled.

"What, you doubted me?" Jayd teased her.

The girl frowned at them. "You'll never catch her. I've come to watch you die."

"I fear you may be right." Rayn sighed. "We've met her already; she didn't seem very impressed with us at all."

The girl's eyes lit up with surprise and fear. "You've *seen* the mountain spirit? She is very old, the most powerful of her kind left in the world. She has been here longer than my ancestors have memory, longer still. She has not been seen in a hundred years! How can you claim to have met her!?"

They didn't answer. Rayn began to wonder if this girl was exaggerating or if perhaps the dragon they'd met wasn't the one that lived on this mountain. Then he wasn't sure if that was good news, or bad.

Rayn continued. "We don't want to hurt her, child. We only seek her counsel."

The girl looked surprised, then doubtful. "In my father's day a wiseman like you came saying the same thing. They say the dragon tests all who enter this mountain. The wiseman came back, but would no longer speak. He died three days later in my mother's house. We only know he never saw the mountain spirit. He didn't and neither will you!"

"She seems awfully protective of this 'mountain spirit', doesn't she?" Jayd smiled.

The dark haired girl stood up to her full height, her pale skin seeming to echo the white peak of the mountain. "She has protected our house, our clan, for as long as we've lived! She chases away the hunters and keeps the curse away from our sheep. We let her take any that wander onto her mountain. To us, she is sacred. I will *not* let you harm her."

"We do not intend to harm her in any way," Rayn repeated.

She still looked like she did not believe him.

"In the light of Divinity, I will not harm this dragon," he promised.

"You say that today..." she disagreed.

"You should come with us," Pure offered.

Rayn was bothered but not offended. It was becoming obvious that he was not really in charge of this expedition. That was only an illusion they kept up for public appearances. To be honest, he didn't know who was in charge; they were just four friends with the same goal, going in the same direction. Besides, he had to admit, it was proper tradition to share the journey with any found on the same path.

"Oh, can she, Rayn?" Jayd begged. "See, she is dressed for travel and I'll wager she is packed with food for three days at the size of her pack."

Rayn nodded, he had already noticed the bags she was carrying. He still wasn't sure and this was the kind of personal decision he wasn't supposed to use the staff for. "I don't know. Rhoc, what do you think?"

Rhoc just looked confused.

Rayn sighed. "I suppose he doesn't mind... and neither do I."

The girl folded her arms. "But I don't *want* to travel with you. You're all *going* to die."

Rayn shrugged. "Suit yourself. You're welcome to share our fire with us or not. We are going up the mountain. And we will speak to your mountain spirit, come what may."

She stood there, thinking for a moment.

"I am Snow," she said, "after the snow that falls softly and turns the world white in deep winter."

"Snow, nice name," Jayd said, then turned to introduce them all.

The girl seemed to cheer up considerably and, despite her words, after a short while was walking with them. She confirmed that they were indeed on the right path. The three girls chatted happily all the way up the mountain until they reached the edge of the tree line and made camp. Then they continued to chat inside their little tent well into the dark hours. Rayn began to wonder if they would attract some form of wild beast with their noise. Yet as he drifted off to a restless sleep, the weight of the world heavy on his brow, he heard something from Snow that would trouble his thoughts for the entire next day.

"The dragon will test you. She always does. I think they *all* do. They are angry, angry at humans for something that happened long ago. You know, in all our stories I know of only one that gained the dragon's trust, a child who was lost hundreds of years ago and whom the dragon took pity on. But the mountain spirit is not to be approached; all say so in my village! She causes the storms, her moods are sudden and unpredictable, she sends forth nightmares and can cause the earth to shake. *I* do not want to see the dragon. But if you do, I know only this – she will test you. And NO ONE has EVER passed those tests…"

Tested

Snow left them at the cavern's entrance.

It was probably the wise thing to do; it was clear that a dragon lived here and that the dragon here did not want to be disturbed. In the day since they'd left the tree line, Snow had made fast friends of Jayd and Pure. It was clear she also had a very practical side to her that Rayn admired. What Rhoc thought of her was a mystery; he kept his thoughts to himself, though he seemed happy to carry things for her.

The four of them stood now at the cavern's edge, staring down into the darkness. The cavern entrance was strewn with men's bones, and a deep, unsettling smell of the earth wafted from the darkness.

Rayn watched the cavern nervously.

"Whose dumb idea was this?" he asked.

"Yours," Jayd reminded him.

"Oh, yeah," he muttered.

It sounded suspiciously like a conversation they'd had only six months ago. Rayn shook his head in astonishment and Jayd's mouth curved into her knowing, crooked smile.

"We cannot turn back," Pure closed a determined fist. "We said we'd come and now we are here. We will go in!"

The wind blew, dragging with it the unsettling scent of the cavern below.

Pure paused. "But perhaps, bold wiseman, you could go first?"

Rayn nodded. There were no words of self-praise this time, no bold proclaiming of his manhood. He was afraid and there was no shame in any man fearing what *they* were choosing to do.

He started walking. A test. A test from a dragon. What kind of test could that be?

The tunnel went in, and down: down for many paces. They were led only by the light of his staff. Soon the huge tunnel branched.

"Which way now, good wiseman," Pure whispered.

He looked at the tunnels.

"This way," Jayd said, pointing left.

"How can you tell?" Pure asked.

"Because it's the way the dragon would go," Jayd replied.

"How do you know that?" Rayn asked.

"Look, it's larger than the other tunnel. Dragons like big things, ok? So it's left. Just go left."

In the end it seemed as good a choice as any, though the staff was silent. Rayn realized her wisdom had led them this far without fail, thus, they went left.

They approached the darkness, making their way through several other intersections. Soon the tunnel began to open out, lit by a dim red light. As Rayn studied the ground he began to make out the tracks of the creatures of the night; lizards, some snakes. They clearly found this place welcoming. But to him, there was something deeply unnerving about the cave. It had a sense of age, and deep wisdom about it, as though his whole heart was laid open for the cave itself to read. He wiped the sweat from his brow again.

Suddenly there was a hissing sound from the other side of the wall, like a giant snake rattling across enormous boulders. In their sullen rattling, Rayn heard the words, *Look to the roof above you.*

It was silently splitting apart.

"Look out!" he shouted, pointing to the roof. The far wall began to crumble before their eyes. Just in time, the others dashed out the way. All except Rhoc, who hadn't heard him and didn't have the speed to move at all. A giant boulder split from the ceiling and fell towards him. Pure squealed in frustration as she tried and failed to turn it from its course, while Rayn prayed in desperation for his friend.

Yet in that next instant, Rhoc looked up and caught the boulder, equal to the size of his body, in his bare hands.

Rayn gasped. He'd never seen anything like it.

Rhoc had been bearing his burdens without complaint but this new strength was inexplicable. Unless… *The curse!* With a roar of fear and panic, Rayn readied to swing his staff around. At least in its fire he would know if his old friend was cursed. But the girls held him back.

"No, Rayn, what are you doing?" Jayd squealed.

"It's Rhoc, Rayn," Pure tried to reassure him.

But tears stung Rayn's eyes. He knew what had to be done. "It's the curse. It's the only reason he could be so strong now. We have - we have to kill him."

"What? No, Rayn, this is madness!" Jayd insisted.

Rhoc just stood there, holding the massive boulder aloft, a look of confusion on his face. Rayn knew it was the last he'd ever see his friend. It might be the last he'd ever know of himself, for in that moment he realized he would die if he ever had to kill his best friend. Tears flowed down his face.

"No! Rayn, I forbid-" Pure began.

Rayn flung her from him, pushing his sister aside as well. In fear and rage he pointed his staff right at the maiden's heart. "You! *You* command *me*! How dare you! I am a wiseman of the light, a Shepherd of the people. I hold the staff … you dare…" he stuttered, lost for words.

She lay on the ground, covering her mouth in fear, eyes brim with tears.

Trembling in fright.

Rayn could say no more.

"Test it yourself," Jayd said, a cold edge to her voice. So even she disrespected him in her heart. "Ask the Divinity you claim to serve, see if Rhoc has acquired the curse."

Rayn looked at her, fallen to the ground as well. He shook his fist in rage. "You dare as well! Who are you to doubt *my* authority!" He wanted them gone. He wanted them out of the way…

… but they had a point. He knew his duty was to serve the light before his own desires, even if it hurt.

He held out the staff, ready to plunge it into Rhoc's face, the boulder he held would surely crush him.

Rhoc just stood there, confused, yet trusting.

"Is Rhoc now taken of the curse?"

No.

Definite no.

Rayn shook with fear and in that revelation all the insane hatred, jealousy and pride fell from his heart, leaving him weak. He knelt on the floor. He could not believe what he'd become, what he'd almost inexcusably done, if it weren't for the counsel of friends.

Rhoc shoved the bolder aside and Rayn wrapped his arms around him, sobbing with joy that his friend's life had been spared.

"I'm so sorry," he said to Rhoc and to them all. "I don't know what came over me."

Rayn helped them to their feet.

Pure looked at him nervously but she held her head up.

"Stop being so scary," Jayd told him.

Rayn couldn't help but smile. He turned to apologize to Pure again. They might have embraced but suddenly Rhoc said, "Oorm!" and he turned to see a massive cavern had opened up. They entered the cavern, and there, lying among what was an impossible array of beautiful crystals of purple and yellow and blue, was a dragon.

Not the dragon of the woods; this was the largest dragon Rayn had ever imagined. There was no way that she could fit through any of the cavern here, she was simply immense. Her head was as large as the entire village square. Her teeth were the size of swords. Her silver scales gleamed in the scattered light that shimmered around her cavern. She lay twisted and curled around the room so much that it was impossible to tell which part was joined to which.

Her head rested on a stone dais near the center of the room. A small flight of stone stairs led up to a platform that one ambitious soul might use to speak to her.

Rayn took a hesitating step forward but faltered. It did not feel right. Even his staff felt uncomfortable, a sure sign he was stepping outside the path of Divinity. He was not the one that should speak to the dragon.

It was Pure.

They all seemed to know it.

He turned and looked at her. She looked out with a strange look of confidence mixed with fear. She laid a hand on his arm, forgiving him. For a moment he held it gratefully.

He stood back, and let someone else be first. *So*, Rayn thought. *That is what it means to be tested by a dragon.*

Pure approached the platform, her pace slow but her head held high. The dragon seemed asleep, though it probably wasn't. It was so large there was little doubt in any of their minds that it could spring to life in a heartbeat and swallow her whole.

Rayn could hear Pure's nervous breaths. She stood alone in the crystallized cavern, the first person in who knew how many eons to have done so. For a long moment, Pure was silent. Then she spoke and her voice was quiet.

"What happened, dragon?" She spoke the truest question in her heart. "We used to be friends, your kind and mine. What happened?"

Her voice was hardly a whisper.

The dragon did not stir.

"Listen to me," She pleaded, "I need answers. There is a plague, a new plague of the Perish. It is coming across the land and it can heal and it can *think*. This is the worst thing! And I don't know where or when I am, and I don't know what happened to my family. Please, Please! I need answers!"

The dragon stirred, opened one eye, then closed it with a huff.

For a second there was silence.

Then Pure screamed. "Get up! You lazy monster! Get up! I command you to speak to me!"

Then the dragon did move, its entire body of coils stretching and scraping in great sparks along the ground, its gigantic wings flexing slightly for they would otherwise sunder the cavern walls. It opened its enormous mouth, yawned widely displaying its hundreds of blade sharp teeth, and spoke.

"It's about time." Her voice was as an old woman's: slow, creaky, yet alive.

Pure almost choked in surprise and relief, smiling at her companions, then bowing to the floor like Rayn's people did when begging for their lives.

"I... I'm sorry. Please, please, mighty dragon," Pure said, "we need answers."

Rayn found himself gasping with relief and pulled himself together. It was a dragon. It was a real live dragon once again.

The dragon yawned again and lifted up her mighty head to look over her. Her eyes were piercing and old. "Come forward, young ones.

You *all* are brave to have passed my tests," she said, resting her mighty head on the stone dais by the platform. She seemed old and tired.

"All? I thought I alone had been tested," Rayn pondered out loud.

The dragon laughed. "Children. After all this time and they send children to me? And you? Why are you wearing the robes of a man, and a wiseman at that! Never mind, I know why. I see far in this cave, much more than any of my kind. It keeps me sane in a world gone mad."

"What tests?" Pure asked.

"First, to you, fair human. What gave you the courage to command a being a thousand times your size?"

"I… do not know," she replied.

"Oh, stop that," the dragon insisted, "have you no idea what you are? What *courage* it took to speak to me? And in so doing you have found your dragon's gift. You are of the royal house that founded the original settlements of Pearl. I recognize it in your voice, in your walk, in the way you stand. You, young princess, have the power of commanding dragons."

"What?" Pure said in disbelief.

The dragon laughed. "Is it so hard to believe? And as for you, bold warrior," she said to Rhoc, "know you your gift?"

He nodded, somehow understanding what the dragon was saying, and held out his fist.

"That is right, the rare and precious gift of great strength. I am impressed, I have not seen that in some time."

"What of me?" Jayd asked, not waiting for an invitation.

"Can you not tell?" The dragon asked.

Rayn was taken aback. He'd expected a much more formal, or frightening conversation with his first dragon. Instead, this was more like a backyard chat with a grandma.

"She's... very good at finding things," Rayn offered, he did not want to be left out of the conversation.

Jayd shook her head. "No, I'm not, I just *think*."

"Actually, that is part of the gift," the dragon explained, "you have a gift, a very precious gift. Your heart is a compass that will guide you to anything you seek, all are, but your heart is well calibrated. You are gifted at *finding*. You are a navigator."

Jayd was silent, but she still didn't look like she believed the dragon.

The dragon curled its lips, perhaps it smiled? Then Rayn sensed his time had come.

"Please, good dragon, will you not tell me..." he began, bowing to one knee.

She snorted in frustration, and Rayn sensed he'd offended her. Then her great coils moved. A massive, sharpened paw lifted from the ground and she stood up on her front legs, spread her wings out as far as they would go, and moved her head till it towered above him.

A sulphur breath of acid and flame struck the ground in front of him, and Rayn trembled. Then she held her head up and roared.

"So easy is it?" The dragon said in disgust. "To bow and apologize and plead before one who is obviously more powerful than you? And why did you not show your sister the same respect when you knocked her to the ground in your pride! Hypocrite! Think yourself wise? Divinity respects *truth*, not merely authority. All lives are equal. You wisemen walk the lands thinking you alone are the hands of the Divine. But you are not – all are an expression of the Divine. I am glad your culture gives such authority to men, for I would be loath to see a woman so *corrupted*."

Rayn didn't know what to say. He'd only ever been chastened a few times in his life, for he was so very careful to be well behaved. Even after he'd promised himself never to let pride get in the way of truth, Divinity had still found pride in his heart. The dragon was right, and it really hurt, yet he did not feel any guilt. It was odd. He almost felt - inspired. Liberated from living lies. The dragon didn't want to harm him, only help him be his best. He was in awe of her wisdom and perception.

"I…" he stumbled. Then stood up to face her. "You are right. I will hereafter heed the wisdom of all life, and not my own." Then he paused, that did not feel right. "No, I am a part of the Divine as well. I will heed all truth, regardless of the source, and never let pride be in the way of doing what is right."

The dragon nodded, as one warrior might to another. "Your lessons are harsh boy, they need to be. For you have so very little time. Your challenge must be overcome quickly and while you are still young."

"But…" Pure wondered aloud. "What about his gift?"

The dragon spoke kindly. "You mean he doesn't know? I find that humorous. But you all have a trial, as well as a talent. There is need of both to help you fulfil the purpose of your life. The trial will likely be with you your whole life, for most of you, and it keeps you humble and open. You, wiseman, are charged with pride, and must learn humility. As for you others, your challenges are not yet revealed to you. But they will be, and I have given you clues today and in your path up that mountain. Even you, the little one they call Snow."

Everyone turned, and there was a frightened squeak from the cavern entrance. Sure enough, Snow was there too. Pure held out her hand for her to join them.

Snow rushed down, her pigtails flying out behind her, and threw herself face first onto the ground. She spoke in a trembling voice, "Forgive me, great one. I only... I just *had* to know."

The dragon laughed again, a solemn and gentle sound. "I see you have chosen to have a part in this, but your time is not yet, but soon. Return to your village and have them prepare for war. The curse will reach this land in three days."

"Yes, mountain spirit."

The dragon smiled and breathed on her. Instead of sulphur, the breath smelt like smelted iron and the dew on grass. Rayn straight away knew it was a blessing of some kind.

Snow rose, smiled at them with trembling, clutched hands, and ran out.

War? Rayn pondered.

"Now, for some answers," the dragon said and laid her head down on the dais. She sighed, as though tired, and suddenly two crystals by them flickered with glowing light. Inside, pictures began to form. Pictures that helped tell the story she now related:

"Four thousand years ago a mighty people came to claim this land – barren of all but the most shallow forms of life at the time. They brought seeds and beasts, and taught the land how to rain. They were your people, the people of the white maiden, though you were only a child at that time and cannot remember. They are the ancestors of all who survive in this land today."

Rayn saw boats, so many, and so large they could scarcely be imagined. They set about the tasks of preparing a great sphere, as if it had been a world.

"Then came the Perish. I know their origins but will not speak it here," the dragon continued. "They are a disease, tiny animals that can live inside a person's blood."

And here Pure hid a victorious smile but caught his eye.

The dragon continued. "This disease causes life to change, perverting them into unspeakable abominations – even perverting dragons. But then something happened that had not happened before. Somehow they learnt how to take over the minds of men. When they did that, they gained intelligence. The man who hunts you is not the first of this thinking disease. With the cunning of men at their command, they began to develop tactics and the entire empire of man was laid waste in a year. Thousands of worlds were returned to dust, even this world was almost destroyed. Yet some scant samples of life remained, tiny fragments with a natural immunity to the plague. They grew and as they did, so did the plague. Every few years it gains a new adaptation and then nature fights back with newer and stronger life. It is a war that has seen no end yet."

She sighed a tired breath and continued, "But one thing was clear from long before: the plague was using the dragons to move between the stars. When we learnt that this was happening we all made a pact to stop travelling between the worlds. The plague was stayed. We dragons swore to never again leave 'till the plague was destroyed from this world. That was four thousand years ago and we have not succeeded yet. As far as we can tell we are the only world that remains and also the only world on which the plague still lives."

Pure sobbed. "Then my mother, my whole household? They've been dead four thousand years?"

"You are of the royal house Oordu," the dragon said, "a princess. The only one left standing. I thought your people's light had been put out forever but you have returned, I do not know how that is possible. We were waiting for the glory of humanity to rise again and had lost all hope. To have you here, returned to us, with the rights and honor of humanity written in your blood gives me hope beyond measure for dragons and humans."

Pure answered, using her own language, but Rayn somehow understood every word once again. "I was placed in an escape capsule by my mother during the last incursion of the Perish. It seems the capsule malfunctioned, failing to awaken me from stasis but fortunate since this may have preserved my life during the outbreaks. However, it also caused me to age, which it was not designed to do."

"Ahh, yes, that would explain it," the dragon said.

"So, every few years," Rayn said, moving things along again, "the 'plague' resurfaces and nature fights it back."

Dr Joseph Ireland

"And never, not in the last thousand years or so, has the plague succeeded in turning a world to dust again," the dragon said in triumph. "Nature grows strong and we feel it will triumph. When it does, we will be free to leave this world."

"But," Pure asked, "what about the bond between dragons and humans?"

The dragon looked sad, then turned its great head about to Rayn. "You will find the answer to that question shortly after you find Rhoc's dragon."

"Excuse me?" Rayn asked. He didn't know Rhoc had a dragon.

"And where will you find Rhoc's dragon?" The dragon asked Jayd.

She paused, like she'd only just caught up with the conversation. "Far, to the east. In a desert by a pool of still water," she replied.

The dragon smiled. "Well done, young one. Your gift is strong. Use it wisely or like all gifts we are given," and here she turned to Rayn, "it *will* corrupt you."

Rayn swallowed hard. Then he asked, "But dragon, what is my talent?"

The dragon almost laughed. "You mean, you still don't know? Good wiseman! You don't know? You cannot tell? You are as blind to your talent as your sister was to hers, as deaf to your own skills as your friend is to sounds! You do not know?"

Then the dragon placed her enormous head right to within arm's reach. "Then I will not tell you."

Rayn gasped. Surely it was important to know?

"I have not told you all your trials; why tell you of your talents and rob you of the journey to discovery? No, bold wiseman. If your gift, so obvious to others, is kept from you then perhaps it is the will of the Divine for you not to know yet. But I will tell you this as I have always known: you will only truly know your talents as you selflessly serve others. That's so important I'm going to repeat that. You will only know your talents when you live to selflessly serve others." She nodded and was silent.

"In a desert?" Pure said aloud.

They waited.

"Great dragon, how will we get there?" Pure asked.

The dragon sighed and lay down. "I will call for my progeny; they will take you. Look out among them; perhaps you will find one that will suit you. Perhaps you may impress them? Perhaps you will pass their tests?"

"But," Pure began, but held her thoughts.

"I know," the dragon closed her eyes. "But I am too old now. I cannot make this journey or any journey. I am over four thousand years old. Even if you *were* to command me, you must ride another."

"Ride…?" Pure said.

"Ride," The dragon agreed. "Isn't that why you came, to become the first dragon riders of Pearl in over four thousand years?"

Her voice was scarcely a whisper but Rayn's skin went cold and he trembled with excitement. The others must have been feeling something similar.

"You'll need the armor and weapons of your ancestors. And young wiseman, you'll need to find the prayers to stay the afflictions this new plague brings, and you will. Too long we dragons have held on to our indignity and wrath with the humans. But it is clear to me now; we are symbiotic species. Even in your banishment we dragons could not leave you alone. The dragon riders *must* fill the skies once more!"

"Then let us do this!" Rayn shouted.

The dragon smiled. "That's the spirit I once knew from humanity: impetuous, curious, without fear! But perhaps I should suggest a course of action you might take? Perhaps finding Rhoc's dragon might not be the wisest *first* course of action. Perhaps if your witless wiseman would make good use of his *tools!*"

Rayn blushed; he knew right away she was telling him to use the staff to reveal the next course of action.

"First, I have but one request," the dragon said, resting her head on the dais once more, "to make of you, white maiden. If you will, would you please rest your hand on the space between my eyes?"

"Why?" She asked, willingly reaching out her shaking hand. Her whole body would fit inside the creature's mouth with ease.

"No particular reason," she said, a hint of sorrow in her voice.

Pure stretched out a tremulous hand, unconsciously squinting her eyes in fear. She didn't seem to notice how fast she was breathing nor how her hand trembled. She looked down at that enormous, ancient jaw, the seething nostrils, the bladed teeth.

He didn't know how she found the courage to do it but as the dragon turned its head and shut her eyes, she reached out to touch the ancient creature. A brilliant white globe of energy began to gather between her palm and the dragon's brow. Neither seemed to notice as the gentle white light surrounded them both, making them glow. The light grew and grew, but Pure did not pause. Not daring to breathe, she touched the dragon.

For a moment there was silence as Pure stroked her brow, tears filling both their eyes. The dragon sighed and shifted her position, and Pure leapt back as the light suddenly disappeared. The dragon hefted her head, then stood up on her front legs and stretched her neck high to the roof.

Then the dragon roared a single, tumultuous sound that blasted off the mountain top with the force of a volcano. In its echoes Rayn heard the words,

"IT IS TIME!"

Dragons

When the dragons came, they came quickly.

The one first to arrive appeared in only seconds, simply materializing in a thunderclap of red and angry smoke. One moment it wasn't there, the next it was.

The others took only a few breaths more. The first few flew in through to the cavern now open to the sky. They were red and green and blue. There were some as small as a man. Most were as large as a house and could have borne a man with ease. More and more of them poured into the open mountain, roosting on the cliff sides or by the crystals the old dragon used.

At first they were silent, then one arrived and his first words were ones of war.

"What are they doing here, Matron?" he demanded in a harsh voice. His form was spiked and scythian, as though the bones that extended from his skin were made of a silver metal. "They are *humans*: murderers, slanderers. The glory is *gone* from their culture."

"Enough, Doomclaw," she chided him with a hiss. "Put aside your old hatred, it is time for healing and for war."

He seethed in silence at her rebuke and Rayn knew in his heart that this was one of the dragons that would eat him in a heartbeat, given half the opportunity. From that point on, the dragons were a riot of noise, filling the air with their comments and questions.

"Who are these?"

"Have the humans made amends?"

"Why does Matron summon us to suffer these?"

Then the sky crackled with lightning, but instead of lasting only a moment it gathered in the center of the sky. Then it grew and grew, soon forming a great ring and through that ring a completely different sky was visible, the clouds within darkened as if by night. Then, through the ring of lightning an enormous dragon flew. Larger than any of the other dragons, except the Matron. The dragons called out at his presence, and he lit the sky with lightning that would be visible for leagues.

"Farwing, my old mate," the great old dragon, the one they called Matron, said to him in a gentle voice. "You are not called to this meeting of my children."

He flew down to rest his body on the mountain, waiting outside the cavern as if it were a sign of respect.

"Indeed, Matron, though half those here are my descendants as well. Were there anything so important that you should summon them, I wish to know it, too."

She sighed, as if his words, though unwelcome, were true.

"Indeed, *she* is the cause for which you are called," Matron replied and bent her head down to point towards Pure.

"Is that…" Farwing said, wonder in his voice.

"She is of the royal house. The time has come. It is here at last."

"No human will ever ride the skies with me!" Doomclaw roared and lit the sky with orange flames. His protests were echoed with a chorus of agreement from various dragons.

"No," the Matron disagreed, "the plague has resurfaced. It demonstrates wisdom once again. This is our chance, my son. Soon our banishment to the surface of this world will be ended, once the plague is dealt with once and for all!"

Others cheered.

"Are you certain?" Farwing mused, seeming the only one with authority to speak out of turn to her; Doomclaw was clearly just plain rude.

The dragons erupted in chaos and confusion. Some cried, 'Test her, test her.' Others, 'Eat her!' The sky was almost split with their cries; Rayn found himself following Jayd and covering his ears.

"Is she the one, or will the humans deceive us again!" Doomclaw cried.

"Enough!" the Matron and Pure called out at once. Instantly all the dragons fell into a profound silence. As one, the Matron moved her head and the maiden stepped onto it as though they'd shared the same thought. Without a hint of fear, Pure was lifted up, lifted up many, many paces to stand above the assembled conference of dragons.

"I am Pure, princess of the royal house Oordu. I have seen the Perish take a man, some falcons, and an entire family of wolves. He seeks my life above all others, though I can only guess at why. But this I do know, the plague is coming like never before. It will destroy both our peoples unless we now co-operate. We need your help."

Farwing spoke, "How is it possible you slept four thousand years? None here know the honor of bonding with a human; even the great Matron, oldest on this sphere, was but a hatchling the day this world was first turned into dust. All who fought by your kind are long buried. Now, they have forgotten all that your people were…"

"Then help me remind them," Pure said. "For I remember. I saw men and dragons fighting side by side for each other among the stars. My brother was one of them. I still see his face, and remember him and his dragon fighting as one. As one! We have defeated the Perish before. It is time to bury them in the dust forever!" she shouted.

And the dragons roared their approval, even Doomclaw, as if she had power to command them all.

"But wait," Doomclaw stated, and the Matron sighed her disapproval, "What of the circle? It is not enough that you lead us! What of the circle? Should we all take a rider *war* will be the result as human ambition takes root in *our* hearts. You alone are not enough to command us. Where is the inner circle that will govern the new legion of men and dragons? Where is the inner circle whose power will initiate the great bonding once more?"

The Matron sighed, lowering Pure to the ground again. "I fear my son is right. You must form an inner circle of bonded dragon riders – the dragons that are your own from before your birth. You must find them and thus make yourselves the governing council. When this is done, and only then, will it be possible for the other dragons to feel the innate call to seek out their riders and vice versa. But you have started something that cannot be stopped; in our hearts, we seek reconciliation with men."

Dr Joseph Ireland

"But what happened?" Pure called. "What did our ancestors do?"

"You will know, soon enough."

Rayn could see Pure clutch her fists in frustration. It seemed it was on her mind to command the Matron to tell her, but instead she chose to trust the ancient dragon's judgment.

The Matron spoke. "Seek you out a companion from among my children," she said. "Seek one whose heart will match your own. This will speed you on your quest, and help you to find what you need."

"What of Farwing?" Pure asked. "Who would speed us more than he?"

He and Matron looked at each other but shook their heads.

"Who among you-" Matron began.

"I will be first!" A light blue dragon shouted. His wings seemed tattered at the edges but it took a moment for Rayn to realize he was covered in ice and trailed shards as he flew. "Long have I imagined the company of humans. Too blind have I been without Matron's call to arms. I want to know if there are any of you I may take."

He struck the floor and it shook, a blizzard of ice and snow trailing around them. He was cold.

No one moved.

The dragon sniffed in their direction, indicating towards Rhoc. "This one is strong,"

"Your heart is in the right place, Icewing," the Matron charged him, "but you are too young to bear them all. You will find your rider, soon enough."

He looked hurt and flew away.

Next came one called Hazetail. He slithered down the wall and disappeared into the shadows, revealing himself a moment later behind them.

"Nor I, mother, my rider is not among them."

"You only came to show off your skill." She seemed to smile to him.

Then a white and silver dragon floated down and when she touched the ground mosses sprang to life. By the time she'd left they had bloomed into flowers. She sniffed at them, especially Rayn's staff. She looked in their eyes, seeming to say something but he didn't hear her words.

"Forgive me mother," she said, "I was simply curious."

"That is alright, Treeheart," Matron replied.

"And what of my son, Doomclaw?" Farwing muttered.

If dragons swore, Doomclaw did. "I have nothing to do with these liars," he said, voicing the opinions of many.

But one look from his mother changed his mind. Obediently, Doomclaw flew to stand before them, his steel claws throwing up a shower of red sparks when he landed, cutting great gashes in the stone. Rayn took note of the steel on the ends of his wings as well.

"These are no different," he muttered. "Dragon killers, traitors, they will turn against us, mark my words…"

He sniffed and was about to sneeze, when Pure shouted, "Stop!" instantly he covered his snout and stepped back. It was strange how they honored her command no matter what they thought of her personally.

Their integrity must have been great. Rayn thought he might come to like dragons.

"Enough!" A voice called. Then a green dragon, large, clawed, swooped from the air. Rayn gasped with surprise; it was the dragon they had found at the bottom of the mountain, the one that had given life to a stillborn bird. "Stop toying with us mother! All hearts here know there are none that are meant to be their riders; the connection is far too powerful for these 'interviews'. But I will carry them, since you cannot. I will help them on their quest."

Her mother sighed, "Yes, my child Lifebreath. I knew it was to be you all along, but I had to let it be your choice."

"Mother, we are not as blind as you seem to think. I too have read the signs in the clouds and in the air. I have watched the path of humanity and see new behaviors among them in the last three hundred years. They are returning to what they were. Perhaps if those such as Doomclaw will not forgive them, Divinity will."

Doomclaw scoffed, but held his peace.

"Then you know what to do," Matron said to all her dragons. "Ride to the five continents, seek out the old treasures. Renew the connection with humanity. This is the long awaited day! Once the inner circle is formed of dragon riders it will make it possible for the rest of us to find the riders we deserve. Then once again, if the plague is purged from this land, we will be able to fly among the stars once more!"

Even Doomclaw seemed to approve of that saying. The young dragons took to the air.

"What of you, Matron?" Farwing stretched his great neck into the mountain.

"I will call down the fortress from above the sky; surely four thousand years are enough to purge it of any impurities. I will reconvene the conclave, set up the standing stones once more. This is what I will do. And you? Will you take this news to the eastern continent?"

"Naturally. Those of the northern already know I imagine, given they have one with such a gift. Then I will speak with Gueststone of the western, and Hailbreath from the southern. He is stubborn, but I think he will agree with your assessment, my lady. Perhaps your patience has finally paid off."

"It already has," she replied with her dragon smile.

Then the mighty Farwing reached out and touched noses with Matron. In the moment of their connection Pure gasped.

"What is it?" Rayn asked her.

"Nothing," she replied, though it clearly was.

Then with a roar, Farwing took to the skies. Using wisdom beyond what humanity possessed he made a hole in the sky and flew through it to the other side of the world.

"Come," Lifebreath ordered, "we must begin before the plague takes hold. Its initial progress is slow and several of my brothers have offered to hunt it, but once it takes hold it develops with terrifying speed. We have three weeks, at best."

Jayd

"Go, go!" The dragon Lifebreath ordered. "Get on my back!"

They didn't wait to be told again. They already knew how frightening she could be. They clambered along the iron hard scales, which were surprisingly warm, and held on tight to the solid ridges of plates that lined her back.

"Where to now?" Lifebreath asked her mother.

"I don't know, ask the wiseman. And you have a navigator with you."

Lifebreath gasped. "Is it true? I am glad I did not punish you then. Which is it?"

Jayd raised her hand.

"Oh, you," Lifebreath said with disappointment. She hurried down the cavern and they all had to adjust their grip to stay on. "So, where we headed, Birdkiller?" Lifebreath said looking right ahead.

"Birdkiller!" Jayd protested. "Hey, we needed breakfast."

"Humans haven't changed," the dragon replied.

Rayn noticed Pure looking back, longing and sorrow written all over her face.

"What is it?" Rayn asked again.

"I just... she was so noble, so good. I think I will miss her," she said with tears in her eyes.

"I'll miss her too, but I'm not going to cry about it!" Rayn said, actually trying to just cheer her up.

One cold look from Pure told him that he'd need to work on his humor a little more in the future.

"So, Jayd, where to now?" Rayn tried to change the topic.

Rhoc was gripping with great delight to the dragon's back, his face full of excitement.

"That depends on where we want to go," she replied.

"Oh, that's right. So, that's my job. Hmm…"

Rayn closed his eyes in concentration while the dragon lumbered up the corridor. Her wings barely fit. Who was to be the first to claim a dragon?

Rayn wanted his own dragon. He felt the powerful muscles moving under the steel plates, perfect rumors of moving vertebrae and sinew as she walked. He was riding a dragon, they all were! But it was not *his* dragon. Somewhere in this world was his dragon, it was waiting to be crowned with the glory of a rider, and not any rider, but a wiseman.

And that thought reminded him to be humble. What he wanted was not always what was best. So whose dragon did they need to find first? Whose dragon was the most important that they find first?

He knew the answer as soon as he asked; the staff glowed in support of his decision.

"Jayd," he announced.

"What?" she asked, clinging onto dragon hide, trying to see if she could get a better grip by sliding her fingers under the plates.

"Your dragon is first," he said.

Dr Joseph Ireland

Lifebreath stopped, turning her head on its long neck to look at him. "You're joking, right?"

He shook his head.

The dragon peered at Jayd. "Well then, *navigator*, where must we go?"

Jayd pointed. "South of West, towards some sharp black rocks that rise up out of great moving waters."

"Dead Man's Fingers?" Lifebreath asked.

Jayd shrugged.

Lifebreath braced herself. "Time to get a good hold on, young ones, we have need of haste and now it is time to fly!" She started to run, faster and faster. They were almost thrown off and she sped up. She was running a hundred times faster than any human could, and then she spread her wings, took one great jump from the ground, and she flew.

The force of that jump threw Pure from the beast, Rhoc only just reaching out in time to catch her hand. She screamed and the dragon slowed its flight. Rhoc pulled her back down and she held on tight.

"Do NOT let that happen again!" Lifebreath commanded.

It was a miracle how they flew; her wings seemed more for steering than to actually lift through the sky, so how she held herself aloft was a mystery. The wind whipped past them at their enormous speed and they all had to press their faces to the dragon to keep warm.

She flew so fast.

Yet as the day wore on it was clear that compared to her potential progress, their pace was agonizingly slow. The air high up was terribly cold and neither Pure nor Rayn had any prayer or understanding that could prevent that. Pure's air bracelet was difficult to master and was little help. Lifebreath told them that the dragon riders once had armor that protected them from such inconveniences, but that armor was long lost or hidden. So they had to keep to the lower altitudes. The air down lower was warmer, but thicker and more turbulent, and the dragon had to keep making changes in speed and direction, and with four riders she grew tired quickly. They took too many chances to rest.

By night fall they all were exhausted.

They flew down to rest by a dark river. In a world where the clouds never parted night was always dark. Rhoc helped Rayn light a fire with the tinderbox and what dry wood could be found. They ate their provisions in silence. The dragon drank at the river and filled herself on the dark reeds that grew there.

They were eating the cured meat when Pure stretched her hand in pain.

"What happened?" he asked her.

"Oh," she said, very softly, "I think Rhoc might have been a bit enthusiastic with my hand, it's all bruised up, I'm afraid."

"Here, let me see that," Rayn offered.

She held out her hand to him. Even in the firelight it seemed soft and delicate. He could see no bruise there but holding out the staff, uttered the words of prayer and healing. Then he was shown a vision of the inside of her hand, the twisted muscles and broken blood vessels. He willed in healing. The muscles sewed themselves together; the errant blood became water and flowed away. But there was a problem: there was a broken bone.

He looked at the hand sadly; he had no prayer for broken bones. That had not been discovered by his people even now. It was a burden they had to bear till they knit together again of their own accord.

"Why do you wait, wiseman?" Lifebreath asked him, accusation in her voice.

"There is a broken bone. I cannot heal it," he replied.

Jayd gasped.

"Oh please," Lifebreath protested, "must I do all things for you?"

She walked over to Pure, the ground trembling just a little under her feet. Pure held out her hand in front of the dragon and taking a deep breath in, the dragon sighed on it.

It smelt like wind and rain and… lavender.

There was a pop, and Pure looked surprised.

"You also missed the torn rope inside her hand," the dragon said, and sighed. "Is that what humanity has been reduced to for its crimes?"

Rayn wondered what she meant, but didn't have the heart to ask her yet.

Pure looked out her. "Tell me, good dragon, what did we do?"

Lifebreath looked into the dark night. "I do not know myself. The Matron is the only one who saw those days and she was just a hatchling. But hidden in our minds is a shared memory that in the midst of the last war with the Perish, humans and dragons turned against each other. We are told it was the humans' fault. As the alliance broke down, both were torn to shreds by their mutual enemy. That is all I know, but perhaps that might explain the rage of those such as Doomclaw."

"Somewhat," Pure said.

The night fell silent and soon Lifebreath began to sing. It was a slow, sad song and none had the heart to ask what it meant. But it soon sent them to sleep.

***

They woke sometime in the dark night, shuddering awake at Lifebreath's frantic roar.

Rayn swung around with his staff, trying to disentangle himself from his night cloak. The sky suddenly lit up with Pure's bright flames. In their brief and flickering lights, Rayn saw two foxes, convoluted and silent. They were full of the curse or the plague, depending on your point of view. They were trying to sneak up on the girls, curled up by the dragon's flank. As soon as the light struck their eyes, they leapt.

And were struck aside by a sweep of Lifebreath's tail. Instantly they stood up, prowling about, barking in the night.

"They are alerting their fellows!" Jayd explained.

Rayn lit up the area with the blue light of his staff.

Rhoc threw an axe and it severed a foreleg of one of the abominations, but it still stood there and looked set to leap again.

Rayn held out his staff, Jayd her swords, Rhoc his double bladed axe, and Pure held onto her fire.

And Lifebreath suddenly breathed over the top of them and right onto the foxes. Caught somewhat in her breath, Rayn felt suddenly salubrious, full of life and health. Like he could run a league with ease and still not stop.

The foxes, however, felt much different. They howled and fell to their sides. Their bodies twisted and bulged, pustules leaking fluids all through their hides. They twisted and cried, their flesh dissolving, leaving little but skin and bones in a matter of seconds.

"What was that?" Jayd asked.

"Get on, get on now!" Lifebreath ordered.

They scrambled on.

"What was that?" Jayd insisted.

"My life breath," the dragon replied. "Now hold tight!" She screamed, and a moment later they rose into the cool night air.

It took a moment for them to catch their breath and let the dragon explain. "My breath brings life, and those creatures are already dead. I re-life-ed their body's natural defenses and it kills them along with the curse. Though, to be truthful, one in every thousand will actually survive the process, most are dead in seconds."

"But how?!" Pure shouted. "How did they find us so soon? And we had the help of a dragon!"

"Indeed." Lifebreath agreed. "The plague is spreading much faster this time, even with the dragons hunting them. It has been many millennia since we took a stand against the plague. I can only assume many hundreds of beings are already infected and that these two were just two lucky scouts that have happened on us."

"But they will bring the others," Jayd said with fear.

"Yes, if it is indeed us that they seek." Lifebreath breathed heavily in the black night air.

But none spoke, for Rayn knew exactly who the plague was seeking to destroy.

Everyone.

Sea

6 The lonely dragon of Dead Man's Fingers

Thankfully dawn came early the next day, though they still hurried with all their strength. If the foxes had found them so quickly, the birds would find them even quicker. Rayn knew that most birds would die rather than be taken with the curse, but those that did succumb would not sleep and would have near immortal strength and stamina to hunt them.

They arrived at the great waters late morning of the next day.

Rayn had only ever heard tell of the great waters; none of his people had ever seen them before. Rhoc was almost drooling with fascination. The dragon flew along the border between the waters, called 'sea', and the land. As a battle that never ended, the waves crashed onto the stones so broken down as to be fine sand in some places but still mighty cliffs in others. Jayd pointed north and they rode that way a while, though it seemed like a few moments, the great dragon taking full advantage of what she called the updrafts between the sea and cliffs.

Soon great black rocks were visible, rising high above the waters like the fingers of a dead man clutching in vain for salvation from a cloud filled sky. And perhaps, in some way, they were; many times travelers must have perished on the sharp and unheeding stones.

And there, resting on the highest pinnacle was a night black dragon. His bearing was noble, his form lithe and athletic. His horns and claws were a polished ivory and the very edges of his wings ended in shadow. He looked away as though refusing to acknowledge their presence.

Lifebreath didn't rise high in the other dragon's skies, telling them it was important to show him politeness and respect for his domain. She instead pulled alongside the pillar where he sat, her wings beating furiously against the battering winds.

"This, young birdling, is where you get off."

"What?!" Jayd shouted.

"You must face your dragon alone, if indeed he really is yours – I certainly have never met him before. I imagine he's curious about seeing one with riders, unless he's already heard the news. Now get off, I'm getting tired!"

Jayd paused, cringing at the dragon's side, clinging to her scales, not daring to jump the remaining distance. Rayn did not envy her. He knew he could make the jump easily himself. She could too, if she dared, but it was a long way down and there were many sharp rocks.

"Find a way!" the dragon roared, impatient.

Jayd looked like she really wanted to jump, yet her face was pale.

Then Rayn realized something. She had never, never been anywhere without him, or without someone. To face a dragon alone, to be the first to win a dragon and ride it? How would she -

"Just jump already!" Lifebreath screamed, losing height.

Jayd turned white with fright and held on even harder.

Then Rhoc reached over to her, grabbed her by the scruff of her shirt and seat of her leggings, and threw her right off. She squealed, turned mid-air and landed first on her feet and then on her butt.

"Rhoc, you monster," she screamed.

"Divinity's light be with you," Rayn shouted a blessing at her.

"You can do this," Pure shouted.

"Aaaargh," Rhoc said in encouragement.

"Finally!" Lifebreath breathed with rude impatience. "Hurry up, birdling. You must face him; alone."

***

"Hurry up, birdling! You must face him; alone!" The horrible dragon said, teasing her again.

Jayd continued to sit down in a huff while the others fled to safety, high above the cold sea spray, far away from the sharp sea rocks.

What am I doing? Jayd wondered to herself.

She put her face in her hands. She didn't want to be here. It was hard enough to ride a dragon in the black of night with nothing but your bossy half-brother's glowing stick for light, and a living cauldron that hated you personally for warmth.

And now she was expected to walk up and meet a dragon alone?

What IDIOT made up that rule?

With her face in her hands she saw her mother's features, and wondered how she was doing. Did she miss her? They'd never been close. In fact, her mother, Rayn's stepmother, had always seemed to act as though Jayd was some kind of accident that wasn't supposed to happen. But she had happened, and even though she knew her mother loved her, she didn't have much time for her either. Never treated Jayd like she would amount to much. She talked so much about marrying her away one day that Jayd couldn't help but feel she was counting the days until she received a dowry for her. There wasn't much to live up to with a mother like that.

Rayn had even less to do with his stepmother but that seemed to suit them both quite well, and Jayd supposed neither of them had ever thought about it.

What Rayn obviously was thinking about was his new non-girlfriend, the white maiden. The hottest girl in the whole country that he alternately treated like a queen before whom he was a wilting fool, and a willful child for whom he didn't want to be responsible.

But, of course, he would have no idea.

No idea, either, of how much she herself admired and, yes, *liked* him. He was her first crush and though she *knew* it was silly to like your half step brother in that way, it certainly wasn't illegal to marry one, among her own people. But she kept all that in her heart, sure that one day she'd outgrow that and move on. He was bossy and self-absorbed, loved to show off and be the good little wiseman everyone admired. But she knew he was just as ambitious as any man, he just showed it differently.

She sighed.

They'd all be dead in three weeks if she didn't start moving up this cliff.

She had no trouble finding the best way. None at all. Now that the Matron had pointed out her gift, she knew exactly what to do. She wanted to find the safest, fastest way up and knew just which way to go. She walked to the back of the grotto and climbed through a hole in the wall. Clutching desperately to the wet, crumbly rocks she climbed along the wall. She refused to look down at the crashing waves. They made her dizzy and she knew falling would kill her.

After she had rounded the wall, she was relieved to see a short, level path of moss, the kind of place that a bird might roost in the spring. In spite of what the annoying dragon had said - Jayd liked birds. She would watch them often and envy their freedom. She'd always wondered what it was like to fly and was sad to find out it was pretty awful on Lifebreath.

So why was she trying to find a dragon of her own?

Oh yeah, save the world and all that, she thought.

Jayd sighed. She continued to make her way up in much the same manner. At times walking along what might have been paths, other times clinging with all her strength to the rock face. Some places were quite tricky and without her gift she would have needed help to make the climb. But she was a guide: a 'navigator.' She could find anything, anywhere!

But finding the pinnacle of the rock took far *too little* time.

As soon as she'd poked her head up over the top and spied the back of the dragon looking out towards the sea, she ducked back down again.

Dragons didn't like people. Dragons ate people, or so the legends told.

But there was a world to save.

But how could *she* save the world? She'd seen what the curse had done to Hak and the wolves and the falcons. It was only a matter of time before it came for them all. Perhaps it was already within them and it was only a matter of time?

In spite of her thoughts and because no one was watching, she curled into a ball and allowed the silent tears to run down her face. *Why does it have to be me?* She wondered.

Suddenly she heard a dragon give a snort of derision above her. She almost fell off the precipice right there and then – that would serve them all right. She turned quickly and looked up at the beast. It was black, with a twisted mouth that looked ready to turn into a grin at any moment, two teeth sticking oddly out of the left side. He was smooth, dark, and muscled, like a well-trained warrior. She felt a connection right away.

But he did not look impressed.

Again he snorted and began to walk away.

"Hey!" Jayd shouted. "Hey! Don't walk away!"

But the dragon continued to walk.

Jayd got up and ran after it. "Get back here, Darkwing!" She shouted.

Oh, how did I know his name? She wondered.

Suddenly the belligerent animal spread its wings and allowed the sea breeze to lift it high above the rocks. In a moment, it had flown clear away off the precipice and onto the second most tall Fingers of the Dead.

"You stupid, selfish dragon," she shouted into the wind. "Get back here, get back here now!"

Immediately she thought about the fastest, safest way to get over there and saw in her mind a deep green line that involved going down the precipice the way she came, allowing herself to be swept out to sea and then back again to coil around the other precipice.

Stupid, stupid dragon!

There had to be a better way.

Suddenly a glint of light caught her eye and she turned to see a strange contraption lying on the ground, packed down among other glitters between the rocks that might have been part of this dragon's hoard. It looked like a wide, jeweled bracelet, made of bronze and decorated with many ornate symbols, some of which she recognized as protection from her own people. In the center lay a beautiful green stone, in the appearance of emerald, a carving underneath it in the shape of a winged boot.

And since it was just the sort of thing she'd do, she put it on.

"Now wh-" she wondered.

Suddenly the bracelet transformed, and in a moment each of her arms was covered with a translucent bronze wing. From her back flowed a flared tail, like a dragon's. It was a Man-wing!

"Oh this is-" she was going to say 'cool' or 'interesting', but the words were lost as she found herself swept by the winds and thrown screaming into the air. The word that actually came out might have been 'stupid', but it was difficult to tell.

Jayd screamed again and again. She tried to bend over to grab a hold of the rocks but that only made matters worse; the wings seemed to grab hold of the air instead and lifted her high above the safety of the precipice.

This was her worst nightmare – realized.

Jayd wailed with something between terror and excitement as she hit some kind of updraft that lifted her even higher. It very soon lost its interest in carrying her up and as her stomach seemed to lift into her mouth, she hovered high in the air like an angel, lost between heaven and death.

So she screamed again.

Then she fell.

The sea seemed so far away, far enough away as to make waiting for death painfully long. Jayd screamed and screamed until she had to take a breath, and that made her think – if she was going to die, why not die fighting?

Frantically she flapped against the rushing winds, hopelessly tumbling in the turbulence. It was clear that there was nothing she could do and in the silence, she prepared to die.

Looking up at the skypearl clouds, she found a moment of peace before oblivion, a moment strangely broken by a single black gull floating peacefully in the winds. She wondered what it would be like to be that gull, free and at peace with the air. Then the gull dived towards her.

Like a rock.

A rock that was growing very quickly. Its size was *enormous*.

She realized with a muted start that it was actually the black dragon, racing down towards her. Without fear, she saw it look at her but it did not try to save her. Instead, in the silence of the wind, Jayd watched it as it pulled along beside her and spread its wings strong and wide, level and true. It caught the invisible wind and was lifted safely back into the air.

It was showing her how to survive.

There was still a chance!

She turned; the crashing waves were so close now. But she hardly noticed them. Copying the dragon perfectly she spread her copper wings…

… and flew.

She was too surprised to cry out and a moment later the dragon pulled down alongside her again. It flew a little ahead, showing her how to move its tail to catch the breeze and steer. She followed its lead as it led her along the sharp stones of Dead Man's Fingers with ease.

She lived. She let out a squeal of triumph and relief, and was amazed to hear the dragon echo her cry. She followed it as it flew right towards the cliff that marked the mainland and it slowed down its speed by flying upwards, landing a moment later on the cliff top with ease.

Jayd couldn't mimic such skill, but set down on land again in front of it safely. Her wings folded back into the bracelet in an instant. She was breathing heavily but had never felt so alive.

She had survived.

She had flown.

She looked at the dragon. He seemed … shy yet also driven by curiosity. For a breath they just stood there, looking at each other.

"Hi," she said.

The dragon bowed his head. "Greetings, rider, I *am* Darkwing. You survived..."

"Yes, well, first time flying, what did you expect?" she joked.

He smiled, apparently he shared her sense of humor. "I didn't think you would, you seemed so afraid."

"Well, saving the world takes courage," she replied.

"Courage? I don't think there is courage, only faith. I could not let you ride me without a test."

"Do you dragons always test people?" she asked.

"We must, we are driven to. Besides, too many that might claim to be my rider are either liars or fools. But now the test has brought you wisdom. Do you know what your trial is?"

"Flying?" She asked.

He smiled again. "Not flying."

"Being ready to accept death then," she offered.

"Actually, you seemed quite prepared for that as well. No, I sense your trial is having faith in yourself. You cowered when we first met; you almost didn't make it up here in the first place. You were going to leave me on the far precipice once I left you until an accident drove us together again. If I had to guess, I would say you lack faith – that you've always lived in other people's shadows, that you doubt your personal ability to fulfil your destiny. That you're always waiting for others to make things happen for you. That is what I think."

She pondered those words, and for some reason they weren't the least bit offensive. They were just … helpful.

"And what of you? Do you lack faith?" She asked.

"No, it is my strength. Riders and dragons often share complementary qualities. What you lack in faith I make up for. I have … other faults," he sighed and looking away.

Somehow Jayd knew this dragon well enough that she could already tell what he was feeling. He was *lonely*. Hiding all the way out here in an inhospitable and damp climate didn't seem like a very dragon thing to do. Even in their banishment, Lifebreath had told them, the dragons tended to hide in view of a human settlement. So why was he all the way out here? Didn't he know how to make friends?

Yet being social was one of the things Jayd knew she was really good at. Even public speaking didn't scare her, though she knew of others who would rather die. She reached out and held the dragon by the jaw. She felt the enormous power rippling underneath the stone hard scales.

"Don't worry, you won't be alone anymore," she said, feeling such pity and affection for the powerful, lonely beast.

It bowed its head to her and without knowing why, she reached out and patted it on the forehead. In that moment there was an enormous crack, like the world splitting in two. The wind curled around their ankles as a sudden unbreakable bond was formed between them.

They had become dragon and rider.

The first in four thousand years.

7 Darkwing, Lord of the Night and wielder of Black flame.

Dr Joseph Ireland

On dark wings

Rayn was pacing with worry, so when Jayd finally returned, riding up on the back of a large, thin black dragon, he almost died. Yet there was such a huge difference about her. She seemed confident, utterly unafraid, almost arrogant. She was smiling her twisted smile brightly. She was also wearing a strange jeweled bracelet and he wondered where she might have stolen that from.

Lifebreath immediately stood and bowed. "Rider and dragon, I greet you as one. This is good news. I sense many changes in you, young rider. And Darkwing, though I know little of you I sense you have changed much as well."

"Thank you," they both said at the same time. Jayd continued, as though speaking for them both, "But we cannot tarry for compliments. The world needs saving, remember?"

"Indeed, we must-" Lifebreath began.

Suddenly there was a loud thudding sound and the curl of red and angry smoke, and out of the mist popped a dark red dragon, the one they'd first seen at the great council not two days ago.

"Stormclouds!" Lifebreath called out. "What news?"

Stormclouds stayed aloft, hovering slowly with his four wings. When he spoke his voice was calloused and dark, like an old man with who'd spent too many years shouting. "I have searched all day up and

down this coast for you. Here, I bring a gift unveiled at Vipertail's lair."
To the ground he threw a large, leather package.

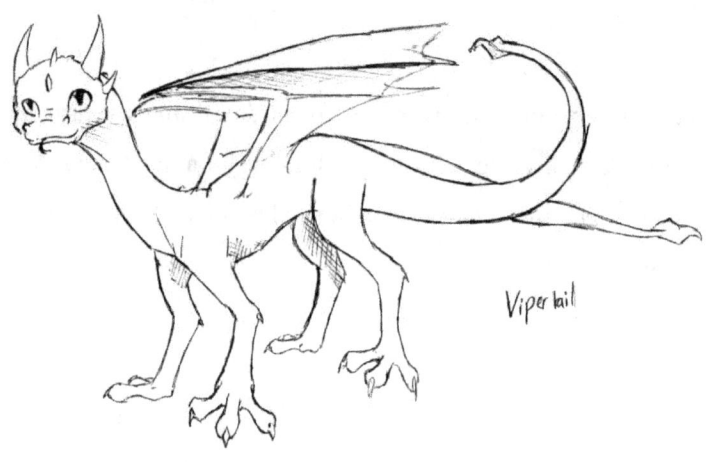

8 Vipertail, keeper of antiquities

"What is it?" Darkwing asked.

"A saddle?" Jayd guessed.

Lifebreath gasped in hope. "A saddle! As worn by the noble dragon riders of legend?"

"The same," Stormclouds replied, his voice husky and unpleasant. "Located just recently. We thought you could use it, and after the Matron ordered the treasures be found, it seemed appropriate."

Rayn walked up to the bundle of leather and steel. There were hooks, straps and a flat leather saddle. All were of excellent make, well-worn but in astonishingly good repair.

Dr Joseph Ireland

"It is said," Lifebreath began, whispering in Rayn's ear as though sharing a secret, "that the humans had mastered time, thought and matter so that the dragon rider's equipment would not wear – very much like your staff there young wiseman. Useful, no? So tell me, can you fit the saddle? Who should be the first?"

"I will," Jayd and Darkwing spoke at once. She laughed, and he lowered his head so that she could pat it.

They were pretty close already.

It took almost an hour and Darkwing seemed unwilling to allow any near him but Jayd, who he did not let out of his sight. But with some comforting words from Jayd, the great black dragon allowed Pure to assist in fitting the strange dragon saddle as best they could. Horses usually needed a blanket under the saddle but the strange device seemed to have all the features built in.

"It seems ironic, my rider," Darkwing humbly observed, "that a saddle such as this will never let you fall, and you have only just learnt to fly."

She smiled. "Look, it has this latch here, I can set myself free whenever I want. It seems the saddle can somehow detect when I am sitting on it and it tightens the belt immediately. I wonder how it does that? You don't suppose there is any demonry..." she asked innocently, looking over at Rayn.

"I sense no evil about it," Rayn confidently proclaimed, as he already had checked. "Yet no real wards, runes or command of the Divine either. Perhaps it is simply, as Pure says, just a complex tool of some kind."

"Yes, that is all." Pure smiled. "I could show you how it worked if I studied it, I am sure. But I was only four when I lost my people and I never really learnt much of such tools."

Rhoc was eyeing the self-tightening belt with suspicion.

"Even so," Rayn said, "I don't know how we will convince my people that there is no demonry involved."

"Show them this!" Darkwing roared, and with a squeal from Jayd, lifted his head high into the air, breathing out tendrils of pure darkness that thundered like flame. "I AM DARKWING!" He roared. "Ridden by Jayd of the Celtwyld, I am a protector of men, of nature, and a servant of the Divine! Who will challenge *me* and say if I am possessed of any demonry!"

Rayn found himself gasping in fear. An angry dragon was a terrifying thing and no one could answer.

"Easy, boy." Jayd grinned.

"Forgive me, my rider," he said wryly, "your presence gives me confidence I have never known."

"As does yours," she said and hugged him tight.

***

So, Jayd had a dragon. If it were possible, that left only himself, Pure and Rhoc to find a dragon.

They spent the night in peace, Darkwing bidding his old haunt goodbye before the first light sang across the ever clouded skies of Pearl. He told them his speed was vastly increased in the darkness.

Pure had them up early. "All right then, navigator, where to next?"

"I don't know, that's Rayn's job, remember?" she said with sarcasm, resting her body on the muscled arm of her dragon.

Pure looked at her, annoyed, then turned to Rayn, waiting for him to reply.

"That's right," he remembered, "I say where and she says how."

He knelt to pray, expecting to be in prayer a whole hour. Yet the answer came soon and strong, there must have been a great need to rush.

"Rhoc."

As soon as he told them, Jayd pointed. "A desert, westward. Little grows, and the stones there are as tall as a man and round."

"I know not this place," Lifebreath said, and Darkwing nodded. "But since it is there we must go, let us get a head start!"

Just as they were about to take wing, Pure sitting on the back of Jayd's saddle, the boys still clinging to Lifebreath's back, Stormclouds returned. Again, he refused to land.

"I bring dire tidings," he spoke in his coarse voice.

"Speak," Lifebreath spoke, still apparently the one truly in charge of their expedition.

"Dothmere and Fireyes have fallen to the plague."

They all gasped, except the dragons, who seemed to seethe with rage. Rayn felt Lifebreath's body become dangerously hot.

"How?!" She demanded, watching him as he slowly circled overhead.

"It seems the plague has grown wiser this time. They sent a horde of afflicted beings, men included, to a small human town. Dothmere and

Fireyes were sent to assist. However, someone had placed infected men's bones, sharpened into spikes, inside some of the plagued sheep. When they bit down on them the bones pierced the inside of their mouths. They would have been taken by the plague in a day but we have saved them that horror ..."

Lifebreath gasped. "You *killed* them?"

"In *mercy*," Stormclouds growled. "Had you been with us it might have been a different story, your... gift... is sorely missed."

She prowled the ground. Rayn couldn't guess what she was thinking.

"Bring forth a great vessel of water," she said, "and I will fill it with my blessing. If any, man or beast, are touched by the plague it will help them. At least it will give them a fighting chance."

Stormclouds nodded without a word, and disappeared.

"There was a time," Lifebreath said sadly, "it is said, that the wisemen had the faith and prayers sufficient to heal the plague. I don't suppose, young man, that you know any of the old prayers?"

Rayn knew many, many prayers: For helping to start fires, for naming children, for mending a sprained wrist or a gash given by a dog. But he had no prayers for this new plague, just like he had none for broken bones. Perhaps... there was a chance, an ancient ritual. But it required special circumstances and surely the other wisemen were attempting it even as they spoke. Rayn wondered if humanity had ever had such prayers, for none spoke of them as having had a more golden age than the current one. Had they really built boats that could fly?

Deeds that could earn them the trust and respect of a being as powerful as a dragon? Prayers that could stay a plague?

And if so, why had Divinity allowed such to be forgotten?

He shook his head.

In the next moment Stormclouds reappeared, carrying two great barrels with water. He set them on the ground yet refused to touch it himself.

Drawing in great breaths, the deep green dragon, Lifebreath, exhaled on one of the barrels. They seemed to grow stronger in her presence, the wood darkening, unseen mosses on the barrels springing to life. As her breath swirled in the air, Rayn caught a sense of it and it filled him again with health. Yet in his body he knew she could not cure the plague, only strengthen others against it. Immediately he added his own water containers to the last barrel, as did the others. She filled them with her life breath without question.

"You know, Stormclouds," Pure said, her voice soft and respectful, "our journey would be much hastened if we had you to bring us along."

"No," he said, his voice harsh. "I have no rider. I need no rider!" And snatching up the barrels with such haste it scattered their water containers, he was gone.

"He is not impressed with us," Rayn assumed.

"Nor the Matron's call to arms," Lifebreath whispered.

The cave of wonders

Jayd was in trouble again.

A day later, heading towards the desert, Rayn had been stretching his legs while the dragons slept peacefully, and naturally Jayd had taken that as an opportunity to go wander off again in search of the 'most interesting thing nearby'.

He'd told her to stay near. He'd told her to stay safe. And now he found her, standing completely alone, on a small hill covered entirely in fallen branches and moss covered foliage…

… a pair of black forest tigers slowly sneaking up behind her.

"Jayd!" Rayn shouted.

She whirled around, less than a moment from death. The first leapt at her and she had her swords out only just in time, gashing one across the teeth. The other one tried to surround her but Rayn pushed it away with his staff.

They stood back to back, waiting for them to attack on the unsteady ground.

"What in Divinity's name are you doing out here alone?!" he shouted.

"No harm done," she replied in a quivering voice.

The small, black tigers growled, circling them as though trying to find a break in their defenses. Rayn reached inside to find a way to drive them away, and he found it.

Their fear.

His staff glowed as he worked a small miracle, pushing fear into their hearts. It was the same way he'd seen his mentor drive away an angry bear one evening, so long ago it could have been another life.

He watched as their growls turned to yowls of fear, their ears flattening, their eyes widened.

And as one, they ran.

Rayn sighed with relief.

"Well that was easy," Jayd grinned.

Then he felt angry again. "Jayd! You could have died! We have a whole world to save here, you can't just go wondering off when I tell you not to!"

9 Arguing, again.

"You don't tell me where I can go," she told him, hand on her hip as she sheathed a sword.

But his rage did not subside, "There are more important things here, Jayd! Why don't you *ever* listen to me!"

"I don't *have* to listen to you!" she shouted, poking him in the chest. "Just because you're a man, doesn't mean you make all the decisions for *me*."

"I'm not trying to make all the decisions for you!" he protested.

"You're always trying to make the decisions for me. It's, 'Jayd do this,' and, 'Jayd do that.'"

He was so mad that he couldn't speak.

Then she noticed he was standing on one of her swords and without thinking she just shoved him in the chest. "Move," she told him.

He shoved her back.

Her mouth opened in surprise, then her eyes flared with anger. "Don't touch me!" She shouted and leaping forwards, shoved him back in the chest with all her power.

He was immediately stunned at the force of the blow and a blind rage gathered inside him.

"Right," he said, throwing aside his staff. *So she wanted a fight, let it be.*

He pulled up his cuffs and she curled her hands in fists.

Then the ground collapsed underneath him.

Branches snapped and he realized he was falling. With a look of pure panic, Jayd reached out to grab him and, to his chagrin, Rayn clutched on for his life. He dragged her with him and they fell into the hole where the ground had opened up.

Rayn roared in fright, the world seeming to spin as he fell. Thick roots and choking dirt cut against him as darkness quickly gathered. He heard Jayd screaming in fear. A moment later all the wind was knocked out of him as he hit the ground painfully on his side.

"Rayn!" Jayd squealed in desperation. "Rayn, oh, Rayn. I'm so sorry!"

He tried to say something but his lungs weren't working. The sky looked so far above. He saw Jayd in the dim shaft of light that filtered down from the roof.

She buried her face in her hands. "We brought that on ourselves..." Then she whispered, her voice almost too soft to hear, "Oh, please, Divine - don't let those be the last words he ever hears from me."

Gasping for breath, he banged his fist on the ground to get her attention. She gasped then cried out with relief and scurried to him on hands and knees, wincing as though her ankle had borne the worst of her fall.

"Oh, thank you," she said relieved, holding him.

He patted her hand gratefully.

The darkness seemed to grow around them. They had fallen a very long way.

"Just breathe," she told him.

It made him laugh, as best he could. Just breathing was all he was trying to do right now.

Then she started laughing too.

Suddenly the argument of only a few moments ago seemed so very foolish. Like children quarrelling over a toy, they had been worrying about something neither of them could really own – another person's choices.

Forgetting there were much more important things.

A moment later there was a shout from above.

Rayn looked up and saw the outline of Rhoc.

"Hey!" Rayn shouted, much less than he wanted to say, but all he could manage right now.

Jayd limped up, struggling into the light. She waved and he shouted back. Placing his hands out in front of him in a 'stay there' kind of gesture, he turned and ran away.

"Well, I guess we wait it out," she said, turning to face him with a limp.

Then Jayd began searching around.

"What are you doing?" he asked.

"Trying to get some light. Here, this should burn, do you have the flint?"

"Yes, right here," Rayn replied, pulling it from his pack, grateful to see it was not too badly damaged in the fall. He turned the handle which spun the rounded flint against the hardened stone. Whatever Jayd had rustled up burnt easily and soon they could take a look around.

"What is this place?" Jayd asked.

They looked around. He saw they had landed on some debris, probably fallen branches and mold. It was a cold, damp place. A natural cavern of some sort.

The way out was at least thirty paces above. Tree roots and crumbling earthen walls lined the exit. Unless someone threw down a rope or a very long vine, it would be impossible to climb out, especially with Jayd's ankle.

"Hey," she said, "I see… a light."

"Oh no, don't you go exploring again, you hear me?"

She turned to look at him, hand on one hip, belligerence on her face.

"I *hear* you," she told him and turning, began to limp away.

Rayn looked up, begging Rhoc to return. But he didn't. Surely they would hear him calling if he returned with Lifebreath.

But he couldn't leave Jayd alone to wander in a cavern.

With all his heart he wished he'd never set his staff aside to 'teach his sister a lesson.'

But he couldn't have her wandering into the darkness alone.

He stumbled along on the uneven ground to catch up to her, torch waving aside the thin fibers that cluttered their path. He tried not to think of them as spider webs but there was little else they could be, except perhaps a strange effect of the fungus. He held on to that latter thought with intense devotion.

After a dozen paces and with his eyes adjusted to the dimness, he began to make out a faint light in the distance. The cavern curved ahead and from there, a light.

"Hold the torch down," he told her.

She did so. There was indeed, a light of some sort.

She held his arm tightly and pressed on. He knew he had only one weapon now, plus the little knife. He hoped she had her two blades ready and noticed her hands close to her hips.

It would have to do.

The tunnel grew in brightness until they found themselves squinting in mottled, many colored light. Images seemed to shift in the silence of the cavern as though speaking in light. He didn't know what to think.

He paused and Jayd steadied herself on his arm. Then, pulling his arm, she urged him on.

Bracing himself, he stepped with her into the blinding lights of the cavern beyond.

The story

The cavern of lights was a miracle to behold. Scores of giant crystals, similar to the ones at the Matron's cavern, glowed with Divine lights. There was every color of the spectrum and the lights reflected against the wall.

"Look," Jayd noted, holding out her hand, "no shadows."

Rayn raised his hand to confirm and indeed, they cast no shadows on the far walls. It was as if the light passed right through them.

"Perhaps there are too many lights to make a shadow?" Jayd said, seeming hopeful.

But Rayn knew it was more than that.

"What is this place?" she said in wonder, stepping forwards.

He didn't even bother telling her to leave it all alone. She would know he was thinking it.

She turned to face him, smiling with wonder at the amazing lights. Then the smile faded from her face as she looked behind him.

Rayn whirled around, expecting to see a demon from the deepest pits. Instead, he found only a shadow. Or was it? It was moving, forming dozens of shapes in the glowing light. There were… men… yes, it was clear now. Men and dragons.

Jayd moved to join him, transfixed by the images. In the light that made her shadow it was clear now that some kind of message was being conveyed.

"It's a story," he realized.

Jayd and he continued to watch the story unfold as they walked around the chamber. By the miracles of the crystals they found the entire narrative being told within their hearts, intricate details of the story appearing inside them as though spoken by a wiseman, though they heard no word.

They understood and felt: Long ago, a union was forged between men and dragons. Though at first wary, each learnt to trust the other in time. Together, men and dragons were able to do far more than the other had ever imagined alone. By dragons, men learnt how to travel between the stars with ease. By men, dragons found an answer to the loneliness in their souls. Together they built the greatest empire either had ever known, founded on justice, opportunity and freedom. Together they lived in peace.

And together they warred. Small, insidious shadows of black that lived between the spaces, primal demons as Rayn and Jayd knew them. The dragons and men fought them back. Then, centuries later, massive beasts, the size of large cities, flew between worlds on lines that looked like golden threads. They would swallow dragons whole and could lay waste to great swathes of the cities of men. Great battles were fought to drive the beasts away and while many dragons died, the alliance between men and dragons prevailed.

Dr Joseph Ireland

But their battles were not done. Rumors became horrors and terrible hunters in the shapes of beasts tormented the peace of men and dragons. It seemed little could be done but the knowledge of men and the might of dragons prevailed when they forged new weapons. The hunters were vanquished in a mighty war, set on a desolate landscape on a faraway world.

Then the union of men and dragons turned their attention to a little orb, set like a pearl in a glistening backdrop, like a sheet of satin strewn with glittering grains of sand. He felt his heart reach out towards this image and knew instinctively it was a symbol of his world. A council was held by the ancestors of the dragons and humans who walk the land today. Together, with the wisdom of dragons, they built great boats that could ride above the sky. Together they came to a giant pearl of white and together they began to bring life to its surface. They brought plants and animals and something that breathed new life into the air.

The Pearl grew and grew, filling with life and civilization.

Then the story grew dark. A new threat filled the air above Pearl. Animals, men and dragons were falling victim to a new threat to which none could defend themselves. It was *the Perish*. It turned men into monsters and drove them insane.

Cities fell from the sky, dragons died of sorrow, and the royal houses of men fell, every one. Men lay dead in the streets only to rise again as mindless minions of the curse. Darkness gathered around the beautiful Pearl and in a moment, it seemed utterly alone in the universe.

Rayn felt the depth of the suffering tearing at his heart and for a moment he honestly believed he could watch no longer.

But then a small spark of hope kindled in his heart, echoed in the faint lights that glistened on the walls. A few survived, perhaps twice a hundred. Families, children, men. They had lost their dragons, they had lost their homes.

They had fled to this cavern, far from where they had once lived.

Even here, they knew, the curse would one day find them. So they made a decision. They took upon themselves a change. A permanent one. One that would mean their deaths, but through it, their stories could live on forever.

Living as memories in a cave made of wonderful lights.

It touched his heart, knowing these his ancestors who had lived four thousand years ago. They had faith and held on to that faith that one day, perhaps long after the ages of men and dragons had fallen from the worlds, someone would be around to hear the story. That, someone, somewhere, would know what lives they had lived.

Jayd gasped.

He turned and saw her looking at the crystals.

"I see them now," she whispered. "I see them dancing."

Rayn turned, wondering what she meant. Till he then saw them too. The people, his ancestors, had *become* the crystals. The light seemed to reflect the peaceful acceptance of their fate, their acceptance of their empire's fall. But they were not sad. They were happy. He saw them now too. Crystals like an old couple, holding hands, children playing with toys, a woman dancing.

In a sense... they lived.

Their stories lived on, though they had passed away. As a miracle beyond imagining. And he saw them too, a hundred million stories hiding in the shadows on the wall. All one had to do was to ask and to listen. And they would live a story too, any one taken from a twice hundred lives, maybe more.

Jayd sank to her knees, "They *are* dancing."

He joined her, watching as the stories waited to be played out once more along the walls. "They are at peace."

She nodded, tears falling from her eyes. "So… that's how it all started. Not like the old stories, is it? I like this version better."

Rayn thought how the story he had just heard differed from the stories the wisemen learnt about their past. They were not so different, he thought. Not in heart, not in meaning. They had come from far away. Many had sacrificed much so that he and his sister could be here today. The stories were not really that much different.

"I want to come back, often," Jayd told him.

He had to agree.

"Did you see how we didn't have to hear?" she told him. "We only had to listen. Do you understand?"

He did.

"I wish you would listen to me," she told him gently.

He wondered a moment what she meant, until he realized she was reminding him of the argument that had got them into this place. Then he wondered why she was accusing him of not listening to her, hadn't it been the other way around?

"I *do* listen to you," he countered.

"But you don't, you don't listen to me," she said. "You only hear what you want to. I have many important things to say and I don't think you realize that yet. And you think I never listen to you but I do, Rayn. I may have been raised in your father's home, but that does not make me your property."

"You... you're still my responsibility. Oh Jayd, can't you see I care for you, I'm not trying to take away your freedom. I don't think anyone can do that. I just... need you to listen to me."

She paused. "I do listen to you, Rayn. I listen to every word you say. Even the nasty, stinging, back stabbing words you use when you complain about me to my mother. I listen to everything. But that doesn't mean I'm going to do what you say."

He stopped and was lost in thought for a moment. He realized that he had assumed if she was listening, his thoughts made such sense that anyone would just do them. Now he realized she might have heard it all and still not wanted to do what he thought was the right thing to do. He sat back, and was lost in thought.

"Well, thank you Jayd. I... didn't know. I am glad you listen."

She unfolded her arms. "And I'm glad you talk, sometimes. You're not all bad, you know. Sometimes you say some pretty sensible things and I guess... I guess I am just too proud. I do the exact opposite because I don't want to look like the little girl who is too easy to push around. I'm... foolish like that, I suppose."

He put his arm around her. "Not as foolish as I am."

Dr Joseph Ireland

She squirmed, yet stayed. Together they watched the magic lights dancing on the roof an hour more, until they began to hear Rhoc's worried cry from down the corridor.

But there wasn't time to show him the cavern yet.

The dragons were rested and it was time to flee, lest death find them as well.

Night of miracles

The journey to the far desert took two days. As ice slowly formed on his nose and eyelashes, Rayn found himself desperately wishing for some famous weather resistant dragon rider armor but none presented itself. The gear from the town near the Matron's mountain was helpful, but not enough. They took turns with Pure's bracelet that kept the air around one of them, as it helped them stay just a little warmer without the wind always striking against them. Jayd was best at it, but it was still only a temporary solution.

It was as they rode the second day that Lifebreath presented Rayn with an interesting question. "I notice, young wiseman, that your companion there seems unable to hear."

"Yes," Rayn shouted against the wind. She was getting stronger each day and they were flying more often now, "since birth."

"Intriguing," the dragon said. "Why do you not use your faith to heal him? If he is only deaf."

Rayn was struck. He had never thought of that. In all his life the wisemen had told him that one was to accept their lot in life, that deafness was given as punishment for the parents' sins. Rayn had never even thought of healing Rhoc's deafness one day, let alone *asking* if it were desirable, or even possible.

He thought about it for the rest of the day, watching with fascination as Jayd again and again leapt off her dragon in free fall. The first time Pure screamed, only to see Jayd open out a set of dragon wings and tail of her own, flying recklessly around the sky. Her dragon responded to her adventurousness with glee, terrifying the poor white maiden with antics of his own to match his rider. By the time they set down, Pure gave him a look which so clearly said, *Get me away from this crazy pair!"*

They set down near a deserted place, towards the edge of a desert. The air was so dry it split Rayn's lips and made them bleed often. It was not a place he was looking forward to going. The ground was dusty red, covered with termite mounds and small, twisted trees.

They lit a fire and sat around it telling stories. None were more eager to the task than Jayd, and her dragon seemed perfectly caught up in everything she had to say. Lifebreath also spoke great stories. One story stood out to Rayn forever, for it was the last he ever heard from her:

"In the time before men walked this land, even before the land before this one, dragons lived in the halls of the Giants. It is said that we were their pets, made by them from fire and clay. We lived, we learnt, we loved them. We do not know why but as the ages continued the numbers of the Giants steadily fell. Then came the time when the last of the Giants' children were born. Within a scant thousand years, the dragons were left alone. Abandoned by our creators we attempted to forge a world of peace but division and war held us back for millennia."

"Then, as it is said, by happy accident we found the humans. They were small, weak and physically frail. Yet their minds were great, almost infinite. Instead of looking within for power, they looked without. Instead of developing lungs that could breathe water, or skin that could survive the unshielded light of a sun, they developed external means; amazing machines that they used to explore the worlds. They were to us very curious creatures indeed."

"In them we found kindred spirits, though they were very small. Kindred souls born on another world. Together a quick alliance was formed, and it was soon found that men and dragons could forge an unbreakable bond that would transcend life and meaning. Within that bond, both humanity and dragonkin took to the stars, fought back all chaos and won the light of the greatest empire either had ever known. That is the true story of our shared heritage. It was told to me in the egg and was once told to men within the womb. It sad that you have forgotten this," she concluded.

"I remember the story," Pure said, eyes shining with tears in the firelight, "and I will live to see the sky filled with the alliance of dragons and men once more."

"I hope so," Lifebreath whispered.

That was an amazing story. So amazing yet it saddened Rayn that Rhoc couldn't hear any of it, as he sat in his own thoughts, brushing mud from his boots.

That was when Rayn decided something had to be done and in that moment a prayer sprang to his mind, unusually, as a poem:

"Anvil, hammer, stirrup, drum,
Let the damage be undone,
Let silence leave and music shine,
A purer praise to light Divine."

Rayn said the prayer in his mind, holding out the staff while it glowed a gentle blue, his heart filling with compassion for his friend.

Rhoc looked up, not seeming to understand, and smiled.

Then in the darkness Lifebreath began to sing again, humming to herself in a tuneless melody.

For a moment the sky filled with respectful silence as the night listened to her.

Then Rhoc roared in fright and nearly leapt out of his skin. He was banging his ears, roaring in fright and wonder.

Lifebreath stopped humming.

Jayd ran up to him, holding his hands down from beating himself. "Calm down Rhoc, what is it? What is it?"

He wailed in confusion.

Rayn could only guess what was happening and wished he'd thought of asking his friend first. Or at least giving him some warning.

He lit the staff and as Rhoc watched, walked up to him calmly. He stood so the boy could see him in its light.

"Rhoc," he said.

The boy cried out in wonder and fear, banging his ears.

"Don't worry, it's all right. I just learnt how to heal your ears Rhoc. You're not under your parents' curse any more. You can hear. You can hear because the Divine made it so, not me. I am Rayn. Rayn."

"R ... R ..." Rhoc stuttered in confusion. Then he laughed, a healthy rigorous laugh that Rayn knew well.

Then he roared in triumph.

Throwing his arms around Rayn he almost crushed the life out of him, he was so strong! He kept on groaning and singing and shouting for almost an hour in the darkness. He listened to Jayd speak and laughed. He listened to Pure speak and seemed most unimpressed. He listened to Rayn again and hit the ground as if to say, 'I knew you sounded like that!'

And as twilight turned to dark, Rhoc listened to Lifebreath sing. By the time the night was late and Rayn could hold his weary eyes open no longer, Rhoc was still listening to the night time and probably didn't sleep at all. Rayn had never noticed how noisy the night was. He fell to sleep, grateful for a wiseman's staff and careful to write the new prayer down immediately. This was a night of miracles. This was a good night.

The clay

10 Lifebreath

"Dragons, you know, were first made from clay," Lifebreath told Rayn as they set down at Jayd's command some time near lunch the next day. "Clay like this, rich and brown."

They were in a deep trench hidden well within the dusty desert, three days out into the warm land. Sparse, prickly brown bushes grew, as well as tall, thick cactus. So finding a deep ravine with bright green vegetation and running water made Rayn all the more grateful for his sister's talent. The dragons drank deeply from the waters while the humans prepared to search out berries they knew.

"What was that?" Jayd suddenly asked.

Rayn looked around. "What?" he asked.

"What?" Rhoc smiled. His voice was still nasal and droning, as it had been before his hearing had been born. He'd spent the whole morning talking gibberish to himself while they rode through the sky. It had driven Rayn to distraction.

"Up in the sky, I thought I saw Stormclouds," Jayd said, sounding hopeful.

But something about that name made Rayn feel very, very nervous. He did not know why, and didn't know if it was Divinity speaking to him or just his own worried mind playing tricks. They were hunting dragons and fleeing the plague; this was not a good environment for inspiration.

Suddenly Jayd stopped.

"She's here," she said.

"Now what?" Rayn asked.

"Whaaaaaat!" Rhoc offered, smiling and trying to be helpful. Rayn shushed him aside.

The two resting dragons raised their heads.

"Her, Rhoc's dragon," Jayd said.

They waited in silence, broken only by the tinkling of the whispered brook.

"Where?" Rayn asked.

"I can't tell," Jayd replied. "Do you suppose she came by herself? Perhaps she was looking for us as well?"

Rhoc looked at them, confusion on his face. When Jayd spoke to him, it was in front of him so that he could read her lips.

"Your dragon is here," she said.

Rhoc turned pale and Rayn suddenly had the thought that Rhoc might not have known they were looking for dragons at all, let alone thought that they were looking for one for *him*.

"Don't worry Rhoc," Rayn assured him, "you can find your dragon."

Rhoc let out a worried yell, something between a howl and a whimper. He might be able to hear but he still had to learn how to speak. He fondled the handles of the axes at his side but did not draw them.

They looked out of the ravine, across the beautiful ferns and flowers that grew there.

Rayn raised his staff, hoping to help but it stung him and threw itself to the ground.

"Fine, this is Rhoc's test. I get it."

Rhoc looked around, determined, frightened and confused.

And alone.

Without explanation, he splashed across to the little stream to stand on a flat boulder that protruded from the waters. Little flies spun around him but he ignored them. He seemed to be praying, kneeling down on the stone. Or was he listening?

A moment later a glowing white light, like a little fairy, spun around him. He swatted at it and it dodged away.

Then it swung back, by his ears. He looked to be getting angry at it.

But it didn't seem to want to leave.

So he smashed it between his mighty hands.

There was a large clap sound and instantly they all felt the most horrible feeling inside. Rhoc had done something terribly, terribly wrong.

He opened his hands and cried out in horror. Somehow Rayn was able to tell exactly what he said even without words.

"My dragon! My little fairy dragon!"

Jayd screamed in dismay and Darkwing hissed. Rayn began charging towards them to see if he could help but Lifebreath was even faster.

But not fast enough.

Suddenly a huge, black and silver dragon landed in the stream between Lifebreath and Rhoc, throwing up a shower of red sparks as he hit the soil. Rayn saw from the corner of his eyes two more dragons take up positions on either side of the ravine and in the distance, at the very edge, Stormclouds hovered.

Doomclaw paused before speaking. "Hold Lifebreath, this quest is not yours. It is not mine. These humans have brought upon themselves the curse anew. They deserve to die by it once more."

Lifebreath slinked sideways, her head low, her razor sharp claws fully extended. "What madness drives you, Doomclaw? Has the plague already taken you?"

"NO!" He roared. "But it claims the lives of Draytooth and even Everclaw! The battle goes poorly. A battle that isn't even ours. We are dying for a race that no longer honors us, that cannot even remember their crimes!"

"Stand aside Doomclaw," she shouted. "A shapeshifter is wounded, struck by this boy–"

"You see!" Doomclaw roared. "What need have we of more proof? Leave off this quest right now and I will spare your life."

Lifebreath stood up, apparently unable to believe what she had just heard. She looked over at Rayn and Pure, for Jayd was nowhere to be seen. For an instant, for just a moment, Rayn thought Lifebreath might even concede to the tyrant's request.

Then she growled her denial. "I will *never* go back on my word, unlike *you* Doomclaw. And what have Shrieker and Enfathomer to do with you? Have they come to make death of me rather than see the Matron's will done?"

"She has abandoned us," Enfathomer shouted, "caught up in her studies, she cares nothing for her own children's dying in a war she refuses to participate in!"

"Impossible," Lifebreath shouted back, "she is trying to save all our lives. This is not the plague we know, it is coming for dragons too, the old places will not hide us."

"And how can you know that?" Doomclaw argued. "All I know is that while these humans live, other dragons will follow you. When these humans are dead we dragons will leave this world to its fate-"

"Coward!" shouted Rayn unintentionally, realizing in hindsight that it was not the smartest thing to do.

The black and silver dragon turned on him. "How DARE you!" He hissed, his red tongue and sulphur breath almost baking him on the spot. Doomclaw stood up, arrogant and proud, keeping his eyes ever on Lifebreath. "Then let me enlighten you in the ways of *cowardice*. Do you know from whence the plague springs? Do you know what the humans did to dishonor the dragons? Do you know who *killed* the old alliance?"

"Those are just rumors!" Lifebreath said, positioning herself, watching carefully a silently weeping Rhoc holding a fading light.

Doomclaw continued, reveling in his cruelty, "Long ago, dragons and humans were allies, the best, or so it is said. Together they formed an empire that filled the stars. Then humans grew jealous of the dragons' power. They began to fear those that needed no external help, those who didn't need machines, to traverse the great distance between the stars. They began to *fear* us. So they developed a new machine, a new form of life. A disease intended to slay the dragons should they ever turn against their allies, forged from the immune system of dragons themselves! These 'leukocytes', however, showed that they could infect *any* living being. In their stupidity and pride, humans allowed this disease to escape containment and it became the plague. A plague that ended both our empires!"

He was so angry he almost breathed fire over Pure and Rayn right there and then. But his desire to gloat held him back.

Pure was holding Rayn's hand. She was saying nothing.

"These children are not guilty of their parents' sins, even *if* they are true," Lifebreath said, diplomatically, trying to calm things down.

Rayn looked over at Rhoc. He didn't even seem to notice anything that was happening around him.

***

Rhoc was in more pain that he'd ever known before. In his hands he seemed to hold his very own life. But it was not his life. It was someone else's. A dragon. His dragon.

And, once again, because he was stupid and careless and strong, he'd destroyed something beautiful.

Rhoc looked down at the fragile creature. He could clearly see it was a dragon now. She was small and golden and had wings just like a dragonfly. Her scales reflected the filtered light like a rainbow. And her eyes, her little, half closed eyes, looked just like a person's.

She was alive but she was dying in his hands.

He looked at his hands. Tough, calloused. So used to holding axes. So used to destroying things. Like cutting trees to the ground. Like splitting the backbone of a cursed trapper.

Like killing dragons.

Suddenly there was motion around him, motion almost too quick to see. The beautiful dragon, the one who sang all the time, had charged the black and silver dragon. But he must have expected it and with a slash of his tail brought her down to the ground, red sparks flying where he struck her side. All dragons had talons sharp as steel; this dragon's must have been a thousand time sharper.

It was difficult to see through his tears, even harder to see through his pain. But Rhoc numbly watched as Rayn moved forward and tried to strike at the black dragon with his flaming blue staff, but it did little but annoy the beast.

Then the white maiden stood up and she was about to speak when suddenly the air was split with a cry so hideous that they all cringed.

But not he, he was already in too much pain.

It was one of the dragons up on the ledge. While it cried out, the white maiden could not speak.

The black and silver dragon was about to charge Rayn when Lifebreath grabbed his legs, cutting into his flesh. In response, he stabbed her in the neck with his tail, and Pure's screams were matched only by the ridge dragon's inhuman noise.

Tears flowed freely as Rhoc watched the singing green dragon. She was wounded to death and could not get up.

It was time to die.

At least that was something Rhoc was good at.

With as much care as if he were carrying a snowflake, Rhoc placed his little, dying dragon down on the stone. He folded her wings, and said goodbye.

With a roar, he leapt off the stone, part of it crumbling under the force of the blow. He felt himself flying through the air like a catapult stone, high up and right onto the black dragon's head. He'd drawn his axe but it splintered against the huge creature's iron plated skull. So he bashed it with the hilt instead, repeatedly pummeling down on it again and again. He felt the armor plating buckle under the fevered blows. He heard bone splinter.

The dragon roared and tried to throw him off but he held on with ease.

Then Rhoc saw the mighty bladed tail swing around and he ducked off, clinging instead to the dragon's arm. Without thinking, he wrapped his arms around its forearm and hugged with all his might.

He felt the bones crack and split, and the dragon roared in pain.

Rhoc leapt off, jumping back towards Rayn and Pure.

Then the great dragon drew a breath. Rhoc suddenly realized there was nowhere to go. Even if he jumped, his two friends would be slain in the fire.

Pure was about to speak. Rhoc thought it a brave way to die especially seeing the screaming dragon would probably stop her.

But the scream never came. Looking up, Rhoc saw to his amazement that Jayd and her black dragon had seemingly walked through the shadows and grappled the screamer from off the cliff.

It was not a tactic that would last long, for even as he watched, the dragon that travelled through smoke and flame appeared at Jayd's side, attempting to wrestle her dragon from Screecher's back. But it was enough time for Pure to speak, and with loathing reluctance, the dark one seemed forced to swallow its flames.

Suddenly, in the next instant, a billowing plume of life and health covered the black dragon. Lifebreath had breathed on him as her dying act. His arm bones mended, his skull stood whole, his plates were healed.

Rhoc felt like he died inside. How could she be so foolish? They were losing this battle and she had handed it right to him?

Inside his heart became stone, dark. Evil. He would kill this black dragon and every dragon he ever met. It was what he was good at. It was *all* he was good at!

"Fool!" the dark dragon called. "Why heal you me?"

"I wasn't aiming at you," Lifebreath replied.

Rhoc almost jumped right at the black and silver dragon when suddenly he felt something stir in his heart.

It was hope.

The other two dragons had Jayd and her black dragon pinned to the earth. Dark one had them cornered.

And the little light on the rock suddenly brightened. Then exploded with light.

And all the hate and self-loathing within him was replaced with unimaginable hope.

Suddenly stone boulders began unfolding themselves from the air and the little light began to turn into a dragon made of stone. Solid stone. Huge, solid stone twice the height of any other dragon there. It had short wings of stone and probably couldn't fly but its tail was a massive club.

"What?" the dark one called.

Rhoc fell to his knees.

"Go!" Pure ordered. "Report your failure to the others!"

The stone dragon roared and the other dragons fled, except the dark one. It took a stone wallop to the head, then to the side, before he decided it was time to go. He clawed at the stone dragon, his metal bones bouncing off her armored hide and left as soon as he could.

"You've not seen the last of me," he promised.

A moment later the stones began to fold into nothingness once more and the little dragon light was left.

It alighted on the fallen form of Lifebreath.

They ran to help her but it was too late. Rayn was an amazing wiseman, one of the best Rhoc had ever seen. But even Rayn did not have a prayer to bring others back from the dead.

Lifebreath was dead and her talent with her. She had died to bring him his dragon, Fairystone. So while Pure and Jayd wept, while Rayn uttered prayers for a peaceful transit to the afterlife, Rhoc held his little dragon. She was small and weak. She would need all his protection even as he realized he needed her to protect him from losing hope and becoming a monster himself.

You are good, little Fairystone told him in his heart. Don't lose hope, don't ever lose hope. Everything will always work out all right in the end and if it isn't alright yet don't worry, it isn't the end. You'll see. Don't lose hope my beautiful boy. Don't ever lose hope.

11 Fairystone, a shifter.

Life

The hardest thing Rayn had ever done was to cremate Lifebreath. In all his life he'd never, ever wished for a prayer to bring one back to life more than today. But the staff and his heart were silent. Either it was not the time or he lacked the faith, or it could not be done. Death was so very permanent, a journey no man or dragon had ever returned from.

Rayn sighed as the flame finally leapt high into the desert sky. He'd had to light it himself without Pure's help, she was too upset.

Jayd approached him. "Do you think Doomclaw was telling the truth?"

Rayn sighed. "Probably, hoping that in so doing he would do us as much harm as possible. This curse, this plague, my heart tells me will be the worst we've ever seen."

Jayd sighed. "I will miss the flowers," she said, and Rayn wondered what she meant. "So," she said, not waiting for the flames to burn any lower, "Where to now?"

"Oh," said Rayn, but even before he'd formed the question the answer had arrived, "Me."

Phew.

"My turn at last-" he began.

But Jayd cut him off. "There," she said, pointing down and towards the left.

"There?" Rayn asked.

Dr Joseph Ireland

"Yes," she explained, seeming annoyed at having to make the effort of explaining, "inside the ground. Deep within. The most direct route there is to dig."

"Dig?" Rayn asked. He was stupefied. "Dig? For a dragon? Why, is it already dead and buried?"

Jayd shrugged. "I'll go pack the stuff. I don't think Rhoc is in much of a state to help."

Rayn sighed. She was right. Rhoc was holding his little fairy dragon and not saying anything at all, just watching the dancing light as though they could somehow communicate without words, though at least he'd told them her name.

Suddenly Stormclouds returned.

Rhoc roared a warning and Pure lit two great flames in her hands. She must have been angry; they lit the ravine from one side to the other, so much more than the funeral pyre.

Stormclouds said nothing, but flew closer.

"Get away, traitor!" Pure shouted, throwing a roaring column of fire at him.

He dodged it by disappearing, reappearing behind her. Then he threw a leather bundle at her feet– another saddle, and disappeared before she could turn around.

His voice echoed around the ravine. "Doomclaw's rebellion runs deeper than you imagine, young princess. I brought you a gift, in case you one day prevail. But I have one other thing for you, if you will stay your flames?"

"Show yourself," she ordered.

Stormclouds appeared, hovering in the air, his head bent low as if bowing. He was close, well within arm's reach if Pure had decided to reach out and touch him.

He paused there a moment, flying in the air, looking at her warily. Then, from his other paw, he cast down a helmet.

It was gold, or brilliant bronze, simple and without a visor. Along the sides it had great wings, like a dragon, flowing backwards. It was an elegant and intimidating helm.

"What game are you playing at, Stormclouds?" she demanded.

He scowled, as if he were not in any game of his own choosing. "I do not ask your forgiveness, nor will I. But here is another saddle and helm if you like, though I doubt you can use it now."

She glared at him with tear stained eyes. "How goes the war?"

"Poorly. Doomclaw spoke the truth. The plague took a town called Shenswold before we could notice. All were slain and the plants destroyed. Even life was taken from the soil so that it all became as dust. What remained living was given over to the plague. We burnt it all, Doomclaw first among us to take charge of this. There were no survivors and we fear other outbreaks are soon to follow."

Jayd stifled a sob. Shenswold was not a day's journey from home.

Then she spoke. "Is what Doomclaw said true? Did we humans really create the curse? I mean, the plague?"

Stormclouds paused. "Yes, as a way to defeat the dragons. Ask Matron if you do not believe me. Now we turn again to defend you with our lives? I know not why. But I fear your existence is too tied up with our own now. If humanity dies... I fear we will as well."

Dr Joseph Ireland

"Then why," Darkwing finally spoke up, "why not join us? We could use your help."

Stormclouds hovered up, looking over at him but turned and spoke to Pure.

"I will help where I can but for now you are on your own. I saw your guide-ess pointing and I am... unwilling to travel understone."

With a rumbling thunder, he was gone.

Fairystone whispered something to Rhoc and he nodded, but Rayn couldn't tell what she said.

"Well, Darkwing, we are glad you are here," Rayn said, "and Rhoc's dragon too. Jayd tells me my dragon is down there."

Fairystone made a peep, Rhoc nodded and she floated up to Rayn where she rested on his hand. He had to hold her up to his face so that he could see her. She was little more than a dragonfly, so small and fragile.

"Master tells me you are in charge of this quest," she said.

Rayn shrugged and nodded.

"I am Fairystone, a changer. I can take us under the ground, it would be my pleasure, if you will follow close behind?"

"Certainly," Rayn replied.

"Stand back then," she said. She truly came across as a very cheerful dragon, in spite of the circumstances which now included a dragon uprising and, potentially, all their deaths.

Stones again began to unfold themselves from the air as Fairystone became a massive dragon made of stone once more.

Rhoc cheered and clapped his hands with pride. The shape shifting Fairystone roared in approval and struck the ground, burrowing down at an angle. As she went, at about the pace a man could comfortably walk, the stone seemed to part aside as if by some miracle.

"We'd best hurry," Darkwing replied, "I suspect the tunnel will revert after us."

Rhoc snatched up the second saddle and Pure handed Rayn the helm. He looked at it as they slowly followed Fairystone. Then he handed it to Jayd.

"Here, you alone ride a dragon today."

"Cool!" She shouted, putting it on immediately. It seemed to resize to fit her head but still looked out of place. "Whoa, this is so weird! I can see all around me, in every direction! Ooh and I can make out details so very far away! Sooo Cooool!"

Then Jayd sighed.

"But it's not for me," she said. "Too *manly*. Euch!"

Darkwing smiled. "And she is not going to ride for much this day, is she?"

Rayn agreed and tried the helm himself. It did make him feel more confident but his vision was in no way improved.

"I suspect its workings are only allowed for dragon riders," Pure suggested, walking along as the tunnel began to cover them. "That way the items are not coveted by those not called to the great honor."

"I suppose not," Rayn said, a little regretful. He had hoped it would help him. But the tunnel was sealing up already. Bidding Lifebreath a final farewell he lit the staff and stowed the helm in his pack. He would look intimidating in it anyway.

***

They walked for three days, accompanied only by the thunder of Fairystone burrowing through stone, or profound silence. At first the journey was cold and damp but it soon grew warm by the end of the second day. By the third day, it was growing uncomfortably hot.

Then, for no apparent reason, they emerged into a huge natural cave. It was refreshingly cool and a stream ran down the center.

"Let us refill what water we can," Pure announced.

"But not the bottles that were blessed by Lifebreath," Jayd reminded her. They each had a full water skin of her healing waters and each had refused to drink them. So by now they were very, very thirsty.

The others rested, Fairystone resuming her natural form and chatting with Rhoc. Jayd and Darkwing dangled claws and feet in the stream, and Pure tried to lift up the waters using whatever skill she called understanding. They seemed busy so Rayn left them to their diversion, and wandered up to explore where the waters came from. There he found a dark cavern, so small he'd have to crawl through, entering into the cavern from what might have been the north.

He was a wiseman, expected to be a man. Required at all times to comport himself with dignity. But what he *really* wanted to do was get down on his hands and knees in the mud, feel it squishing between his fingers and toes, and crawl up the little tunnel while the waters poured all over his grateful head and tired legs.

So he just sighed and stood there.

"Rayn!" Jayd suddenly shouted.

He turned around and ran down to where she could see him. "Look at this, what is that in the water?"

They all ran down to look.

An otter swam about in the water and for a moment Rayn wondered where it had come from, till it occurred to him that Fairystone was missing. Either that, or Fairystone could become an otter too. And the little otter, with a questioning expression on its face, was holding on to the unmistakable glimmer of bronze in the dark water.

Without waiting he took off his robe and sash and dived down. It wasn't very deep but there in the mud was an iron gauntlet, badly rusted away. He was about to give up in disappointment when his eyes caught on a strange glimmering reflecting from his staff. Reaching down into the mud he felt something cold, hard, with the feel of metal. It took a good minute, his lungs burning for air but he was an experienced swimmer. Eventually he realized it was a large breastplate made of solid bronze. His heart leapt in his chest. Rayn knew only one race of man that made breastplates of metal and not leather.

Dragon riders.

He grabbed the breastplate, seeing with delight that it still held on to its back plate. With a moment of regret, he looked around for a previous owner, but he was long dead or had left the armor here a long, long time ago.

He swam to the surface, hampered by its great weight.

The others were cheering when he surfaced, and Rhoc lifted him out of the water like a child. They set the plate down on the ground.

12 "Look what I found!" Fairystone thought out loud.

"So ornate," Jayd gleamed.

"Aargh, wow, oooh, wow," Rhoc said.

It was a real, valuable dragon rider breastplate made to protect the heart and, if legends were to be believed, the integrity of the rider.

"Look, I see writing!" Pure said.

Rayn looked down at where the writing ringed the circle where the rider's heart would sit.

Pure tried to read it, "Honor, doing what you say you'll do, h… hope. Um, oh, what's that one again?"

"Love," Rayn replied.

"Rayn, how can you read that?" Pure asked him.

"How can you not?" he said. It was written as clear as any spoken language to him.

"I have not seen this writing since I was four and did not know it well then either. But it is written in a language you have never before seen, so how can you read it?"

"How… can you not?" he said. He looked down. He read the whole plate. He made clear sense of the picture in the middle of it with just a glance. He even knew the triple lines along the edge of the plate symbolized the protection of the Divine, though his people had never used that symbol.

And he'd never held that breastplate before.

"And what I'd like to know," Jayd said, "is how you always seem to know what the dragons are saying, even when Pure is speaking to them in that strange, growly language."

"Yes, growly language," Pure said. "Yes, like 'look you've found a breastplate'," Pure said, and Rayn jumped.

He'd heard her say something in another language, yet he'd understood it perfectly. For the first time, he realized he'd understood anything anyone was saying in any language.

And, apparently, could read it too.

"I…" he said, a bit lost for words.

"You don't suppose it's his wiseman's gift? I've heard of that happening," Jayd said. "But it has only happened once or twice, on special occasions, to very faithful wisemen. Not to an over-ambitious one *all the time*."

"You're a speaker, aren't you," Pure said in their common language.

"I..."

"He's lost his gift," Darkwing joked, sending Jayd into gales of laughter.

Rayn stood and with conscious intent, spoke to Darkwing in his native tongue, "I still have my gifts."

Then he turned to Pure and with deliberate desire to speak her language, said, "I think you are right and I am glad you are travelling with us."

She gasped. "It has been a long time since I heard that speech," she said, voice quiet. "I expected to never hear it again."

She looked like she wanted to hold him, to welcome him to her home. But Rayn was too enchanted with the revelation she had given him of his gift. Besides, she wasn't even a woman yet and he wasn't supposed to hold one too young to marry anyway. She was always overlooking his traditions like this.

Then he turned to Fairystone and found himself forming words made of chittering and clicks, "Thank you for saving us and taking us to meet my dragon," he said.

"Thank *you!*" she replied.

Jayd slapped his shoulder, breaking him out of his wonderment. "Now I know why you two understood that Matron so well. I didn't catch a thing she didn't say to me directly."

"Really? How about you, Rhoc?" Rayn said.

Rhoc was smiling, as if to say, *I told you so.* Rayn realized Rhoc was still deaf at the time; he would have heard nothing.

Yet Rayn was touched to his heart. All his life he had been the only one who seemed to know what Rhoc was saying. Others thought he had no words because he had no thoughts, but Rayn had always known that was not true. By his gift he had given Rhoc a voice all his life and protected him from the indignity of not being able to communicate his wishes. It was what had brought them close and protected them many times.

Rhoc walked up and gave him a gentle hug. It said, *Thank you.*

Rayn pushed away tears of gratitude to Divinity's benevolence. "Well, enough of this. Jayd, what other pieces of dragon armor do we have around here?"

She immediately began searching, sending Rhoc or Darkwing looking through mud and stone. But they found only two more pieces: a greave for the lower leg and a guard for the left arm.

"Selfish rider, why would he only place such trinkets around here for us to find," Jayd complained. "I cannot find any more; unless I am being blocked somehow, the rest of this armor will never be found."

Rayn sighed and took to cleaning what he had. It took a good while but finally the temptation to try it on was too much. The padding within the armor would protect his clothes and skin but he took off the cloak, it would need to go over the armor.

"Looking good," Jayd praised him as he donned the robe over his armor like a cloak. "We might make a warrior of you yet!"

"Perhaps," Rayn agreed but shifted uncomfortably with all the weight of bronze over him, "but if this is what a warrior must wear into battle, I am disinclined-"

"Oh!" Rhoc grinned. "T ee try!" *Let me try,* he attempted his first spoken sentence. He'd been trying phrases constantly over the past three days; Rayn knew that sentences were soon to follow.

"Oh, hang on," Pure disagreed. "Try the helmet on as well."

"But..." Rayn said but even Rhoc insisted. "All right," he said, and taking the helmet from Jayd, slipped it on his own head.

Instantly Rayn knew something had happened; he felt lighter. There was a solemn hum and the dirt and grit flew from the armor, leaving it gleaming like polished silver inlaid with gold. The writing seemed to write itself anew, words glowing with renewed power and faith.

"I had hoped so," Pure said in their common language, "The helm still holds a working source of power, unlike the rest of the armor. Now they are sharing their strength. Now they are all awake."

"What?" Jayd asked.

Pure repeated herself in her native language but just to Rayn, since she couldn't possibly make it any simpler than in her native tongue. "The residual power source within the helm has successfully reactivated the entire suit of armor. The parts are acting as a synergistic whole." Then she continued in the common language, "You have a new suit of armor, future dragon rider."

Rayn stood in gleaming wonder, his great blue robe flowing like a cloak down his armored back. His breastplate, greave and arm guard reshaping themselves to fit his young form perfectly, their weight almost leaving them completely until they were little more than reeds in effort to lift. Each glowed with light and protections.

His staff arm felt strong, his legs as though they drew health itself from the willing earth. And inside his heart he felt such indomitable courage as he'd never known, a faith and conviction that all could be done if he willed it.

"Divinity again approves our cause," he muttered.

"Let us hope," Jayd whispered, "it is enough."

Stone walls

They had not gone another hour before Darkwing asked them to stop.

Fairystone curled into a great semi-circle as she did when they rested, preventing the cavern from sealing down on top of them. Since gaining part of a dragon rider's armor, Rayn had grown more confident than ever and his pace was greatly quickened. He was impatient to get where they were going and to pause now just provoked his wrath.

But he suffered it. Dragons were sometimes wise.

"I do not like where we are heading," Darkwing said.

"Explain yourself," Rayn replied.

Darkwing raised an eyebrow at him, as if mildly bothered by his tone, but continued. "If I have my bearings right and I think that I do, we are arriving at a place most fearsome. There is... a prison. The most isolated and feared prison of all this world, for it is a prison for dragons..."

His words hung heavily on the air. No one spoke.

Then Darkwing sighed and it broke the mood. "So, if we're going where I think we're going, it's probably not a good idea to go *right* there, if you get my meaning. We should probably head for the front door instead?"

"Why?" Rayn asked.

Jayd was nodding. "Because if we're heading for a prisoner dragon we'll end up right in his cell. We should be careful to ask more questions next time, Darkwing could have flown us here in a day overland. Instead we headed directly."

Rayn pondered. "But what if they do not give us the dragon? And what if it is evil?"

"It might be a guard," Jayd reminded them. "Still, we should go through the front door, don't you think, Rayn?"

He shrugged. It was so obvious that it was silly of her to ask him.

Still, he had the staff. He checked and the strong answer seemed to be the front door. Then he did wish he'd thought of asking before. They could have saved two days of darkness.

But then they might have never found the armor…

More thought was required here.

***

The guard was picking at his claws. Guard duty was insanely boring; get a more *stupid* dragon to guard the doors, that's what he said! Anyone with half a brain was driven insane with all the pointless waiting. There were no visitors to Deepstone mountain. There were never any successful breakouts. All the visitors were well appointed and known in advance. This was no a chance to be a hero.

Now, if he was out, fighting the plague! *That* was a chance! News had reached them that another human town had fallen and eleven dragons were slain now, including that Lifebreath he'd heard so much about. That was their mistake, staying so close to humans. They were like an addiction to most dragons. They'd just hung around them hoping the little humans would get their act together one day, and suddenly the Matron up and announces their banishment is over? Strange days, strange days indeed.

For a moment he pondered whether he, too, would seek out a rider. None had felt the call yet. None of which he knew. And certainly none would that lived inside these walls. Twenty dragons in all, all murderers and liars. Lost souls that had no hope. It was once told that all dragons were honest and true. So what had happened when they'd banished the humans that had driven one dragon in every million mad? He might never know.

He rolled onto his back and sighed. If the head warden caught him here, like this, there would be trouble. *But I am a dragon too and needn't listen to any, for who could command me?* He twisted on his back, allowing the dark stones to catch against the scales that itched. Being able to see in the dark was his gift. Not much of a gift, but some envied it.

Then he heard a sound. Like someone else was scratching.

What was that?

He pulled his lazy head from the silent rock and listened.

Nothing.

He yawned. He'd almost wished it *was* something so that he'd have something useful to do! He-

There it was again, unmistakable this time. Something was stirring underneath the rock.

He sniffed the ground. What could it be? Not a Slugdragon, that was impossible. The rock here was too full of stone they did not like, besides the protections the warden held here.

But there it was again.

He barked a warning, telling the others inside the jail to look alive.

The sound came again, there could be no doubt: from understone something was headed for the main gate!

He roared. The others were taking too long to come to his aid; where were they? He backed up against the pillars and stone doors that led to the jail beyond. He did not wish to fight a Slugdragon, especially one that seemed to be able to penetrate the defenses thus far. But if it was a fight it wanted, a fight it would get!

***

As soon as Fairystone entered the cavern she transformed back into her natural self, and Rayn was the first to walk into the flat floored cavern beyond. He held out his light. It was clearly of ancient work, with the same powerful runes and words that were on his gleaming suit. He turned around, indicating for the others to follow, until his eyes fell on a mighty door of pure stone and its single guard. A large, and very nervous, dragon. It was pressed up against the stone, eyes wide, trembling with fear.

"Greetings," Rayn said to it in the language of dragons, now he knew he could.

"You..." it stuttered, "you are a man, in the form of a dragon rider? You've come here? What are you doing here? It was lucky I followed my snout and let you stand instead of rending you asunder – you should not have let that changer into this room!" It sighed as if greatly relieved.

"And what form would you have us take when travelling through stone?" Pure asked, walking up beside Rayn. She spoke dragon too, as well as her own tongue, and the language Jayd and all the other villages spoke commonly.

"None, my lady. Whom are you? I mean, sorry. Ahem, I am Nightseer! Guardian of the prison and keeper of the door. State your name and business," the dragon shouted, very commanding, then followed this up with an apologetic, "Please?"

Rayn suppressed a smile.

Jayd came in then, with Darkwing. He was so dark in the cavern it was impossible to make him out. His wing span seemed to increase as well, to fill the entire room with shadow.

"We are here to claim my dragon," Rayn explained.

"What? Here?" Nightseer sneered. "I doubt that. There are murderers beyond. You ... you shall not pass."

Rayn opened his mouth to speak but Pure cut him off.

"Stand aside, dragon. Let us pass."

The dragon obeyed as if it had little say in the matter but then hastily explained, "You bear the mark of royalty within you, young maid. I would gladly honor that. But this seal is unbroken. Only those with the high warden's gift may pass, unless your changer there turns back into stone form and rends the door, but then that would set off all the alarms."

"Perhaps you can inform the high warden–" Rayn began, until Pure cut him off again.

"High warden, I command you to appear!" she shouted.

Rayn was going to question her tactics, but it seemed to work. Slithering from the rocks themselves another dragon appeared, deep magenta or purple in the dim cavern.

"Enough!" he roared, his voice efficient and demanding as one accustomed to giving orders and keeping law. "I see the rumors are true. The royal house of Oordu yet stands. The royal houses have not been seen in four thousand years and many had begun to suspect them but legend. Yet not I. Still, I fear you have come in vain if you seek a dragon. I sense a bond with none of you and the gate guard here is unlikely to ever find a rider, methinks."

Pure was silent but she looked angry. It was clear that things still weren't happening fast enough for her and she was probably still annoyed that they'd taken the long way to the prison.

"Good high warden," Rayn continued, "We are honored to be here. If thee and he are all the free dragons here, then I fear Divinity bids me claim my dragon from among the chained. See, I am a wiseman. Perhaps if he is indeed a prisoner, he may repent?"

The high warden growled deeply. "You would trust a dragon at his word, even as a man? We are little better at keeping our oaths, I assure you! You would do better to have your princess use her… formidable… talent to force him to obey."

Rayn shook his head. "It would not be a lasting solution. Please, let me see my dragon."

The high warden paused, the gate guard looking over him. "I am aware of the Matron's command and of the presence of the plague again upon the land. But no dragon ever entering this most sacred of places has ever left, you must understand that. It will take months, weeks at best, to convince the high conclave of the dragons that one can be allowed to leave. I doubt they will make an exception, even for you."

Rayn nodded. "Then you'd better let them know right away."

The high warden huffed. "You haven't even found your dragon yet."

Rayn looked at Jayd, and she pointed towards the prison.

"Perhaps, but it will be soon."

The high warden looked at him darkly, slithering forwards *through* the stones at his feet until he towered over Rayn's head. Rayn looked at him, hoping the fear he felt in his heart was not showing in his eyes.

But it probably was.

"Come," the high warden said, "but the others stay here."

"But-" Pure began to protest.

"We're not coming, are we?" Jayd assumed.

"Better get comfortable," Pure replied to her in the common language.

Rayn was swept up by a dragon's claw and carried through the stone as if it were no thicker than water.

The room within was strange beyond compare. Torches burnt around in sconces, lighting the scene. Everything was dragon sized.

There was a large bed of gems and gold, a desk, and a large, still pool that might have been a mirror.

The high warden did not pause, throwing himself and Rayn with him through stone doors with impunity. They passed into another corridor, a large brown rock with a huge glowing red rune on its surface.

"Hailpaw," The high warden hissed, "used his powers to cripple other dragons and claim their treasures. It took seven to bring him in and all still bear their wounds."

They passed a black door with a golden rune. "Svengnok, took to farming humans and having them do his bidding, stealing. His empire fell six hundred years ago; now he waits for the darkness to claim him here."

A green door, made of wood. "Highvoice, temptress, murderess: a liar." The high warden hissed with particular spite. From beyond the door Rayn sensed a tremendous sorrow and regret that pulled at his heart and begged him to set that dragon within free. But he chose to side with the wisdom of the dragons on whom to imprison for life.

Finally, deep within the crypt, they found an iron door with thrumming blue runes. Runes very similar in color to those on Rayn's staff.

"Ironfang, the first of the worst three. It took seventeen years and more than forty dragons to bring in this fugitive. In the end he took to 'preserving' a lost town of humans and for threat of destroying this town, the hunters lured him into a trap. He has been here only sixty years, but many rejoice at his capture. He is dishonest, a lost soul; watch yourself. It was only by the aid of a wiseman such as yourself that he was taken prisoner. Ironfang had opportunity to slay the wiseman but did not, none know why. I can only assume he might have a soft spot for humans who bear the staff such as you do."

Rayn could not reply. He was having trouble speaking. His mind was full of confused thoughts and overwhelmed by random feelings. It was as if a part of his own soul was behind that door. Yet it was a lost part. There was irrational anger at what this dragon had done, letting the 'team' down, as it were. Then there was overwhelming pity, followed again by an insane rage that wanted to split the earth from here to the sky and set this great beast free.

But he could say none of that.

"Let us go in," he said, after he had steeled himself.

This time the high warden didn't walk through the walls. He spoke commanding words of authority and asked the door to open. The runes flashed bright blue, a similar light reflecting in his own staff, a familiar light touching his soul. This was Divine power very, very similar to his own.

And the door opened.

***

Inside, a pitiful creature crouched on the ground. Its wings were in iron chains, chains which wrapped around its paws and tail. The dragon was large, larger than Darkwing, larger than Lifebreath. Even larger than Doomclaw. But it looked tired.

Its forehead was pressed to a giant stone pillar with glowing runes that ran down it. The dragon seemed as if it could not move its head from off that pillar, leaving it forced to stand continually.

Rayn was expecting a riot of emotions to overflow, but instead, he felt nothing. He was calm, almost beyond normal. As if he came to talk to this dragon every day. And with his first glance he knew two things:

This dragon was his, and –

This dragon deserved its punishment.

For a moment, there was silence.

"Well, wiseman, have you come to mock me?" The dragon asked, in a voice that moved and sounded, well, in the same way his voice did.

"This is not the way I expected to meet you," Rayn answered.

The dragon's eyes widened with surprise, then narrowed. "So, a rider has arrived to claim me? Am I now to be tortured as someone's little pet-"

"Silence," Rayn ordered. The dragon's voice was strange, like a part of himself. And it was as if he was telling an annoying, immature part of himself to shut up and stop playing silly games.

The dragon was silent a moment. "I see a broken suit of armor, and the staff and robe of a wisemen. So why are you here, human?"

Something touched Rayn's heart. It felt like sympathy.

A vision opened up, and he saw the dragon's past fly by in a matter of moments. It felt like this noble beast was created as a creature of purity and light. Then one day it had found itself in a broken world, a world that was dying from the plague. A world where nothing was the way it was supposed to be. A world where a part of his soul was missing.

The dragon felt it too and struggled to hold back tears, loathing the sobs that wracked his form unbidden in the presence of true understanding, and the infinite compassion that flowed from Rayn like a storm.

Rayn was flooded by new memories. A noble soul, making mistakes in a confusing world. He thought he was making a point but he was only making enemies. He thought he was keeping his word but he was only bearing a grudge. He thought he was righting wrongs, when he was only plotting revenge. Light had turned to darkness and soon he was running for his life.

Rayn fell to his knees as a hundred lifetimes of regret and sin flooded through him. Then he saw the real darkness. The self-loathing that led to mistakes and broken laws and pain. He saw how this dragon had created crime upon crime not to see what he could get away with, but because he couldn't understand why he kept getting away with it at all.

"Stop!" the dragon begged, even as a new flood of memories flowed from him. He could not hide the truth from Rayn, not with all his strength, because it was his own heart that sought forgiveness and he had no power against himself. This was a truly dark dragon, who had hidden his light deep within. And now it burst out like fire.

"You…" Rayn tried to say. But he didn't need to know any more. He had seen inside this dragon's past. He knew what he was and why he'd done everything he'd ever done. And he knew he had to be freed to make amends for his past.

And he needed to be free NOW.

"Wiseman, no!" The high warden shouted, leaping towards him.

But there was no way he could be fast enough. Rayn knew the words of ending, to put aside an old prayer that no longer served its purpose. The runes of power switched off, from the tip of the pillar to the roof. And before the high warden could draw a breath, Ironfang had reared up away from the pillar. Snapping the chain around his tail with impunity, he swung it around and smashed the pillar to dust.

Rayn covered his eyes as the smashing and snapping of chains continued. They were as nothing before Ironfang's rage and renewed strength. As the dust settled, Rayn could feel the high warden cringing in the stones behind him.

In the settling cloud a dragon stood, high and noble. His eyes glowed red, a deep rumbling as the fire inside him reignited for the first time in sixty years.

Rayn considered running but a strange calm in his heart held him there.

Then Ironfang; murderer, criminal, lost soul, bowed his head at Rayn's feet and shut his eyes in meek submission. "It *is* you." The dragon explained. "*You* were what was missing."

Neither could prevent the tears or the sobs that stole from a forgiven murderer's soul.

Rayn touched his snout and on impression, rubbed his brow. In that moment the bond was made complete. He not only knew Ironfang's thoughts, he could feel his body as if it were his own. But it was not overwhelming; he was still very much his own mind and person. It was like having a best friend, only that friend was as long as a river and had claws of iron.

Dr Joseph Ireland

"Come," said Rayn.

Rayn got up on Ironfang without hesitation, as if they'd both shared the thought at the same moment. The dragon had to tilt his neck earthward and Rayn had to reach up to his full height. Grabbing hold of the scales, he pulled himself at the same moment Ironfang pulled up and he almost went flying through the air yet, as one, they moved so that he landed almost softly. He grabbed the stone hard scales without thinking.

"Ah, no?" The high warden whimpered.

Rayn looked at the high warden, fearfully peering out from the stones.

I could blind him. Ironfang joked in dark humor. Rayn could feel, deep in his heart, and perfectly knew his dragon would never willingly break a law again, as long as he rode with him. But Rayn also knew he was the only one who knew the depth of this dragon's repentance and regret.

He only wished each and every human, and every dragon, could share this bond.

"I am sorry, high warden," Rayn apologized. "Our cause is more necessary. We are going to stop the worst plague this world has ever seen. Please, you need to let us out."

"But I can't!" The high warden begged. "Not without the conclave. They alone can sign a prisoner's freedom."

"Then…" Rayn began, but there was a loud crash.

It seemed Fairystone and Rhoc were on their way after all, with Jayd to guide them no doubt.

"No, no! You can't come in here!" The high warden said, cringing in the stone.

Rhoc and Pure were riding Fairystone in her stone dragon form. She apparently had little trouble ripping apart stone barriers four paces thick.

When Pure spoke, it was with her commanding voice. "High warden, stand down. What has happened here?"

"He's trying to steal the prisoner." The high warden whimpered – all traces of power and dignity gone.

Rayn said nothing.

Pure looked at him, riding Ironfang as one.

"Can you vouch for your dragon?" She asked.

He wanted to. But he knew him better than that already. "Whether or not he is redeemed, he is needed. He *has* to come with us."

She paused. Then nodded. "High warden. Let him go."

The high warden hissed, somehow finding the strength to resist her command but he still honored her authority. "The high conclave *will* hear about this. They will be *very interested* to hear about the first breakout in millennia."

"Be sure you tell them," she ordered.

And the high warden disappeared.

"Come," she said to Rayn and Ironfang, "we should hurry."

***

They travelled in a sheer chasm up to the light, and Ironfang looked out at the windswept plains for the first time in six decades. There was a part of him that wanted to run, to break free. To go far away. But Rayn could also feel a deep need to redeem himself, to answer for his crimes, to reclaim his title and name. Rayn found it ironic that a dragon so strong and powerful should want to run away instead of facing justice.

Ironfang would stay.

Rayn breathed a sigh of relief. He knew this was in Ironfang's heart – he was glad to see he'd just passed his test.

"So," Jayd asked, squinting in the light, "where to now?"

Fairystone was buzzing all around her head, making it even harder for her to see.

"My dragon?" Pure asked. "I have none to claim yet. Tell me, wiseman, it is my turn now?"

Rayn smiled. He almost didn't need to ask, but he did anyway, just in case.

No.

Rayn blinked at the forcefulness of the reply. It was not Pure's turn. He looked at her in surprise and confusion and she read his face immediately.

For a moment she paced in frustration.

"Very well then, wiseman. Tell me there is a more important mission then! Tell me what we are to seek now and have your sister find it."

I take it, rider, that that young one with dark hair is your sister and she is a navigator? Ironfang asked him in his heart.

Indeed. Rayn replied.

"Well?" Pure insisted.

Rayn stood down from Ironfang's back and was sorry to feel the distance between them. But he needed to think and to pray. *Where are we to go next?*

He spent an hour in prayer, fervent prayer, while the others patiently waited and watched the sky. Pure filled Ironfang in on much of what was happening and it was interesting to see Ironfang was glad to hear Doomclaw was still around. But that sounded more like he wanted revenge than a reunion.

Yet as the day aged, no answer came. Rayn pled with even greater fervency. The curse was spreading. Dragons were dying. They had to hurry! They had to-

Then Stormclouds appeared.

"Ho, Stormclouds," Pure said, and her voice fell silent.

Something was very wrong.

His skin seemed dark, stretched. Covered in blotches. A great welt full of pus ran along his flank and his eyes were possessed orbs of milky darkness.

The plague had found him.

Everything happened at once. Pure lit her fire as a great circle around them all and Fairystone assumed her stone dragon form. Rhoc leapt at him, axe drawn and Jayd ran to Darkwing's side.

But none were faster than Stormclouds. He leapt through the air itself, circling them with thunder and smoke. With a single talon or spiked tail he lashed out at them, while they swung around striking him

many times. He cared not for flames, or wounds, though Ironfang clearly broke bones. He even ignored Maiden's calls.

Within seconds, each of them was covered with numerous wounds and scratches. The tactic was obvious; the plague was seeking their bodies, not taking their lives. Even if they won they would be cursed before the next daybreak, their talents and gifts used to serve an insatiable enemy.

Unless they took their own lives before then. But Stormclouds, enhanced in fortitude by the plague, was taking a terrible toll. If they were overcome...

Suddenly he felt Ironfang's fear. Terrible, irrational fear.

He was about to run.

Rayn said nothing but willed his peace and hope into his dragon, *Better to die fighting than trapped in a cave.*

Ironfang agreed. *Have you no cure for the plague yet, wiseman?*

Then Rayn remembered. They did. They stood back to back, watching the smoke and thunder. Rayn was watching, looking for a pattern. There didn't seem to be any but perhaps a wiseman's heart would succeed where well thought out plans might fail. With nothing but faith he took a full water skin of Lifebreath's gift and turning around, threw it.

His aim was miraculous. The entire water container slid down Stormclouds' throat even as he appeared to take a lash at Ironfang. His dragon grabbed Stormclouds' leg and threw him towards the ground, yet Stormclouds was gone before he'd even touched it.

They thought themselves free when Fairystone called out. Stormclouds had moved to the other side and was raking her stone flank. He seemed so intent on it that he fell from the air and touched the ground.

Fairystone swung about and struck him, knocking the wind from him. He stumbled about, preparing to charge her but swayed as though confused.

Ironfang charged but Rayn stayed his dragon. He wanted to save Stormclouds, if it were possible. There was a ritual, a hope, he needed to know if it could be done.

"WHAT?" Ironfang shouted at him.

"Yes, what?" Pure asked.

Rayn held his hands up and made them wait.

Stormclouds stumbled where he stood. He tried to disappear, but the wisps of smoke did not form properly. He cried out and stumbled again as if walking was something he never did, like an ill man.

He roared at them and Ironfang laughed.

"That bottle, what was in it?" Ironfang asked him in the language of dragons.

Pure gasped. "You used part of Lifebreath's water?" she chided him in the common language.

Jayd turned, watching them glare at each other. "Perhaps we'd better all use some of her water," she said.

Pure looked at her in surprise but nodded and took her water skin out with such fervor she almost dropped it.

Stormclouds stumbled and fell to his side. He was breathing heavily but already his eyes had begun to clear.

As quick as they could, they applied the healing waters to all of their wounds, binding them in soaked poultices. By the time they were done there were only two bottles left.

"What of him?" Jayd asked, pointing at the sweating and struggling Stormclouds.

"Bind him," Rayn ordered.

Ironfang obliged and while Stormclouds struggled and tried to disappear, yet Ironfang held him fast.

"His strength is still enhanced," Ironfang told them.

Rayn walked up. He looked at Stormclouds' great wounds. Yet he was still alive. Alive, in spite of Lifebreath's deadly gift.

He knew why they'd had to wait this long hour now. He knelt down in the dragon's reach. He carefully prepared a ritual that had been taught to him since he was a young student of the wiseman. It was one that had been known for centuries and was said to bring resistance to the plague. But it would only work if they found one who resisted the plague already, as those slain by it had no blessing in their blood.

He got his bowl and took some blood, tears and bone from the screeching Stormclouds and, feeling prompted, he added a few drops of Lifebreath's gift. He worked the ritual, scribed the symbols, spoke the long poem. In the fading light of the day, while the sun still shone, he dipped the staff in the bowl.

"Will it work?" Pure asked him.

"We will know only in the morning," Rayn replied. He was tired.

The gate guard had mercifully come to the surface, bringing Ironfang's old chains, and Ironfang himself used them to bind Stormclouds more permanently. They had used the last of the waters to heal Stormclouds' broken bones, and to ease the terrible scar on his side after they had purged it of the curse. Their efforts were apparently having great effect since he was now asleep.

"I think he will live," Jayd said.

They shared a sleepless night in shifts, a dragon and their rider struggling to stay awake while they waited to see if the Divine would answer their prayer for a cure or to see if they would turn themselves. Those that tried to sleep were woken only by the gentle movement of the chains as a cursed dragon slept.

The change within

A new day dawned and Rayn held out his staff to the earliest morning light. When it burst out blue, he breathed a sigh of hope. Finally, they had a weapon against the plague.

He approached Stormclouds while all others watched on. At the sound of his footsteps, the dragon opened his eyes, deep brown at last, yet bloodshot and pained still. Ironfang stood guard over the fallen dragon.

He spoke, his voice even more husky and deep than before, if it was possible. "Wiseman. I remember you. Ahh! Have you come to end my life in mercy?"

"No, Stormclouds."

"You are wounded? Are you... oh, it was me, yes, now I remember."

"How did this happen?" Rayn asked.

"I, ooh, the pain is great young man, are you sure you won't end my life?"

"Please, I seek answers first."

Stormclouds huffed, the fight gone out of him. "We fought against the plague as it massed its first horde at Ferriswold of the Celtwyld. No further dragons had fallen and I felt myself always very safe. But a cursed hawk carried a snake and it pierced my armor just the slightest here. I almost did not feel the bite and paid it no heed. My folly was my own! They are led now by a man, a man I have never seen, but he wears the robes of a trapper of your very people, wiseman."

"His name is Hak," Rayn said.

"Little good that knowledge does us now," Stormclouds coughed, "but he still bears all the tactics of a sober mind. The plague seems particularly cunning this time."

"Wait, didn't we kill him? Didn't Rhoc put an axe in his back?" Jayd asked.

"That might explain his healing," Stormclouds said, "he is a misshapen individual now, hunchbacked and crippled, a crocodile's claw as his right hand. The plague may have healed him but it does so poorly. And I, how am I alive? However imperfectly you have healed me wiseman, I thank you. I think within the next month I will be able to stand again."

"We have need of you much, much sooner than that," Rayn replied. "I have learnt a new prayer; do you want to be the first recipient of it?"

Stormclouds huffed. "Yet you are not cursed? Are you sure I am the first?"

Rayn put his staff to Stormclouds' brow. "Living Divine, bless this creature to your glory – his time is not yet come."

Even as he said the words, Rayn knew he had missed something in the ritual.

Dr Joseph Ireland

While he still thought about it, Pure piped in. "Your powers are best at water, and Lifebreath's gift was given as water that you made the plaguecursed to drink. I am guessing you need to bless water instead."

How could she know that? Rayn was bothered but still wondered if there wasn't an element of truth in what she said. Besides, if she was wrong, perhaps she would cease to council him all the time.

Again Nightseer, the gate guard, was summoned and he brought up six great barrels of water. The high warden had not yet returned so he was alone. And really, really, anxious to see that no plaguecursed would find their way to the gate of his prison.

So Rayn blessed the water instead. Taking the largest of the water containers, Rhoc's, he anointed Stormclouds and poured the rest down his parched throat.

He swallowed and coughed. Then he roared and his voice was his own again. A second later, he appeared up into the sky, hovering for a moment before falling to the earth.

His healing was truly miraculous. Taking Rayn's leave, he pushed his face into the barrel and drank all that remained.

Then he roared in victory again, the pain filled scar on his belly fading.

"This is what was needed," he roared. "I must take you back to the battlefront now. Oh." He was unsteady on his feet. "Or later today, I think."

"I'm sorry, but I feel it is more important to engage this quest," Rayn said, smiling through tears of victory. "However, bring six barrels each morning. I can fill them all. And if you bring another wiseman's staff, I will share my blessing, thus they will have the prayer as well. This is a good day. This is a very good day indeed!"

They laughed at the reckless abandon with which their past foe drank from a second barrel.

Then, just in the instant in which Stormclouds thrust his head down again, Rayn clearly saw a vision in the waters. It was a mountain, covered in snow. And in that vision Rayn knew exactly where the Divine was sending them next. They needed to meet someone there. Someone who had something they needed, who completed a circle...

"Wait!" he shouted, but it was too late. Stormclouds took a quick gulp and sat up again. "Too late," Rayn replied.

"You saw something?" Pure asked.

Rayn nodded.

"That way," Jayd pointed further south, without even needing to be asked.

They were gone within the hour, leaving Stormclouds resting by his barrels, waiting for the hour his strength returned enough to carry them, one at a time, back to the battlefront. This water would save humans and dragons.

This water was a gift of the Divine, the last gift of Lifebreath.

***

They flew with all their speed, which was considerable in Ironfang's case. However, even he was no match for Darkwing's speed at night – he seemed to take great leaps through the darkness itself. Jayd had no trouble finding opportunities to practice flying with him. The group shared a warm fire each night and there was always wood since Rhoc had learnt how to uproot trees. He was stronger than a dragon, for his size, and they regarded him with wary respect.

Pure was sitting by the evening flames, causing them to dance in strange patterns and different colors.

"It's so amazing how you do that," Jayd said to her. "I wish I knew how."

"You can, I can teach you," Pure offered. "It is a skill that one can learn, not demonry. What is demonry, anyway?"

Jayd turned unconsciously to Rayn. Telling stories was his job. Seriously, only the wiseman was supposed to know and tell the old stories around the firelight at night. Rayn liked it how Jayd respected that.

"It is said that by faith, all things are possible," Rayn replied. "But that is more than mere confidence; it is being able to see your outcomes before they occur. It takes great patience and power."

"That's true," Pure interrupted.

Jayd coughed to suggest she should be listening instead. Pure nodded and looked at Rayn.

Rayn continued. "Now, the Divine knows what is best for us and is made up of all the wisdom in the universe. When our souls die we return to the Divine, gaining great power, and serve it. However, there are some who do not have a change of heart and hold on to this world instead of moving on. Those people can misuse the Divine powers to influence events among the living. They are lost spirits and unclean souls.

Sometimes they actively strive to destroy that which is good, using their Divine knowledge and powers for evil. They are the demons, seeking always to destroy the works of goodness. They use truth and power to deceive and destroy all that is good and kind and true. Their power is known as demonry."

He paused, allowing his words to sink in. He thought he'd told the story rather well.

"Yes, that's pretty much the gist of it," Pure agreed. "Though our people called it 'treachery', not demonry: Perverted truth. It did not cause much trouble in our day because the people were very well educated. Now that humans are so much more ignorant, I'm not surprised you struggle so much."

Rayn was bothered by that suggestion; she was always comparing her people to his and making his people seem primitive and uneducated.

"But what I don't understand yet," she explained, "is why you are so *good* at what you do Rayn? There were wisemen in my day but it took many of them working together to achieve what you do alone. Are you a particularly gifted wiseman? I have not met any others. Has humanity perhaps changed? Or does your ignorance increase your faith?"

Ironfang shifted his stance, unconsciously preparing for battle since that last question had sounded like an insult. Rayn assumed that, ironically, Ironfang couldn't even tell he was doing so and chose not to point it out to him.

Darkwing answered instead. "A caution, your royal youth, you speak of the wiseman in such casual tones. Wisemen are invested with all the faith of their people. To insult them is to challenge their entire culture."

"I only mean to instruct," she argued in the common tongue, "and … to answer my own questions."

"I am sure," Darkwing replied, "that a budding woman of your intelligence and charisma can find more constructive means of challenging the deeply held beliefs of other people?"

Rayn could tell it was flattery, but Pure seemed taken in by it. "Yes, good point Darkwing. I am sorry, Rayn, if I give offence. I am… too curious."

It was like a weight off his chest but he didn't really know why. It was good that Darkwing had stood up for him, for all his people. Rayn had wanted to say, 'show some respect' for ages, but didn't know how. He hadn't even thought of just asking for it. He was thankful for Darkwing's tact.

"Curiosity is no crime," Rayn said, sincerely, "and I enjoy your questions. I do not think I am of any particular talent among men, other than I am under a far greater weight of responsibility than most. As are you. I mean, not to tell you what to do it's just I know it's big for you too. Um. Ugh!" Rayn found himself falling over his own words when trying to talk to her, again. It was a peculiar effect she had on him. "Perhaps we know truths even your people did not understand?"

"Oh, that's not likely," she said without a pause.

Here we go again, Rayn thought.

Ironfang laughed at him on the inside.

Rhoc huffed; Fairystone wanted to speak. She stood up on a log in the fire, on the unburnt section. "Men aren't fools," she shouted, but it sounded like the tiniest bell far away tolling in a thick fog.

"I agree," Darkwing said. "I do not think it is any ignorance on the part of men, for is it not told among the ancient Oordu that faith must be based on truth to be real? Belief in something is not power 'til it is belief in something that is true."

Fairystone shouted. "But that man has changed in the past years is true. If you had the eyes to see, you would see what I say is true."

"Mankind has changed then?" Pure wondered aloud then pondered in silence for a moment. She looked up at the stars. "Hmmm... I wish I had a teacher," she said, and turned over to go to sleep.

***

Late the next day, Rayn pressed his nose further into the ruffled folds of his cloak, trying to warm himself against the heated body of a dragon. It rarely rained on Pearl, in his experience. Instead, the ground was watered by the mists. On cold days like today the clouds would become heavy, reaching down to touch the earth, covering it with a thick veil. Countless tiny droplets of water would float in the air, sticking to everything they touched. Over the hours everything unprotected by sealed doors or a warming fire would soon be dripping wet; a slow drenching of water that stole away all heat from his body and from which there was no other protection.

Dragons labored against the thick air, growing tired. "I think it wisest if we end this day early." Darkwing suggested.

Trembling from the cold, Rayn could only nod.

Her hands pale, Pure refused any help starting a fire, though as much as any apprentice Rayn knew the prayers to drive away the water from the wood. They ate their rations in silence, resting under Darkwing's enormous wing. Though he provided no more protection from the drenching mist than the fire, his service kept the warm air close, and allowed them to dry off their bedding just a little before they headed off for a brief sleep in the darkness.

"We'll need to snuggle up," Jayd announced.

Rayn said nothing. It was the only thing to do when camping out in the mist. Pressed between the bodies of dragons, a tangle of limbs and soggy bedding, Rayn expected it would be many hours before he fell asleep. But it wasn't.

***

Rayn was awoken sometime in the dark night. Ironfang had stretched out, Darkwing had curled up. Jayd and Rhoc were still lying back to back against him.

Immediately Rayn saw what had awoken him. Pure was up, and had left their sorry, wet huddle. Instead she sat alone, staring into the fire. He wondered what she was doing. Was she trying to keep away the cold with her old friend the fire? It seemed an odd thing to try to do when there was a camping huddle nearby.

Then he noticed a gleam in her eye, a glistening of water. Was she crying?

Rayn listened to the patter of the drops as water fell from the trees and dragon wings, the only light the dying fire before him.

Pure said nothing, and neither did he.

She was pulling away again, keeping her distance from them all physically, and socially. He wondered why she always did this. She was always the last to embrace when offered, the first to seek solace. He wondered what she was thinking.

He looked at her, silent in the darkness as she stared into the dancing flames. She didn't reach out to move them, or change them into miraculous colors. She didn't move at all, and he wondered what it was that her heart was looking at.

For a moment the thought occurred to him that he should probably speak to her. That he should, as his father had so often done for him, sit by him and say nothing; filling silence with the warmth of his affection.

But she was Pure, and in one week she had gone from being just another young girl, to being the sole surviving princess of a forgotten empire. It was a lot to process, and she would probably need time to do it.

Rayn sighed, and turning over fell straight to sleep.

The teacher

They flew the next day over broken scrublands as the air grew colder, heading up and into the continent. The mountain was still a day away. They had two saddles, so Rayn and Rhoc rode Ironfang, while Jayd and Pure accompanied Darkwing. Fairystone rode in Rhoc's pocket, and seemed very happy there.

In the late afternoon, a dark mood swung over Ironfang and his strength slackened.

What is it? Rayn asked.

What? Oh, I forget, he lied, and sped on.

Rayn watched closely; some darkness had arisen from the past to trouble his dragon. He'd probably forgotten the event but not how it made him feel. And that feeling was upon him and would cloud his judgment. Ironfang was too troubled by the past to deal with the present.

Rayn's spirit grew in hope; he was a healer and a wiseman. Surely he could help? *What darkness conceals your path?* he asked his dragon in as soft and gentle manner as he knew.

He felt an odd tug and knew a part of his dragon's heart had suddenly hidden itself from him. It was a lonely, almost painful feeling.

Nothing I would trouble you with, good wiseman, Ironfang replied.

Rayn waited.

Ironfang sighed.

I can see there will be little hiding the truth from you. And the hidden part of his friend's heart began to open up to him once more. *When I was young, I often watched how men suffered. How wives lost husbands and children died of plague. I watched them suffer and would often ask myself, 'where is the Divine'? How can they allow this if they are loving and just?'*

Suddenly the anger surfaced anew and Rayn felt it come dangerously close to his own heart. Ironfang continued, his voice coarse, *and I decided that if Divinity did not answer there was none, or no final justice for the wicked. Only what justice could be imposed by others. Tell me, wiseman, if you have faith, what evidence do you have of Divinity? Your staff, did you know, is just a machine, a very clever machine. The faith you claim is just a natural power of all life. There is no final justice.*

Suddenly they were struck by a great wind, Rayn had no time to reply. *If Divinity chooses to answer, then so be it,* Rayn thought to himself.

Ironfang was thrown off balance. He was a large dragon, and very strong, but the wind had caught him, throwing him about. Rayn was almost thrown off; fortunately the saddle was very good. Within seconds, they fell clumsily to the ground.

"Is that your answer?" Ironfang roared, his voice angry, his heart in pain.

Rayn picked himself up from the sand. "Ouch," he said.

Ironfang walked over, putting out his claw to help Rayn up, watching the sky warily. "Just a freak sand pillar," he insisted.

Then Rhoc cried out. It sounded like a confused groan but Rayn understood that he meant, *'Hey come check this out guys!'*

Rayn wasted no time. It was a strange statue, half fallen over in the dust, covered with long dead weeds. It looked like a man's head and torso, arms and one eye missing.

"What is it?" Rayn asked.

"Curious indeed," Ironfang said with a smile. "I think the woman you like would want to see this," he said, referring to Pure.

"I don't *like* her," Rayn protested, "and she's not a woman, yet."

"How do you define women then?" he mocked. "Is it a ritual you need to do? Or a special age at which womanhood 'happens' to a girl, eh? You humans are always making up the strangest laws. But then again, that's what led to your technologies. Technologies that resulted in the invention of things like *that.*" He pointed to the man's head.

By then Darkwing had joined them.

"You all right?" Jayd asked them.

Pure leapt from her dragon and ran over. "A *teacher!*" she shouted. "Here, in the middle of nowhere? What is this place? Look!" She said, pointing out other stones which, now to the aided eye, began to mark out what may have once been pillars in a large hall.

They were standing in a room.

"A teacher!" she said, kneeling down to the ground. She brushed the stone statue's face and head, but then grew sad. "He is asleep," she announced.

They were silent.

"We dragons have no need of teachers," Darkwing explained. "All our knowledge is hidden in the ribbon of life inside every part of our bodies, and all we learn passes to our children. It has made us strong, but you humans, for all your physical weakness, are very clever."

"We stored our knowledge here, in the teachers," Pure explained. Borrowing Rayn's little knife she then pulled the dark, black rock from its right eye. It was not likely to be valuable, it was so dark and faded. But she collected her treasure nonetheless.

"Wait!" Rayn called. In the distance, his helm had just spotted three dark, winged creatures. And they were flying towards them at great speed.

Dragons? Ironfang asked.

"Dragons, with riders!" Rayn said in disbelief.

"We should meet them here on the ground," Darkwing explained. "It is peaceful in dragon culture to do so."

"And besides, if they do not know we have a changer with us, it will be better should they prove to be foes or cursed," Ironfang replied, a keen mind for any tactical advantage.

Fifty breaths later the other dragon riders flew up. Even before they arrived, Rayn could see they were from a faraway land. Their manner of dress was strange yet well suited to those that might fly often, and very high in the colder clouds. Their helmets were peaked with strange plumed points, and they bore spears of such a great length they could be used from a dragon with ease.

Their leader dismounted and saluted Rayn and his companions.

"Hail!" He said. "Does any speak the tongue of Venfirth?"

"I do," Rayn replied.

The man looked surprised, "Good. Very well. I am Norvich, and I come in peace. We have a gift for the dragon riders of the central continent."

Rayn relayed his words,

Be wary, rider, they have daggers in their boots and their helmet plumes likely conceal knives as well. Ironfang informed him.

He inquired of the Divine, yet felt the men intended no harm.

Rayn stood forward. "I am Rayn, wiseman of the Celtwyld, and I am a dragon rider. What gifts do you speak of?"

The man ran forward and bowed, indicating towards his companions to unpack. "Two weeks ago this day, the oracle of Venfirth spoke of the rise of the dragon riders again! She bade us take you provisions and tools of our trade. We... I cannot believe it! You are real? You truly do claim your dragon?"

"And he me," Rayn explained. "As does my sister here, with her black dragon." Then he took a moment to catch her up on what was being said.

"I don't understand," Jayd said. "If they're so glad to see dragon riders, what are they riding?"

Rayn looked and immediately understood, he turned to Norvich for confirmation. "You are not your dragon's rider? I mean, you ride together but you are not bonded?"

Norvich cast his eyes down. "No, we are not. But we have been great allies to our dragons for many years, we call ourselves 'dragonfriends'."

It's one of the things we disliked about those southern dragons, Ironfang explained. *Thankfully dragons that will take a rider are few and far between. You are probably looking at all the dragonfriends in this man's entire kingdom.*

Are you always reading my thoughts? Rayn asked Ironfang.

He seemed offended. *Whenever you allow me*, he replied.

But Rayn didn't mind, and it had been useful information.

"Please, goodman Rayn, priest of the central continent, the oracle has spoken. You must take these gifts off us. She speaks of a terrible plague that will touch the land as a sign that the dragon riders have been found. Once the inner circle is formed, the other dragons will feel the call of their riders and soon many thousands of us may take to the air as one!"

Rayn rejoiced at the thought, even as a sobering idea pressed against his heart. "But what if your dragon does not bond to you?"

Norvich looked around nervously, then cast his eyes down again and whispered. "It is still a very real concern. Yes. Perhaps he will claim some small child that cannot hold his reins? I don't know."

"You see, we do not ride with reins; hands are enough," Rayn encouraged him, but then he realized that probably wasn't what Norvich wanted to hear right now. He wanted him to say, *There's no way your faithful friend there would ever take a rider other than yourself!*

"Please, good priest Rayn, accept these gifts as sacred from the lands of the south. We fight with you against the plague!"

They laid out great saddlebags of food, clothing and bedding. The gear was crafted with great care and concern, and designed to fit dragon and rider perfectly. They did, however, have no use of the bridles and, as

Rayn was soon to realize, that made the southern dragons jealous and anxious in the extreme to have him complete the first dragon circle. There was also a compass and spyglass in each pack, rare items of extreme value to Rayn's people.

They received the gifts with gratitude, laying two loads on the mighty Ironfang.

"Now, if you will, you may receive a blessing from our priestess?" Norvich requested.

"What is a 'priestess'?" Rayn asked, and was introduced to a young woman, only a year or two older than he, pretty, with long brown hair and hazel eyes. She was holding a wiseman's staff and Rayn realized she was a wiseman of her tribe. How strange these people were! But Rayn was wary; he didn't know the priestess at all, nor the tenets of her faith. It could taint his cause… although Norvich's gifts were well meaning and would keep them warm in the higher air, which meant they could travel faster now.

So at his suggestion, they performed a trusting ritual, which was odd since the priestess didn't do it exactly quite right. But whatever she did, it seemed to work and their staves resonated with a brief white light of Divine blessing on their respective works. The priestess' staff was green; that was fairly common color for wisemen. Rayn decided they could trust her.

"Rayn," Pure said. "Why don't you teach them how to make blessing water? They can stand better against the plague in their own lands, as they surely will need to."

He was struck with the truth and simplicity of her suggestion, and proposed it immediately to the priestess.

She prayed about it, and looked enthusiastic, telling Norvich, "This is no doubt the blessing we seek to pay us for our labors." So Rayn taught her the prayer and passed his blue light to her, and her staff glowed blue too, for just a second, indicating that the sacred truth had been successfully passed to another.

A new wiseman was ready to heal men and dragons from the plague.

Rayn carefully taught her the correct use of the prayer as he had received it and the full story of how it had come about, since that was part of its truth. She seemed to listen very intently. He only hoped she had respect for his stories but then again, a priestess was *like* a wiseman so surely she had to?

"Rayn, there is one more thing I wish to give you," Norvich said. "Though I am loath to part with it. But I can see now that it was never mine to keep."

Then Norvich, dragon warrior of the southern continent, pulled from a saddlebag a bronze gauntlet. It was polished and well cared for but the tarnish still clung readily to it.

A dragon rider's gauntlet.

Norvich handed him the gauntlet with almost sacred reluctance. As soon as Rayn donned it, it glistened with new light, the tarnish fading in an instant. He felt the will of a hundred generations of warriors from the southern continent who had held this gauntlet while they warred for the

Divine. This was a sacred object and Rayn was deeply touched by the gift.

He demonstrated his gratitude in a hug, which the man seemed unsure of what to do with.

"I have a question," Pure asked, speaking to both Norvich and Rayn in the language of dragons.

Norvich replied, speaking in the language of dragons though his speech was far from perfect, "Ask, good maiden, my truth will serve you."

Rayn could tell he'd meant to say 'I will answer you truthfully,' but that it didn't translate so well from his native tongue into dragon.

She smiled. "Can you tell me more of this oracle? What does she look like?"

Norvich smiled. "She is beautiful eternally. She sits as one who is wise, teaching the priestesses, for they alone can bear her gaze."

"Sounds like an interesting person," Rayn agreed.

Norvich grinned like he'd managed to keep a secret. "Perhaps, but she is no person, wiseman, she is a soul made into stone centuries ago-"

Then Pure interrupted someone else again. "It's a teacher!" She squealed, and turned on Rayn. "They have a working teacher!"

"What is this?" Norvich said with a scowl.

"Forgive her, she is burdened with too much learning," Rayn smiled.

Pure shrugged off his thin façade of disdain. "A teacher! See, like this statue."

Norvich looked towards the broken statue and his brow furrowed. He looked over to his priestess and she nodded. "That would seem to be in the form of the oracle," he said.

Pure was almost hopping from one foot to another in excitement, her heart still young. "I must - please, can you let me speak to your oracle? As soon as we are able we will journey there! Can we leave *now?*"

Norvich was silent a moment. "We would be honored to see you again, young woman, with your companions. Your priest can test our priestess' knowledge of your prayer. We can show you our great cities and you may ask of us any gift you seek."

"You are too kind," Rayn said, wondering if the southern people really were so generous or if they just say things like that. "And we would be honored to travel there. Perhaps when we have done with this business that now presses us?"

"Yes, perhaps then," Norvich said.

Pure huffed.

Rayn held out his hand, and in a strange gesture of friendship, Norvich grabbed his forearm. It gave him a bit of a surprise, but he held firm nonetheless. He sensed in Norvich a strong warrior and a good man.

"I bid you great speed for your task of returning these sacred waters and prayers to your people. Share all you can, for that is the only way we will survive," Rayn said.

"Agreed, and thus," offered Norvich, "let us share a meal ere we depart."

Manhood

They rested well that evening in the company of the southern riders. Rayn lay against Ironfang's warm and muscular forearm, eating the simple soup Rhoc often made, dipping the bread the southern riders had brought. It was a light dinner; it always was while they travelled. Rayn looked at the three Venfirth dragonfriends: one a priestess, one a solid warrior, and Norvich, who stood with all the noble bearing of a chieftain. Rayn marveled how they all obeyed him, their leader, without question. How they deferred to his wishes. How they waited on his words.

He has earned their respect. Ironfang explained to Rayn.

They really do trust him, don't they, Rayn wondered.

A trust he has earned. Ironfang repeated. Tell me, rider, what do you see? Are you so focused on how they obey his commands to be blind to see how he watches over them? What he had done to earn their trust? Look – he knows his people. He really knows them. I bet he could tell what each likes, where they come from, what their family's wishes are as they send a new warrior out to serve in his cause. I wager he knows just how to motivate each one of them and how far he can push them in requiring them to obey. He <u>knows</u> them and uses that knowledge to help them. He does not rule from tyranny – believe me, I know what that is *like. They allow him to lead them because they know that he will do what is best for all, even if that means sacrificing them for a cause they believe in more than their own lives.*

Rayn watched. As he did, the priestess stood up, and he noticed Norvich glance in her direction. What was he thinking? It was impossible to tell. But it was obvious that he was watching his people. A moment later, he offered her the remaining portion of the cured meat he had been eating. At first, she refused him but at his insistence that he was full, she relented.

Rayn pondered; surely he could not have eaten so well on his journey that he truly was not hungry tonight?

He knows her strength is worth more to him tonight than his own hunger. Ironfang explained, seeming the exceptional student of the motives of both dragon and man. *Tell me, young wiseman, do you know your people so well as to earn their trust, as does he? Can you tell what fears keep them up at night or what dreams give them delight in the future? Can you tell when and how a woman in your care best meets the challenges of womanhood each month?*

Rayn was startled. Boys weren't supposed to know about sacred women's business, though the men joked about it often; it seemed to be a time when a husband would run from his wife's sudden onset of insanity. But Ironfang made it seem like a process that could be predicted and assisted, even something that could help win you the respect and... perhaps... gratitude of a woman. He had to admit he was ignorant. He suspected most men were. He had no idea where to start.

Dr Joseph Ireland

He looked at his friends, those he'd known his whole life and those he was only just coming to know. He made a promise to himself that to be a man, he would care enough to get to know each of them truly well, whatever that meant for them as individuals.

Then Stormclouds turned up.

It wasn't good timing, and it wasn't a good way to enter either. The three southern dragons jumped up in fright, hissing and unsheathing their teeth and claws, and it was all their riders could do to bring them to heel again. They were solid allies, it was true, but they did not know their riders' thoughts or feelings.

"You are a surprisingly difficult group to find," Stormclouds said, hovering as was his way.

"Stand down, wingling!" Norvich's dragon ordered, growling in dragon.

Stormclouds stared down at him with disdain. "You are on foreign land, southerner, be careful what you *request*."

The southern dragons roared with contempt.

But they did not fight.

"Southerners," Stormclouds huffed in disdain to Rayn, and threw down a barrel designed to be held by a dragon, and three wisemen staves. "You should have seen the tears and fuss the humans made when I told them I needed their staves! If I do not return in an hour they will be seeking dragon blood, I am sure! And here is a barrel, the Matron bids you bless it now so that she can test the other wisemen's prayers. Set to it, boy."

Ironfang gave Rayn a warning and he turned to notice Norvich slowly reaching for his sword, so disgusted was he at Stormclouds' manner.

"Stand down, man and dragon," Rayn said, turning to Pure in case he needed solid power to back up his request. As it was, things seemed to calm soon; no-one actually wanted to fight with the plague haunting them.

Rayn needed no glory and stood aside to watch the priestess bless the waters well and truly to his satisfaction. Then he bid the southern riders Divine speed and with a noble salute, they rode off, casting dark looks at Stormclouds.

"We *have* to see their oracle," Pure insisted.

"Not today," Rayn replied. He took another hour passing his blessing, as carefully as he could, to the three wisemen's staves that had so faithfully been lent to him. The blessing passed well to each, but Rayn was sorry there was no wiseman present to learn the story, so he told it to Stormclouds instead, hoping it would suffice.

Then Rayn asked, "How goes the war?"

"Not well. Another two human towns are turned to dust, though the waters protect the dragons. We expect to meet our next horde tonight. It is frustrating; the enemy seems to know our minds, gaining in strength each and every night, even as we continue to fight! We can only hope this blessing can turn the battle."

Stormclouds left and Rayn's heart felt riddled with sorrow.

Your Divinity sure has a strange way of telling us to rush, Ironfang joked. Throwing us to the ground like this, then telling us to hurry lest more towns are turned to dust?

Rayn smiled, and explained, *We meet the messengers from the south who bring gifts. We meet Stormclouds and bless not one but four staves of the wisemen? Thank I for the wind that downed us here. Blessed it was, as blessed as the names of the Divine. We even found a teacher for Pure, whatever that is.*

Ironfang huffed, but he smiled.

Rayn continued. *Perhaps there never was a bad thing that happened to man or dragon; only an unwanted thing. But all things are for a purpose. Have faith and do not lose hope, my dragon.*

Ironfang turned, "You have faith enough for us both! And hope. And you are not in want of any compassion. You are a good man, and I an evil dragon… so tell me, do you know what your trial is, Rayn of the Celtwyld?"

He paused. Matron had called it pride, but Ironfang knew him better.

"It is usual for a Dragon and Rider to share complementary strengths. Your weakness, however, matches my own pace for pace. We are arrogant, my young man. Arrogant and proud," Ironfang said and walked off to stretch out on the ground.

Oh, thought Rayn. Ironfang, and the Matron, had both seen right through him.

Then he looked at his new gauntlet. Its grip was true and would never fail to hold on to bridle or weapon. He perceived it had other powers but they too, would perhaps reveal themselves one day.

"We have to go see the oracle," Pure suddenly broke into his thoughts.

"In time," Rayn repeated.

He could see his reply did not satisfy her.

"Come," he said, "let us make use of the early night. We should leave this moment to the white mountain to find the one that completes the circle. To the air, dragon riders of Pearl!"

Regarding dragons

13 Dragons of the far mountain

Late the next day, Rayn sensed there would be trouble before he could see any. Perhaps it was the tingling in the staff? Or perhaps it was the way Ironfang tensed at seeing the far tree line at the distant mountain scorched by recent fire.

Instinctively they rode lower in the sky, Darkwing, who carried the female riders, followed their example.

You don't suppose – Rayn began to ask Ironfang.

The explosion of fire breath from below seemed to answer the question before it was going to be asked. Two dragons, large for their kind, were racing up to meet them. One was smaller, lithe, with the narrower jaw typical of female dragons. The larger was huge, brutish. Not at all like other dragons that Rayn had seen.

Our kind only lives a thousand years, unless we find a compelling cause to drive us. Ironfang explained as he watched the pair with excitement, and rage. *This is what you might term a noble dragon. He is over a thousand and five hundred years, I'll wager.*

And he easily had twice the wingspan of Ironfang.

Rayn felt the heat within his dragon was getting dangerous to touch. His heart was filling with a kind of insatiable battle lust that had clearly once served him to escape all capture.

But not the kind that would help in their cause today.

Darkwing was already taking to the lower air, showing deference to the dragons on whose domain they were trespassing. That, and keeping Jayd and the princess safe.

Ironfang, on the other hand, was perhaps a bit too proud to take the wiser course of action immediately. His delay infuriated the noble dragon.

And his fury provoked Ironfang even more.

The noble swung around, cutting off Ironfang's descent until nothing but a total retreat would be possible.

Tactically, a very vulnerable position, Ironfang pointed out.

The female took up a circling position, watching warily.

Fairystone pressed against Rayn's tunic but did not reveal herself yet.

Rhoc growled.

For a moment Ironfang and the noble just glared at each other, neither backing down, both beating their wings fiercely to remain at the same height.

Let us try talking, Rayn said.

You might as well, Ironfang replied, clearly thinking it would make little difference to the outcome.

Rayn stood up and the noble dragon's eyes grew wide. When the dragon spoke, his voice was deep and old. But it was filled with power.

"Riders," he muttered. "I heard the call."

Then why did he not come? Rayn wondered.

She only called her children to the conclave, none others. I suspect she wanted those she felt she could most trust. The loathing of men runs deep in this world, rider. She is lucky there has not been more resistance.

Why isn't there? Rayn wondered.

Because they're waiting to see if we can succeed, before deciding whether or not to kill us all, he said.

Rayn clenched his teeth. *Dragons,* he cursed.

The noble dragon spat at the ground, flaming spheres falling to the earth. "Your quest means nothing to me," he spoke as though continuing a conversation with someone he couldn't see. "You have transgressed our territory, rider and dragon. I don't care about the bonding. I have never felt the call and I never will. We have risen above that now. You will find dragons far harder to subdue this time, human. We are older, our memories longer. I remember what you did to our ancestors! What treachery!"

"He is not guilty of his parents' crimes," Ironfang argued, dragon teeth grinding.

"Perhaps not," the noble said, settling into a circling pattern. Rayn was just beginning to think the tension was lowering when Ironfang showed him the deception in the way he flew, the tension in his unsheathed claws. The noble was not backing down, not at all.

The huge dragon continued, "But you, dragon, have broken ancient laws of your kind and you know it! We clearly placed our markings, wrote our signatures on the wind. Why do you risk death by your own actions?"

That angered Ironfang, as it probably was supposed to. "Clearly marked?" He was about to launch into a string of profanities and provocations but Rayn held him back.

Let them make the first act of war, he said.

Ironfang agreed.

"I will speak, if you will allow," Rayn shouted.

The noble looked surprised. "And who, I wonder, taught you how?"

"It is the gift of the Divine within me," Rayn told the dragon, hoping the calm in his voice would prevail. "And the ignorance of the signs, which shames me. We will depart hence we came and beg your forgiveness for our trespass."

The noble paused a moment, as though considering a reply.

Ironfang saw it before it even came. He folded his wings in front of himself as a fiery blast stuck them. It would have killed Rayn in an instant, but Ironfang's wings were powerful enough to protect them both.

"You will depart in death!" The noble roared in challenge.

Ironfang thought fast, *Have your silent friend take out the female.* And Rayn motioned to Rhoc. He jumped from the saddle and ran along Ironfang without a hint of fear.

The female was already diving towards Ironfang, hoping to land a telling blow before he recovered from the fiery blast. She paused; a puzzled look on her face, as Rhoc leapt from Ironfang's exposed back and flew towards her. She stopped mid-flight and let him sail right past her. He went screaming towards the ground.

Fairystone will save him, or his great strength, Ironfang decided.

But Rayn had other problems to worry about. The noble was closing. He felt Ironfang's will inside him and chose to surrender to the more experienced warrior's passion. They could not take to the higher air; it would require too much effort and too much time. They could fold their wings and try to evade the attack but the noble had great reach in his ironed talons.

So Ironfang charged him, head on. They grappled claws within heartbeats so that neither could successfully gouge the other.

Flapping furiously, they plummeted through the sky.

The female raced after, but wasn't able to help out in the hurling of wings and claws.

The ground seemed to race up to meet them. Four hundred leagues, then three hundred. Faster and faster it approached, while the fear welled up within Rayn.

He felt Ironfang's determination centered on his claws. He looked down and found his own knuckles white as he similarly clutched onto his staff. Ironfang was not about to let the noble free. He could tell that the older dragon was surprised at Ironfang's strength, but pride drove them both.

They were plummeting to their death and neither would let go.

Please, Rayn begged.

No, Ironfang replied. *I'll not let this fool tell me where I can fly!*

Ironfang roared. The noble tried to breathe fire on them again but Ironfang knocked his jaws away with his own head.

Two hundred leagues, one hundred.

Rayn looked around. No other dragons were in sight.

Fifty.

Suddenly the older dragon released Ironfang with a roar and Ironfang took the opportunity to scratch him badly on the underside of his wrists. Both dragons opened their wings and began to pull away from the fall. The larger size of the noble seemed to work against him and he collided with several trees before regaining his height.

Ironfang veered painfully in the sky and was about to level out when suddenly he turned upside down.

It was only by a miracle that Rayn managed to hang on. Ironfang had pre-empted the female's time of attack and at the last instant, turned around and clawed up at her. She still managed a good pummeling with her tail but it was a clumsy attack. Ironfang managed to gash her underside and put a sizeable cut in her wing. Screaming, she careened into the forest.

Where are the others? Ironfang wondered about the other dragon riders.

Rayn didn't know.

Ironfang was struggling to take the higher air.

Suddenly the forest below was covered in a dark smoke, the sun darkened in its glow.

What is this demonry? Rayn wondered.

It is no demonry, I assure you, Ironfang replied, *but wisdom. It is common for the older dragons to research forgotten lore and often they find old secrets, command of matter and time similar to what men have achieved with their tools.*

The smoke was rapidly growing to envelop them.

Come, wiseman. It is time to use your gifts.

Within heartbeats the smoke had surrounded them. Such was its thickness that he could scarcely see a few stretches in front of him, knowing his dragon's body only with his heart.

Dragon wing beats fluttered close by and Ironfang adjusted his flight.

But they were enveloped in the silent cloud once more.

Rayn knew what he had to do. He reached out to the Divine. He asked for vision beyond his own.

They saw the dragon at the same time. The noble was racing up from below to strike at Ironfang's neck.

Ironfang breathed fire, narrowly dodging the attack while drenching the noble in his toxic, incinerating fumes.

He roared with rage, his female's screech answering him from the sky.

The battle was joined. In an instant, Rayn found himself struggling to hold on as three dragons warred desperately in the sky. He looked about, knowing only that his dragon could see through his eyes, hoping it would do some good.

Ironfang was desperate, and powerful. The rage of a lifetime imprisoned, pent up within, exploded from him in fierce anger. Rayn could only temper it with compassion, striving desperately to turn blind rage into focused combat.

Something must have gotten through. They were holding their own.

Then the female came too close and in a desperate move, clamped her jaws on to Ironfang's wing.

Rayn did not wait for her to tear at the flesh. He leapt from the saddle and brought his staff down on her snout.

There was a blinding blue flash of retribution, and the female screamed and fell from the sky as though unconscious.

The noble roared, and Ironfang began to pull up into the higher air.

Then it betrayed them. A cyclone of wind formed underneath Ironfang's wings at the noble's bidding. It tore Rayn from his precarious clutching and sent him spiraling into the air.

Ironfang instantly folded his wings and went into a downwards plummet to try and catch him. Desperately Rayn reached out for Ironfang, spinning helplessly in the darkened mist.

For a moment, in the cyclonic winds, they lost sight of each other. Rayn held out his staff and it glowed like a beacon. He had no idea how close the ground, and instant death, was.

Then, with a roar of triumph and victory, Ironfang found him. A moment later they pulled out from under the smoke. It did not fade into the forest below.

An instant later Darkwing was beside them. Pure's face ran with tears, Jayd held her knives.

"I thought-" Darkwing began.

Then they turned as the noble and his injured mate descended from the clouds to face them a league away.

"Take my rider," Ironfang ordered, "I end this."

Rayn had no idea what his dragon was planning, some part of his heart was somehow hidden from him.

"But I–" Rayn protested, but a moment later Ironfang simply reached up with his tail and threw him over.

Darkwing caught him easily and hoisted him over to his back.

Ironfang began a rapid acceleration, roaring a death challenge at the noble.

The older dragon simply grinned and began to speed up as well, the female holding back. The clouds above him grew dark with power, seething in his commanded breeze.

Pure stood, the gem glowing at her brow, stilling the cyclone until the dark clouds were no longer of service to the noble. But still it ploughed on.

They met with an explosion of fire. The terrible sound of their collision echoed for leagues. Roaring with vengeance and fury, the two mighty dragons went crashing into the forest below.

The others raced to join them, finding them in the same moment as the female.

Ironfang had the older dragon subdued, the powerful jaws that had given him his name clasped firmly around the noble's mighty neck.

Darkwing rode up, and Rayn ran to the roble. "Surrender, or die," he ordered.

It closed its eyes, and surrendered.

***

An hour later, after healing, they sped on through evening skies.

"I still feel robbed," complained Darkwing, "that we are allowed no treasure for this victory."

Ironfang rode on in silence. Rayn knew his thoughts, that Darkwing had done nothing to earn that treasure. But he also knew Jayd, and if Darkwing's heart was any like her own, it was only said to tease him.

Tell them, Rayn told Ironfang.

"I have simply claimed a life debt," Ironfang informed him. "The two dragons owe us their allegiance now. It is an old law, older than the laws that claim no dragon is to trespass on another dragon's domain."

"That seems ironic," Jayd smiled.

"And unnecessary," Pure chastened them. "We have lost an hour now. I hope you're happy!"

Rayn smiled.

His dragon had just bested two others, and one a noble of air and smoke mastery. Sixty years in prison had not dimmed his battle sense one mote.

Happy?

Yes. They were very, very happy.

The dragon's village

Truly none could match Darkwing for speed in the night; he and Jayd were well rested with camp set up by the time Rayn and the others arrived. They spent a short night resting then set out again before first light. By the evening of the second day they approached the mountain Rayn had seen in vision. It stood out, quite a bit, from the surrounding hills and plains. It had steep sides and a snow capped peak.

Just the kind of place a dragon would love to roost.

"We should make camp," Ironfang told him. "Let us not risk confronting a dragon in the night."

"What fear have you?" Darkwing smiled, for he was strongest at night.

"Fear?!" Ironfang roared, causing Darkwing to cringe. Immediately Rayn pulled him back with his disapproval. "I have no fear. Bring on the night time if you wish."

"Perhaps," Rayn said, "but you have a point. We know nothing of this area. Perhaps we should set down for the evening, find some people to speak to. Perhaps we can find supplies, or perhaps another wiseman to teach?"

"Very well, rider," Ironfang said, glaring at Darkwing. But the black dragon just drove forwards confidently, with a smile – he was not about to let a freed prisoner intimidate him. Yet making others fear him seemed to be how Ironfang approached life, as though it might protect him in some way.

Soon they spotted a quiet human village near the leading edge of the mountain, near the base, and decided that would be the safest place to arrive. They landed quite a way out of the village, since it was likely that they were seen but did not want to cause a panic.

"Let us approach together," Rayn suggested, "as riders and dragons."

Jayd liked the idea but Ironfang wanted her and Darkwing to remain hidden, just in case there was trouble. Rhoc was happy to go wherever he was told. He was practicing talking all the time now, testing his words constantly or enjoying the sensation of humming to himself.

They walked their dragons along a flat riverbed that flowed down from the isolated town. Ironfang was convinced it was a sure way of indicating their benevolent intentions since they were entering from a direction that they would easily be seen.

They were just passing a bunch of huge bamboo plants when Ironfang suddenly turned his head.

What was that? He said.

What was what? Rayn asked.

It sounded like... someone was walking through the bushes. They're trying to surround us, rider!

Then let us introduce ourselves, Rayn said.

And give them the advantage! NO! Ironfang roared and leapt into the bamboo. Darkwing chased after him.

"Ironfang, don't, stop!" Rayn commanded but it was no use.

Suddenly Ironfang tripped. Rayn couldn't see what had happened as he was thrown from the saddle and over his dragon's head, Rhoc roaring as he suffered the same fate. But Ironfang informed him that there were ropes, and they were being held by men.

"Ironfang, yield!" Rayn yelled.

If Ironfang heard it, he did not indicate. A roar and thunder of blackness from behind indicated that Jayd and Darkwing were in a similar predicament.

Sudden ropes appeared and were thrown over his dragon. Rhoc snapped one in an instant but Ironfang reared up with anger, throwing his attackers away a great distance. He flung about, like a man trying to rid himself of ants, and grew angry.

If Rayn didn't stop him soon, Ironfang would harm the humans.

Suddenly Rayn felt someone grab him from behind and pin his arms behind his back, wresting his staff from his grip. Immediately Rayn yielded; he wanted to talk with them, not fight them. Rhoc too was grappled a moment later and following Rayn's example, allowed them to hold him fast. It would be their assailant's mistake; Rhoc was strong enough to break free but he was choosing not to.

Ironfang, however, was entering a frenzy of violence and fear. Rayn tried to break through, to tell him to calm down and submit, to give them a chance to talk. But Ironfang was not that kind of dragon, or perhaps he'd not learnt how it can be more powerful to wait.

Rayn looked around and saw Jayd holding Pure. It looked like Pure had been thrown from Darkwing and had struck her head. At first he was afraid but as men surrounded him with spears he chose to wait instead of rushing to her side. He did not believe she would be truly hurt anyway.

Suddenly a wild wind knocked Ironfang's feet from under him and he tumbled to the ground. Before he could get up, a new dragon simply appeared among the bamboo, merging out of them. She had been perfectly hidden, camouflaged, made unerringly into the shape of her environment. She wore a strange kind of bamboo armor, even for a dragon, and wielded short rods of bamboo, almost as high as a man, in each hand. On her head she had a strange, flat hat of bamboo that resembled a shield.

Ironfang roared a murderous challenge and stumbled to stand up. It was as if she'd done something to his legs, pinched a nerve or something.

He charged clumsily and she leapt nimbly out of his way, spinning around and allowing his momentum to send him crashing into the forest of bamboo. He stood up again, holding his now limp left arm and let out a roar again.

He was going to breathe fire but the bamboo dragon slid down to the ground to stand between Ironfang and Rayn. His dragon swallowed his breath, rather than risk harming his rider and then with an enormous leap jumped high in the air to try to fall on the bamboo dragon from above.

Rayn realized what was going to happen, even if he didn't see Ironfang's clever tail strike that winded his opponent. Yet still the bamboo dragon cunningly clobbered him in the chin and he hit the ground unconscious.

Ironfang was bound, and they tied his snout with smoking reeds that made it impossible for him to wake up. They dragged Rayn, Jayd and Rhoc, along with the roped form of Darkwing, to the riverbed. There they brought down some large, wheeled platforms for carrying the dragons, as though they did this sort of thing all the time.

"Where do you think they'll take us?" Jayd asked him as soon as they were close enough to walk together.

"They're taking us to their village," he replied. A moment later, Pure was thrust into his arms and they allowed him to carry her. She was soft and her skin so white. Without his staff he couldn't heal her but he allowed what goodness he could to flow from him to her. She came half way to waking up, muttering something incomprehensible, but reached up to hold onto his neck so that she was much easier to carry.

"Stay down Pure," he whispered to her in her language. "The dragons are all right. They're taking us to their town. We'll be fine."

No one could understand what their captors were saying, except Rayn. The most interesting thing was how they referred to the bamboo dragon as 'wisest,' apparently a title of the highest respect among them. They were discussing what her will would be for these two dragons, some saying that she would kill them for their trespass, others saying she would set them free as a warning to others. There was only one thing Rayn knew – a dragon would have the final say on whether they lived or died tonight.

***

Dr Joseph Ireland

Jayd looked up at the silhouette that was the bamboo dragon. She was powerful, that much was clear. Using human help she'd managed to best all them and their three dragons, though Rhoc's dragon had done nothing to help them. They were in what must have been the center of the village, powerful drums beating to please their dragon mistress. Dark smoke rolled from two great fires behind her and she looked... well, maybe powerful except the effect was a bit overdone. Really – smoke and silhouettes? Who does that?! Puppeteers?

They were kneeling on a bamboo platform and Rayn had gently placed Pure down. She had no idea he was strong enough to carry her for almost an hour; his arms must have been ready to fall off. They were all unarmed now; thankfully they hadn't taken away her dragon wing bracelet, just her swords, but still she felt strangely vulnerable. At least she also had Pure's air bracelet and she wasn't going to let go of that any time soon! They hadn't used metal chains on her as they did with Rhoc. Thankfully he could tell it wasn't time to break them just yet. She could tell he was following Rayn's example, as was she. Behind them Darkwing waited patiently. He too was bound but not very tightly.

Jayd was working on her own bonds all the way in. Truth of the matter was she'd slipped out of the knot half way into town and was simply holding the ropes on herself so they didn't fall.

These people were in for a real surprise.

Fairystone was nowhere to be seen, probably hiding somewhere in the folds of Rhoc's cloak. She was the wild card, the extra life, the last surprise. Hopefully it didn't turn violent again; this bamboo dragoness was hard to work out.

She certainly had the humans well organized. They were short, with strange, large eyes and big hands. They worked hard under her queenly glare.

Suddenly the drums stopped.

She spoke, in dragon, so Jayd had no idea what she said. But it sounded like a command.

Rayn stood to answer and was shoved back down again.

Pure twitched. Jayd realized she was conscious again and was only pretending to be asleep.

Rayn spoke from where he sat on the ground. After he'd spoken for twenty breaths or so, the dragon turned to deliberate with her humans.

Rayn turned to Jayd and whispered, loud enough for Rhoc and Pure to hear. "I've told the bamboo dragon of our quest; that we seek to complete the first dragon circle and that the Divine has led us here. She is not impressed, having sworn to never take a rider. These people are her servants."

"She's not like the other dragons I know," Jayd said.

"Her name is Windfyrth."

The dragon conferred with her humans in their strange, bubbly tongue. Rayn whispered even quieter, "We may have to show her just what we're capable of; wait for my signal."

"What signal?" Jayd asked.

The bamboo dragon suddenly roared something, bringing everyone to silence in the square. It sounded like a challenge.

14 Windfyrth

Rayn spoke to the bamboo dragon again, though Jayd had no idea what he'd said. It was frustrating not to be in the conversation all the time!

The dragon replied and turned her back.

"We don't have time for this," Rayn growled and got up on one knee, making all their guards raise weapons. He said something angry, then shouted at her as she turned away.

She said something in reply and pointed her nose towards their captured gear. It was as if she'd said, 'Like you can do anything about it without your staff,' to Rayn.

He let her turn away and then held out his arm. Jayd could feel the gathering divinity around him and sure enough, his staff leapt right out of the pile of captured gear, snapping the ropes that held it, and flew towards him.

That, Jayd decided, *is the sign.*

She slipped her bonds and activated her bracelets, forming a small cyclone that brushed away the poisonous herbs tied to Ironfang's snout. In a brilliant moment of inspiration she then turned the cyclone on herself and used it to fly high into the air. Pure was much faster and encircled them with flames before she even stood up. Their bright colors made the guards leap back in surprise. Rhoc snapped his chains like paper, sending several links flying away at such speed that they wounded the guards. Then a little mouse ran out from his boot. Cute little Fairystone, who was just so chatty all the time, burst from his shoe. She began to turn into her stone dragon form, massive boulders unfolding from the air to form a ring around them.

And Rayn, activating his staff, caused water to explode from every water barrel or cup nearby. It became a barrier around them in an instant, turning aside any darts or arrows the few alert guards managed to get off from around them.

People went running and fell back.

The bamboo dragon roared. She sucked in air to breathe on them but Pure shouted, and the dragon choked and spluttered instead. Darkwing slipped his bonds in moments and Rayn, striking his staff on the ground, broke Ironfang's bonds. In a matter of seconds both dragons stood by their side, protecting them from outside a wall of water and fire, stone and air.

Rayn pointed his staff at the bamboo dragon and said something commanding.

She hissed and shook her head, standing low as though nervous.

Rayn shouted, yet Jayd didn't need his gift to tell what he was saying: "You're not going to stop us."

For an instant, there was silence.

Jayd looked hard into the bamboo dragon's eyes, and saw a momentarily flicker of respect. But then it was gone, surrounded by enormous hardness and pride.

There was going to be war.

Without warning, a small human girl ran in between them and the bamboo dragon. She had dark hair, tied in two ponytails on either side of her head.

Jayd blinked.

It was Snow, the little girl from the Matron's mountain, and she stood as though trying to protect the stupid bamboo dragon.

"Stop!" she shouted, and by this time even Rayn had noticed her. "Please don't hurt this dragon."

Rayn looked annoyed, answering her in their natural language. "She is trying to stop us, we're *not* about to be her examples."

"You can't harm her! She is a *dragon!*"

Rayn paused. Then his anger subsided. Clearly even he could see the folly of trying to force a dragon against its will. Or maybe, considering Pure's power, he could - in which case Jayd had no idea why he backed down.

The dragon hissed at Snow and slowly Snow turned around. Then they locked eyes and froze.

Jayd knew immediately what had just happened. They had just found Snow - and Snow had found *her dragon*. Jayd found herself tearing up as she watched the intense connection, which she had felt herself.

It was as if they couldn't stop looking at each other. The dragon hissed and roared, but seemed unable to stop bowing her head. And Snow, both terrified and confused at once, held out her hand.

The proud bamboo dragon seemed to be fighting itself, hating herself even as it seemed to have no power against its own will to be joined. Her people looked around in confusion, unsure of what to do.

Snow just waited, without taking a step forward or looking away, until the Bamboo dragon, scratching against the stones as if she would gladly run away, finally submitted to her touch. There was a crack, like thunder, but it was inside. The kind of noise only a dragon rider would hear. There was a flash of deep green light between Snow's hand and the dragon's brow, and suddenly the struggling stopped.

Pure's flames and Rayn's water had long since dissipated.

Without thinking, she and the other dragon riders immediately bowed at the newly joined dragon and her human.

As one, Snow stepped behind her neck and the bamboo dragon lifted her up.

The citizens roared their protest.

Bamboo shouted at them and they fell silent. While men dropped their weapons and women wept, the dragon said many more things to them.

Citizens warily approached to see to their minor wounds and apologies. Then they began to prepare a hurried feast held in their honor that night, for them, for the dragons, and for the newest dragon and rider of Pearl.

Windfyrth

It wasn't until the festivities and dancing had died down a bit that Jayd finally got some answers from her village wiseman.

"She is Windfyrth, a dragon whose ancestors were born on another world: Thiaz. Do you know it, Pure?"

"Yes, I do," she said, but kept any more thoughts to herself.

"Good," Rayn said. "However, when the banishment began, Windfyrth's grandmother was caught on this world and had to remain. She taught her all she knew, and died here in this mountain passing on to her daughter this town, which held remnants of that world and her rider's children. Windfyrth is angry that she was not able to choose one of the descendants of this village but instead a stranger: Snow."

They looked over at Snow. She was close enough to hear them, patting her bamboo dragon on the neck while they looked out at the entertainment. Neither were saying anything and both looked lost in each other's company. They seemed very much at peace.

It was good to belong to a dragon.

"It is hard for a dragon," Pure explained. "The bonding used to happen just after hatching. It was much easier then, before the mind of man and dragon grew and began to make choices that would draw them apart. Now all is out of balance. The old harmony is lost. Dragons are born out of sync with their riders. It is a terrible thing."

Ironfang, Rayn's scary jail dragon, huffed. He must have agreed.

Rayn continued. "So she's been looking over this village, becoming a sort of lesser deity to them. I am glad we put a stop to that," he said.

"How did she find us?" Jayd asked, wondering if little Snow shared her gift.

"Ask her yourself," Rayn said, being unhelpful.

So Jayd walked over to Snow and asked, "Good evening, Snow. How are you?"

"We are fine now." She smiled, seeming deeply content. Her bamboo dragon looked over, regarding Jayd coldly but saying nothing. Why were all dragons jerks? Oh hang on, Fairystone was cool. It was just Rayn's and Snow's dragons.

"We were just wondering, how did you find us? How did you get here just in time?" Jayd asked.

"I've been tracking you," she replied, "ever since you left the mountain, ever since I ran down to tell my people and the mountain exploded right behind me. I've felt drawn to your cause. I didn't even have my parents' permission. I just followed you."

"Us? On dragons? Over half the continent and over a whole week?!" Jayd said in disbelief. "Can you fly?"

"No! It wasn't easy," Snow said, rubbing Bamboo's snout. Not Bamboo. What was her name again? Windy? Something or other. "I had to use my best judgment, keep my eyes to the sky. I knew you couldn't make it too far in a day and I had help. I made friends with the animals along the way and they helped get me there. I rode a young male

Penbuck for an entire day! I can... I suppose it's all right to tell you, I can speak to animals. I always have. I never told my parents; they would think me mad or possessed of some demonry. So the animals helped me and I found you here. And I didn't expect to find you attacking a dragon since you said you wouldn't! But there you were. And I had to stop you."

"Oh, Rayn wouldn't have harmed any dragon, well, unless it had the curse."

"That's what he keeps saying," Snow said.

"Sooo, are you going to travel with us?" Jayd smiled.

Snow looked hopeful but her dragon said something in her own language. Snow probably didn't speak dragon but naturally she would know her dragon's thoughts so she knew what she was saying.

"Windfyrth insists that we cannot succeed without her. We need to complete the circle."

Jayd sighed in relief. At least that was taken care of!

***

That evening after his companions had fallen to sleep, Rayn sought out a pool of pure water. Finding none, he was able to convince Windfyrth to help him. Jayd, Rhoc and their dragons were already asleep, so she had her people pour pure, clean rainwater from a storage tank into a clear stone bowl, placed deep inside a temple Windfyrth used for meditating. Then she went out to see to her people's needs.

It was an old ritual, one that Rayn had learnt from his master. It was told that it could only be practiced once in a year, unless dire circumstances called for it, else the wiseman might spend his very soul as the price to communicate with the Divine. Tonight was one such night.

He was frustrated. After finding Windfyrth he had asked the Divine if they should now finally go find Pure's dragon, yet again he didn't get any clear response, as though the question itself was wrong. So he'd decided to use a higher prayer tonight, divining in the waters like the old wiseman had taught him. He watched the water an hour in the silent darkness, speaking prayers in his mind. After the hour, he dipped the tip of his staff in the water and the ripples slowly formed images of the clouds – the purest sign of Divinity. Feeling Divinity's presence near, he formed his questions in his mind, knowing that he could get full answers, not just yes and no.

He asked, 'Where should we go next?' and words formed in his mind, like an impression of speaking though he heard no words. Like the memory of language, though he heard no sounds, *That depends on what you want.*

Good point. He asked, 'How do we defeat the plague in the quickest and most effective means possible,' and received the answer *Form the dragon circle*. He already knew that.

'What is the next step in forming the dragon circle?'

Go and see the Matron.

Rayn sighed with gratitude. At least that was a positive step.

He still had more questions, but he decided three was enough for tonight. Thanking the Divine, he shook the image from his mind and went straight to bed.

***

Rayn looked up at the dimly lit morning sky. A night's sleep had once again seemed little more than a brief nap and they were up before dawn to prepare for their departure. It was clear that Windfyrth was well loved and respected of her people. She was bidding them all goodbye, by name, and imparting words of council and command to them all.

Rayn shook his head. Dragons were a creature in want of much study. They were strange, noble, brave, so many different things! All the other dragons had remained hidden, especially Darkwing. Yet none were more public, and more respected and trusted, than Windfyrth. It was amazing and... to be truthful... he wished he wasn't the one who had to bring it to an end. But there was a world to be saved and the tears of a single town could not be counted against the enormous wave of destruction the curse intended to unleash.

Pure walked up to him and smiled. He almost forgot where he was.

"How are you, Rayn?" she asked him.

"Well, well enough. A little light on sleep but nothing compared to those at the heart of the war." He paused, wondering what that would be like, then remembered she was still looking at him. "Yourself?" he asked, remembering his manners.

"Good. Very good," she said, smiling.

There was silence between them.

She spoke at last, "That was very impressive what you did to call your staff to you last night. You progress very quickly."

Dr Joseph Ireland

He was gently flattered. "Thank you, but that was not me. That was the power of the Divine. I could never call the staff to break through fetters like that," he admitted.

She huffed, unsatisfied. "I tell you, that's not how it works!"

He just smiled at her.

She lost the need to argue with him and sighed, looking at Windfyrth saying her goodbyes. "It is a bold thing that we prepare to do," she said.

"Indeed. I don't know what is happening in my home land, yet I roam this world finding dragons in the hope that it will be the end of all our woes! This is not the introduction to adulthood that I expected."

"You are too concerned with yourself." She smiled. "And we are doing good, all the good we can. Is that not what you did with yourself last month, when you were still only a boy?"

His heart softened and allowed some light within. He was worried. He was trying to solve all the world's problems. He was not far off being a boy and didn't need to take on all the traits of manhood in a single day. She'd also just reminded him that he was not alone. In that moment he just wanted to take her swimming in Othlam lake by his town, where they could throw handfuls of water at each other as they'd done before the madness had started.

Adulthood could wait a little longer…

… or perhaps being an adult meant whatever *he* wanted it to. He was a man now and if it meant a swim with his truest friends once in a while, then so be it!

He couldn't help smiling at her. She was good for his thoughts. Then, to his surprise, she actually blushed.

They laughed.

Then the mood broke as Windfyrth stood. "I have said all I intend to at this time," she said, like it was an order to him.

Rayn grew serious once more but kept a smile in his heart. He spoke seriously though; it was what Windfyrth would have expected. She seemed to believe only the most serious matter would take her from her beloved town, so he behaved himself seriously, for her sake.

"Riders, to the skies!" Rayn shouted to the people, and they cheered.

Most of them.

The mountain

15 The mountain

The mountain was amazing, no matter how he looked at it. A huge bluff jutted out from the side, as if part of the mountain had forgotten how to grow up, and had grown diagonally instead. There was no way a natural hand could have forged that mountain.

They were a day into their journey back towards the Matron's mountain. Rayn and Rhoc rode Ironfang, using his helm and the southern riders' armor to survive the thin air. Jayd and Pure rode Darkwing with the bracelet to protect them. Snow rode alone with Windfyrth and had an old suit of fully functional dragon rider armor on. It was ornate, but not very robust or protective – clearly not meant for battle. Windfyrth had been saving it for generations.

He looked out again at the strange mountain, wondering what secrets it must have held within.

He felt Ironfang growl within. He knew his dragon was not happy with his curiosity, or what it meant.

But he did not have to please a dragon. He had to do what was right. *Should we explore the mountain?* he prayed.

A gentle curiosity and hope filled him, a gentle yes, as though it was not a command but rather a suggestion.

Ironfang knew it the moment he did, and began to descend.

"Where are you going?" Jayd shouted.

He pointed and she looked, and said nothing more.

The mountain only grew more interesting the closer they approached. As they drew nearer, Rayn could see the brown stones had clear markings on the sides, as though they had been cut by men. The highest slopes were covered in ice. The enormous cliff, which their dragons rode underneath without fear, was at least a league long. It was strange indeed. The dragons looked at each other in silence. Rayn did not know what secret they shared.

"Windfyrth thinks we should not search that mountain," Snow told him.

"I thought not," he replied.

They circled high in the sky, coming to rest on the far side of the mountain, on the opposite side of the mountain to the bluff. There, a huge cavern was visible, disappearing into its depths.

There the dragons landed in silence.

Dr Joseph Ireland

For a moment they stood there, no one daring to dismount and risk the darkness. Even Jayd was silent before the cavernous night.

"What is it?" Rayn finally asked the dragons.

They paused before answering. In the end, it was Ironfang who spoke. "You should probably go and see for yourselves. We will wait here and gladly rest ourselves. If you need us, simply call."

"Can we trust you to be alone with each other?" Jayd teased the dragons.

Darkwing laughed, seeming in answer.

Windfyrth stretched out her trembling wings. She had been on this journey the least, and yet without complaint. A rest would do her good.

Rayn stood down from Ironfang's back, with his help. His legs were a little stiff from riding but they adjusted quickly. He checked his equipment and his knife.

"It is unlikely you will need your weapons there," Darkwing told him.

He took them with him anyway.

Snow was waiting by her dragon.

"You're not coming," Jayd stated.

Snow nodded.

The four of them walked in. The cavern was at first dark, until their eyes adjusted.

"Look," Jayd told them, pointing to the roof.

At first it looked like it had been a natural cavern, but a few paces in and the walls seemed to change as if smoothed by some hand.

"Or made by men," Jayd suggested.

"That seems impossible; a mountain made by men?" Rayn wondered.

"I have seen them," Pure told him. "This looks like... I best not say. Let us look on a bit more."

They walked on, their footfalls echoing in the twilight of the cavern. The floor was perfectly smooth but sloped upwards as if to follow the curve of the bluff that jutted out from the mountain. Soon they came to a stone door. The caverns continued towards their left and right, curving away and deeper into the mountain.

Pure tried the stone door but it did not move.

"Rhoc?" she asked him.

He sighed and, pushing on the stone slowly, began to force it open. There was a crack and then he shoved it the rest of the way. Within there was an enormous chamber.

Dim light filtered through the cracks in the roof above and water trickled in. Within, the room was strange. Large cylinders of metal and stone, some with the appearance of glass, reached up into the sky as though perhaps they had once supported some great structure. Slick mosses lined the ground and in the distance, small animals scurried from their presence.

"This place is old," Rayn said.

"You don't say?" Jayd grinned.

He shook his finger at her sarcasm. "No, older! This is... this is a tomb."

"Oh, you," she complained, "it's always a coffin or a tomb, why can't you just see with your eyes for once!"

"Jayd, I..." Rayn began, tempted to launch into a lecture how he was desperately trying to do nothing but see *beyond* at all times. But Rhoc touched his arm.

Rhoc looked at Jayd and gave a solemn nod.

Jayd looked down. "I know," she said, "it's just... creepy. I don't like getting the creeps."

So that was it, Rayn realized. She wasn't being rude; she was just trying to be brave.

Pure stepped forward. "I guess this confirms it," she told them.

"What?" Jayd asked.

"This is an orbital vessel. I've seen one before. There used to be hundreds above the skies, raining down life and changing the world. We used them for communication and for protection."

"Then what is it doing down here?" Jayd wondered.

"I don't know," Pure replied. "Actually, I'd like to know how it survived at all." She continued in her own language, "Perhaps the pilot was able to slow orbital entry so as to prevent a cataclysmic collision with this mountain? I don't know. More likely the elementalists were sufficiently skilled to use the mountain to soften the landing. That would explain why the ship was stuck here. But where *is* everybody?"

She spoke as if to herself, though Rayn knew she was aware he could hear her. Even so, the words made little sense.

"Come," she told them.

They walked in the dim light towards the center of the room. It appeared the far wall was curved as well, as though this was simply a massive room attached outside the wall of an even larger, circular room. The inner room must have been truly massive.

Pure seemed to guess his thoughts. "Terraforming devices such as these required extensive planetary machinery to achieve their goals. Thus, all these pillars of stone were once filled with light and energy. They would feed into a central chamber beyond that could work miracles beyond your imagining. Energy and light filling a room like this. I would like very much to show you that."

Something in her words stirred his fears. "Perhaps it is not so wise?" he suggested, eager to leave the lands of the dead to their silent inhabitants.

She looked at him, nodding to acknowledge his concerns. Yet instead she walked on. Soon they arrived at the central pillar in the room, surrounded by numerous others and platforms of stone where people may have once stood.

"I respect your fears, Rayn, but there is another curiosity I must answer," she said in the common tongue. "I must know if there are any escape capsules, or 'beds' as you like to call them, still functioning here. I want to know if anyone survived the fall of Pearl, apart from myself."

Something about all this made him even more nervous but he knew why she needed to do it. He knew he could not deny her.

She stood at the stone and stepping up onto a dais, reached out towards a marble pillar about the height of her hand. To his surprise, it tilted to reach out to her.

"So far, so good," she muttered. She stood there a good ten minutes more, seeming to talk to the stones.

He would have thought her mad but he'd seen what she could do with the elements.

"Rhoc," she suddenly asked.

He jumped.

"Be a good lad and go stand that pillar upright?" she asked.

He turned without complaint, walked twenty paces to where she stood, and hefted a stone pillar from the ground to place it on the base where it must have once belonged.

With a wave of her hand, the stone clicked back into its place and stood whole.

The air seemed to hold its breath.

There was an enormous thrum and a heartbeat later, bright blue and purple lines began to light up along the pillar. They raced down into the earth and began to flow around the room, highlighting every surface. There were simple lines, and areas of great complexity he felt he could never understand. But there were also many dark patches where her repair work could not reach.

He heard Jayd gasp and turned to see her. Again her eyes tracked along the glowing stones and she seemed in awe of what Pure could do.

So was he.

They smiled and Jayd took a step closer.

A moment later the room began again to fill with light, chasing away the creatures of the darkness in its brilliant beam. Stones the size of men pulled themselves up from the ground and floated around before Pure's outstretched arms. It was as if she was conducting them with silent music. The gem at her brow glowed brilliant deep blue. Light flashed between and within the stones, messages too complex to understand. It was miraculous and, for just a moment, Rayn could clearly see how this device may have once flown above the sky.

16 Strange lines

"No," Pure muttered.

"Sorry?" Jayd asked.

Pure sighed, and let stones and her arms rest. "No, there are none. I think the plague got to them all, three and a half millennia ago. This vessel must have survived hundreds of years in space until some internal battle pulled it from the sky. How tragic! To have survived the Perish, only to fall on this world! How–"

She was cut off as sudden footsteps of stone upon stone sounded behind them. Rayn and Jayd whirled around, only to see a huge man of granite, four times the size of a normal man and eyes glowing a threatening green, menacing down towards them.

Dr Joseph Ireland

"Oops," Pure said.

A fist of granite fell from above and almost crushed them where they stood. Rayn pushed himself away by faith, not even knowing he could. Rhoc leapt far away, and Jayd somehow seemed to simply fly.

The creature drew a glowing axe of stone, with a long handle. It stretched it out towards the only being directly in front of it.

Rayn.

"I must have activated the orbital's defenses!" Pure screamed.

The creature swung about but Rayn found its movements slow, as though it had been weakened or damaged in some way. He dodged underneath it easily.

"Make it stop, Pure!" Jayd screamed.

Rayn had his own defenses. "Back! Back I say!" He shouted at the stone statue. "You will not attack us. Return to your sleep!"

For a moment it just paused. Slowly, almost imperceptibly, the gleaming violence in its eyes began to fade.

He heard Pure sigh with relief, then gasp.

The eyes instead filled with a deep red light. In that moment he perceived he had cast out one spirit, only to have the stone monster be filled with another.

"Secondary defenses!" Pure apologized.

Rayn was already running before it had begun to move, it had taken all his strength to cast out the first spirit. It would surely be ready if he tried to do it again.

The ground shuddered underneath him as the monster ran after him. There was a thunderous explosion as Rhoc threw a boulder at it and it smashed it aside with its axe.

He heard Jayd taunting it, the screeching of stone as the monster swung about trying to end her. A moment later Rayn was thrown to the ground as the creature failed in its attempts to swat her and lost its balance, crashing to the ground.

Jayd laughed and helped him up long before the stone monster had time to stand. Another rock smashed against it, but appeared to do no harm.

"Rayn, head up there!" Pure shouted.

They turned and saw her pointing towards a bright light where the sunlight found its way in. It appeared to be at the top of a staircase that wound its way along the outside of a pillar.

Rayn ran.

He heard the machine get up, scrabbling for its axe. He turned to risk a quick glimpse, and it looked as though one arm had stopped functioning. Rather than be burdened, it tore its own arm off.

They arrived at the base of the staircase just as it began to pursue them once more. Breathless, Rayn ran up as fast as he could. He saw Rhoc had already leapt there and was pulling a stone from the wall to hurl at the beast.

Rayn looked back and saw Pure. She was standing in the middle of a huge swirl of air, as though she had summoned the winds around her. The stone at her brow glowed a brilliant yellow. Her dress and hair fluttered violently in the winds she commanded.

"Is she doing that?" Jayd, flying, asked him.

"Pure, run!" Rayn told her.

"I can do this!" Pure affirmed. A moment later the wind threw her, screaming, up towards the light. She hit the roof above the exit quite hard and fell on the floor. Rhoc turned to help her up and they heard her mutter. "I'm all right."

Then the rock staircase in front of him shattered as the monster buried its axe in the stone. Wasting no time, he swung his staff at it in a retributive strike. A ringing sound filled the cavern as wood met stone and the axe fell from the monster's grip. Rayn looked down as it fell and was amazed to see how far they'd already run.

"Come on!" Jayd shouted.

The monster had landed on its feet.

Rayn jumped the gap and continued to run. Jayd flew around its head and a pillar of fire from Pure's outstretched hand scorched its gemmed eyes.

But on it came. In that moment, Rayn began to fear. It knew no pain, it knew no other cause but the defeat of its enemies. It would not stop trying to destroy him. Would it even find him in his nightmares?

Suddenly it jumped from the pillar, climbed up the wall with only one arm and leapt down to cover the only exit. Pure and Rhoc were only paces away from it. Jayd flew up to the exit in an instant, knives drawn.

Then Rhoc grabbed a boulder and, with all his might, threw it back down into the room.

For a moment the creature seemed to join them in watching the lonely rock fly towards the glowing pillars. Rayn wondered why Rhoc had done such a thing. What did he hope to achieve?

Then the stone that Rhoc had hurled smashed into the pillar Pure had made him set aright. In that instant, all the stones in the room went dim and crashed to the ground; the only light was the gentle glow of the sun that struggled through the cracks in the roof.

And two, glowing, evil red eyes.

"Yeah, I was going to suggest that wouldn't work," Pure said.

The room lit up with the monster's dire energy. For an instant Rayn could only see his friends, weapons drawn and battle ready, backlit as though ready to deny the fires of demonry itself. He reached deep within, knowing he could not bear the deaths of any of them. It was not the need of the dragon circle or even the fear of living without them. It was the price of their own lives and the glorious way they each faced death itself with resolution and determination. It was three bold hearts willing to deny death and demonry to succeed at a good cause. It was three very good reasons to live.

And suddenly the wall shattered and the stone monster exploded, showering them in dust and rubble. Pure screamed and Rhoc bent down to cover her.

And silhouetted in the blinding light, there stood a dragon.

Ironfang.

Rayn's heart leapt with joy, tears rising unbidden in his eyes. He raced forward and Ironfang bowed his head so they could press their foreheads together.

Rayn tried to steady his breathing, so none could hear how afraid he'd been.

Rider, Ironfang stated, his voice trembling.

Rayn cleared his throat and leapt up to sit on his dragon's back. He realized in that moment just how close they had become in the time since they'd bonded. He knew with dreadful certainty that while no beast was more powerful than a dragon, no dragon could ever survive the guilt and remorse of having their rider die.

Four reasons to live.

The bitter past

They left the cavern and stood at the top of the mountain. It was clear some structures once stood in the middle, surrounded by a great wall. The entire city had fallen down into the mountain long ago in the pretime, a miracle beyond imagining indeed.

But what was worse was the scene that greeted their eyes in the shadow of the overhanging cliff that was once the mountain's true peak. The bones of men, at least forty, the tattered remains of armor and weapons still clinging to them. And one, whose broken amour seemed most ornate, holding forth a spear with a silver tip that rested in the bleached ribcage of what could have only been a dragon.

"I do not know this one," Darkwing said, having rode with the other dragons to this high place.

The entire area seemed to radiate the reverence that Rayn had first sensed when he stood at the mountain entrance; reverence and regret.

"It is true, you will see," Windfyrth spoke with sorrow. "Men and dragons fought with each other. It was the punishment for the loss of the bonding. This was the result of that endless pain."

"It makes me sad," Jayd confessed. "More sad than I could have ever imagined." A little tear glistened on her cheek.

Dr Joseph Ireland

"Do not mourn, my rider," Darkwing told her, but offered no further comfort.

"Well," Snow said, sliding down from her dragon's back, "I will mourn. This is worse than death – to become an enemy to your own soul? To die fighting that which belongs within you?" Her voice, indeed, choked. "That is worse than to die."

Windfyrth leant her arm against her. Snow turned and, as she promised, began to cry. Her dragon said nothing but could not prevent the tears in her own eyes as well, no doubt overcome by her rider's sorrow that would surely be flowing through her own dragon heart.

They stood in silence.

Soon Jayd began to move as though she would walk among the bones.

"Jayd, don't," Rayn told her, "you must not trespass on this sacred site."

Jayd paused a moment, as though talking to someone inside her heart. "Are you the wiseman of these parts?" she asked, already clearly knowing the answer.

So Rayn did not reply.

She turned. "Then you do not have the authority to command what is sacred here. I will walk, for I feel I must."

His heart burnt within him, in fear for her, but he did not argue. Either she was wrong and would learn from the pain of her own mistakes, or she was right and in stopping her he might prevent some good.

So she walked, stepping over the bones of men and dragon with great care. Darkwing stood forward but did not join her.

No one dared.

"Here," she finally said.

She bent down and spoke again, "Warriors, forgive me, for our need is truly great."

Rayn recognized that prayer. It was the prayer one might give when slaying the family pet in a time of famine, for food.

Then Darkwing spoke as though continuing her prayer, "And forgive me, brother, too. Let your rest be undisturbed."

Jayd continued to search. "Most everything is damaged here," she said. After a breath she bent down, and with as much care and respect as she could muster in this macabre task, began to pull an object from the dust and bones. It made Rayn tremble in fear of what the spirits of the departed may think, despite Jayd's care.

She pulled a broad silver shield from the bones at her feet. When she spoke, it was with reverence. "This helped to slay a dragon."

Rayn half expected the dragons in the room to roar with anger, but they stood silent.

You do not think, my rider, that there are occasionally dragons who deserve death at men's hands? Ironfang whispered to him.

Jayd took the shield, as tall as she was, and after a moment's more searching, found only a left leg greave to her liking. She seemed to become nervous and finally done with her plundering, quickly hurrying back to them.

She breathed as though she'd been holding her breath a long time, but smiled as though she'd done something very brave.

Rayn didn't know whether to smile or complain. He held the shield she'd given him. It was broad and rectangular, not much to his liking. But Rhoc grinned broadly when Rayn showed it to him.

"Will you try it on?" Snow asked.

Rayn looked at her, knowing Rhoc should if it was a gift from the Divine by those who'd gone before.

"After it is washed," he told her, referring to the oldest and most basic of cleaning rituals his people knew.

Snow nodded.

"Oh," Pure began to say, "I don't think, I mean, three thousand years…" she paused. "Yes, after a wash," she finally agreed.

They did so, using the water containers they'd brought. Jayd was happy to submit to a similar washing of her hair and hands just in case. He thought she'd been very brave risking the graves of the dead, but even so, didn't want to give her any more encouragement at breaking the laws older than living memory. Especially when the princess of that lost world was standing beside them.

"It is a protector's shield," Pure explained. "From before. Just as powerful as the staff but made for a very different purpose. I think it will serve you well, Rhoc. And the greave does not match your other one Rayn but I don't think that will matter. Here, try them on now."

Rhoc grunted in approval, insisting Rayn try them both first.

As soon as Rayn donned them the shield brightened as new, and the greave turned about to fit his leg, forming new plates between his breastplate to make a complete leg. He felt strong and well protected, but the shield was just too big for him to use. He surrendered it gladly to Rhoc, who was almost in tears of gratitude.

Then his eyes fell on the silver tipped spear jutting out from the stone nearby. It was long, twice the size of a normal spear. Its haft was polished wood, covered in unfamiliar silver symbols he'd never seen before.

"What is that?" He asked.

Pure answered, "That is a dragon rider's spear – a 'lance'; I doubt any of us could even wield it."

"And I doubt any of us could even pick it up," Jayd said. "Look, it's embedded deep in the stone. I didn't even try. I can't imagine what kind of death would drive wood into solid stone like that."

"Oh, it's not wood," Pure muttered almost to herself. "But, yeah, it's stuck. There's no removing it now."

Rhoc snorted.

They turned.

He nodded at the spear as if to say, 'I bet I could get it.'

"Go ahead then, if you insist," Rayn replied. He reasoned that if Jayd could tread over the bones of the dead, so could Rhoc.

Rhoc stepped carefully over the bones, then got a good grip as his fingers wrapped right around the spear. Rayn winced as he wrenched it out of the dragon's skeletal ribcage. Then Rhoc pulled with all his might.

It didn't budge.

"Come on boy," Jayd muttered, getting up on Darkwing. "Let's leave this sacred place."

Rhoc looked over at her, unimpressed.

He gripped it with both hands, bending right down at the knees. He took three deep breaths, and clutched so tight his knuckles turned white.

He pulled with all his strength.

Suddenly there was a cracking sound as the stone underneath his feet began to give way. Pure screamed and ran to Ironfang, who spread his wings and reached out to help Rayn up. Snow clutched on to Windfyrth but in her eyes there seemed to be a new expression. She was puzzled, and impressed.

The cracking noise deepened, but Rhoc still didn't seem to notice.

The stone split around them, and it budged just a little. Rhoc roared and continued to pull with all his might.

A moment later the entire rooftop gave way, and the spear fell from his grasp. Windfyrth whipped her tail around and caught him about the waist. She lifted him up to safety.

Rhoc growled in frustration.

Pure cried out as the cracks rapidly spread across the fallen city. There was a noise like thunder as the entire area collapsed, then a second roar as half the top of the mountain began to slide down onto the broken city, filling the hole that had been made. Rayn gulped at the enormous destruction they had only barely avoided.

For a moment they watched the mountain in silence.

Ironfang spoke, "So be it. Let the past be buried. Rest under stone, forgotten warriors. Sleep on undisturbed."

They turned, and headed towards the Matron's mountain.

South

By evening they passed over the spot where Pure's broken teacher lay, Windfyrth having better taught them the secrets of the high winds that sped their travel greatly. It occurred to Rayn that it might be as good a place as any to make camp for the night. They were all exhausted, especially the dragons, though Ironfang would never admit that.

Then he saw Pure waving to him from Darkwing. She apparently shared the same thought about stopping for the night.

Good enough for me! Down they went. They would be able to set up before nightfall and perhaps eat a decent meal before resting. They could be up before dawn, Darkwing taking advantage of the twilight to race ahead. With Windfyrth's secrets they might even make Matron's cave before the end of the third day!

"What is this place?" Windfyrth demanded as soon as they landed.

But Rayn didn't know what this place was, so he asked Pure and she answered in dragon. "This was once a school or a temple. They were the same place in my day. We came here to seek the wisdom that our ancestors had placed in these statues here, just like this old broken one."

"That seems of little use to you now," Windfyrth replied.

"It is!" Pure agreed. "But I can repair it. I just need to take this little stone here to a working teacher. I can repair it… I think I can repair it."

Just then, there was a clap of thunder as Stormclouds turned up.

Ironfang almost jumped out of his skin and Windfyrth almost breathed on Stormclouds. Darkwing just yawned and sat down.

"You've added a new rider to your circle," Stormclouds mused and then, uncharacteristically, sat down on the ground.

"I have to learn how to speak dragon," Jayd said to herself, out loud.

"You all right?" Pure asked Stormclouds.

"Fine." Stormclouds grinned at her in the fading light. "Matter of fact, I could not be better!"

"What news from the war?" Rayn asked him.

Stormclouds yawned, crossed his front paws and resting his head down, shut his eyes.

"Answer the wiseman!" Windfyrth demanded, sizzling at Stormclouds' apparent lack of concern.

He raised an eyebrow at her, opening one eye. Then he turned over onto his back and rubbed it against the ground as if he had all the time in the world.

Windfyrth fumed.

Darkwing chuckled.

"Speak, good Stormclouds," Pure asked him, without using her power.

Finally Stormclouds had done teasing them. "Why rush?" He sat up, staring at Rayn. "When it is widely known that Rayn's blessing is going to win this war?" He yawned again.

"I wonder if Fairystone can teach me?" Jayd said, ignoring a conversation she had no access to. "Rhoc should learn too!"

"Speak clearly," Rayn asked him with a smile.

"Rayn's blessing," Stormclouds roared, "which proves so effective against this incarnation of the plague. To spill the blessed waters on the cursed is to watch their bodies burn and melt in a moment, even a drop is enough to slay some! And one in every dozen survives the retransformation and returns to health! What is more, few, very few who partake of the waters are taken by the disease at all!"

"Then that *is* good news," Pure said.

"Good?!" Stormclouds huffed. "We have pushed back two hordes and trampled them into the dust they came from. Each and every human town is protected by a priest and a hundred barrels of the stuff. Some men run into the war dripping wet; the screams of the plague as they touch them is a music of such beauty that no mortal could compose it! The war is all but won!"

"Do not count your piglets before they are weaned," Windfyrth said.

Stormclouds looked at her but didn't disagree. It was clear that he was no fool and was well aware that she had a good point. He nodded at her, and she back. Whatever understanding that had just passed between them was lost on Rayn. Perhaps she acknowledged he'd just tried to make light of their predicament in contrast to the darkness of war, and he acknowledged that he was not blind to the seriousness of that predicament.

Still, the war was all but won! Rayn felt his heart swell with hope. He cheered and the dragons roared.

"What just happened?" Jayd asked.

Pure told her and Rayn couldn't help himself, he danced around the fire with glee. The others joined him, for a moment.

"Enough," Windfyrth warned them, "take your peace, that is good. But don't let down your guard just yet."

"I agree, rider," Ironfang said. "There is much to be done. Perhaps this blessing has bought you some time to form the dragon circle and enlist riders, but it cannot be taken as the final defeat of the plague, not yet."

The dancing stopped and Rayn straightened up. They were right.

Pure squealed. "Stormclouds! Oh, if we've won some time, oh, Rayn, this is perfect. We must let the dragons rest! Hurry, oh!"

She was not making sense, leaping up on her toes. He grabbed her by the arm. Sometimes she was very much like a four year old at heart.

She calmed herself down. "The dragons must rest but we do little but sit down each day. We have time before the night for another adventure... my powers are but a wisp, a fleeting shadow of what they could be! If we can repair this teacher, and awaken all the other teachers, we can unlock hidden powers in my mind – in all our minds! We could teach others how to use this, we could help the children of the next generation become what humanity once was!"

"I, for one, wish to see the glory of men restored," Windfyrth said with sincerity.

Stormclouds huffed. "I am doubtful you would not fall into the same errors…"

Pure shook her fist at him, in good nature. "Humanity has changed, hasn't it, Fairystone? We are not what we once were, well, except for me. And Rayn, whoa, what's with him? Look, it's our chance, all we need—"

Stormclouds cut her off. "Oh, no, this involves me, doesn't it? You want to *ride* me, don't you girl?"

His voice was angry and he sat up. But he did not flee, even though he knew Pure had the power to command him to obey.

It was as if Windfyrth also knew what she was thinking in the silence. "I caution you, young princess, against over use of your authority. You may think you can command dragons out of sheer wisdom, or will power, and there is some truth in that. However, the greater share of your commanding comes from the unbreakable oath of allegiance between the noble dragon ancestors and the humans of the royal houses. Your voice is undeniably one of the royal houses, and our honor to them runs deep, even if their descendants have fallen into disarray. Be wary, a strong dragon committed to their cause may yet prove immune to your command."

Pure looked over at her, and was quiet for a moment. Then she said, "I wasn't going to command him. But Stormclouds, if you will, as we spared your life, will you do this one favor for us?"

"One?" he said, standing up. "No man or child has ever trod these scales! I am a *proud* dragon, why should I submit to your feet?" His voice was coarse and indignant, yet he was clearly hiding a smile. Rayn could only guess his motives – was he getting out of his life debt easily? Or was he glad to help those who saved him, even if he complained about it?

She paused. "Please?"

Stormclouds shuffled about, looking like he was about to ask for some kind of payment. In the end, his conscience seemed to get the better of him and he huffed. "A dark day," he muttered. "A dark day when men and children ride me, ME! Children and a wiseman. Grr, grr, grr."

Ironfang almost hit him, but held his tail in.

"Are you sure?" Snow asked. Rayn looked over, he'd absolutely forgotten she existed. She was never out of arm's reach of her dragon. She didn't speak dragon, but seemed to know what was being said, and they seemed to understand her as effortlessly as well.

"Stay here if you wish," Rayn said.

She talked with her dragon a moment, in the silence of their shared hearts. "No, I should go," she said sadly, as though she wasn't really making that decision for the both of them anyway. Rayn knew just how painful it was to leave your dragon for the first time but then again, perhaps it was wise. Perhaps leaving was just what they both needed right now.

Windfyrth was an interesting dragon.

The five humans loaded themselves onto Stormclouds' back. He was weighed down by the load but did not complain, only asked, "I may need help getting airborne," to Ironfang.

Rayn's dragon was only too happy to oblige and helped throw Stormclouds into the air. Rayn looked out at the dragons just as the red and angry smoke formed around them. Stormclouds' eyes glowed brightly for an instant, looking ahead to check for dangers, then the air suddenly grew thin and they were gone.

And in that moment, Rayn took a longing look at his dear dragon Ironfang sitting beside Darkwing, watching warily at Windfyrth, and his last thought was, "Where's Fairystone?"

17 (Image: Stormclouds as a hatchling – by Snow. Note 4 wings, and the horns have not come in yet)

Venfirth

They took many leaps through the air, Rayn choking in the red and angry smoke, then immediately he felt Stormclouds descending on trembling wings. The sky was much brighter here, the clouds seemed thicker, the air warmer: and the ground was covered with houses.

Hundreds of houses. It was a village, the largest he had ever seen. There must have been hundreds of hundreds of people down there, more than the leaves of a full grown pine tree. He didn't know what to think.

"The city Venfirth – I have only been here once before… in my wild, crazy youth. I must say I am not pleased to be here again. I will come for you at nightfall; that should be late evening back at the place where we left your dragons."

"What?" Rayn said, not understanding. "How can it be day here and night back on our own land?"

"The world you are on is a ball and the light shines on it at different times."

"A ball? How is that possible?"

"Don't worry, I'll explain it," Pure said with a smile.

A ball? Didn't the world just go on flat forever? Rayn wondered to himself. But there was no dragon here to listen to his thoughts.

"If not, I will check in every hour at the tallest peak of the tallest tower, understood?"

"Understood," Rayn said.

By that time the citizens had noticed them and horns blew as people scattered for their houses. Stormclouds landed, reluctantly, in front of the largest building there, right out in the open. He bowed low to allowed them to dismount.

A dozen armed guards with long spears that had blades on the end surrounded them in short order, but not from too close.

"What is this?" the guard captain shouted. "We do not know you, dragon and dragonfriends!"

Stormclouds nudged Rayn ahead.

Rayn looked at the threatening guards, wondering if these people were always so distrustful. "We are from the north, invited here by Norvich, dragonfriend of the Venfirth. Is this your customary greeting?"

The captain ordered his guards to lower their weapons immediately. "Norvich! He left not this morning to see to news of trouble in the western mountains. You honor us with your presence, dragon rider."

Rayn acknowledged his presence with their strange arm shake, and the guards cheered. A moment later a loud call from the sky heralded the arrival of another dragon.

It was the priestess and she was riding her large green dragon.

Rayn smiled; he was glad that someone he knew was finally here.

Stormclouds watched her with great disdain. "I should leave," he said.

As soon as the green dragon touched down, Stormclouds was gone. Rayn bowed at the dragon, but it was the priestess who spoke.

"Good priest Rayn," she said with a smile, leaping from her dragon's back. "We did *not* expect to see you so soon! Come, share a meal."

He glanced over and saw Pure's expression. There was only one thing she wanted.

"I am sorry," Rayn apologized, "but we can only stay an hour, our dragons will be missing us, as do the armies of the central continent. Unfortunately I must insist; we cannot tarry at all! But please, if you can, my friend here wishes to see the oracle, on a matter most urgent."

The priestess seemed unimpressed. Was knocking back a dinner appointment so very offensive to this people? Or was it the request to see the oracle?

"I will see what I can do," the young priestess replied. "But I take it your good friend here is no priestess?"

"What, a Wisewoman? No, they are rare and have very different skills."

"Really? Why would that be?" she asked, looking for a challenge.

"I … do not know," he replied, meaning the Divine had not told him yet, but he was sure it would if it was important. But it wasn't. Getting Pure to the oracle was the only reason they were here.

"Please, come with me," she smiled.

She walked them down what must have been a very important thoroughfare of their immense 'city'. The day was lit by an afternoon sun, which still was very strange for Rayn. And all about them hundreds of the strange people thronged, smiling and staring at them, strangers in a strange land. Some laid down cloaks or blankets for them to walk on,

Dr Joseph Ireland

perhaps honoring his staff? Or more likely their acknowledged status as dragon riders. Did they know he was Rayn of the blessed waters? He walked proudly at the head of his group, nodding kindly at all he could. And he had to admit, he kind of liked it.

After about four hundred breaths they came to a building that stood directly opposite the main building; clearly a temple of some sort. It was set on a hill, and four curved roads of brown earth led up floral paths to the immense structure. At the gates of the paths two green robed priestesses stood, guarding the temple with their staves, all of which glowed green with very little variation between them. It was curious. Rayn noted the temple had the same arrangement of pillars in two straight lines that marked the broken temple where Pure had found her stone, and from whence they'd just departed.

"What a curious thing," Pure said, "stones have been laid between the pillars of the temple so that the building is no longer open to the air. I've never seen that before-"

"Please, we must wait here," the southern priestess explained. "The high priestess alone can give permission for one to see the oracle."

They didn't have to wait long. Soon an old woman, surrounded by four green robed priestesses hastened down the hill. The priestesses were holding a white sheet over her on long poles so that it created a little shadow for their leader.

She looked out at them kindly. "Welcome, welcome all to the glory of Venfirth!" she said, waving magnanimously.

"Thank you, wise one," Rayn replied and inclined his head, as wisemen did when greeting each other among his people.

The old priestess looked confused. "And the others?"

"Oh, I alone speak your tongue," he confessed, then introduced the others. "And please, if you will, wise one, my companion here wishes to consult with your oracle."

At that, the mood changed. The old lady grew stern. "Only a priestess may consult with the oracle," she said, her voice uncompromising and bold.

Rayn wondered what to say. This was not going well. "I understand. Perhaps if I accompany her?"

"Certainly not, you are only a man! And she has not taken the oaths. The schooling alone takes many, many years. You cannot walk in here and see the oracle, what gifts do you bring?"

Gifts? Rayn had not considered that. His work as wiseman often required payment, his service as valued as any hunter or seamstress. He felt ashamed, but then began to wonder if the blessed waters were enough?

They weren't.

Rayn explained the situation to the others. They didn't know what to say either.

Pure was aghast. "I don't understand. Any could see an oracle, or 'teacher', in my day! Please, beg. Beg if you have to!"

He turned but the high priestess didn't even let him speak.

"I cannot ignore the teachings of centuries, even in these dire times," the high priestess insisted, "*and* you bring no gift to demonstrate your sincerity."

He was getting annoyed at that insistence. What did he have to give that was more vital than the cause of forming the dragon circle and restoring the glory of humanity?

Perhaps Pure's quest really would have to wait.

And the staff shook him gently. Suddenly he knew that what Pure wanted *was* important, vitally. And this priestess' blindness and pride was preventing that.

He told the stubborn priestess in no uncertain terms what they needed, and she almost shouted her denial. He shouted back, and Jayd had to pull his arm away before things got even angrier.

In hindsight, he probably shouldn't have shouted at her. Not even Pure's tears, begging on her knees, could soften the old priestesses' heart.

In the end they were dismissed without seeing so much as the dust on the floor of the temple. The young dragon priestess led them back to some tall buildings by the palatial office and suggested they rest themselves. She stayed to talk about the war in the central continent.

Nothing any of them could say or do would convince her, or her people, that Pure needed to see the oracle – he even told them that Pure was asleep for four thousand years and had used oracles before. That idea really got the southern priestess asking questions but it was clear she had no intention of helping them.

"Tell me, please, what is it like to look into the eyes of the oracle?" Pure made Rayn ask their dragonfriend priestess as the sun light drew dim in the sky.

"A mystical experience, I truly spent three years preparing," the southern priestess explained, "and even I was not ready. One must have a strong mind, you must insist on knowing but *one* thing, or the whole infinity of the oracle will burst upon you and destroy you. It has killed many in the past who enter with weak minds or evil in their hearts. It is the final test we undertake to become a priestess," she explained.

When Rayn translated, Pure replied, "It was not like that in my day. In my day there were not oracles. They were the teachers. We would bring children, as young as possible, to see the teachers every day. The teachers would prepare their minds to receive the vast body of human knowledge. But the teachers never harmed anyone! You did not force a teacher to tell you want you wanted. Not ever! That is no doubt what causes the trouble – you just allow wisdom to flow into your mind. No forcing at all," she said and walked off with sorrow to look out the window at the vast city with Jayd and Pure.

"She's upset," Rayn said for her.

"I know," the southern priestess replied.

They were in very fine accommodation, two adjoining rooms, one for men and the other for women. The windows were decorated with fine linen, as were the beds, and they made pillows of linen and feather. The fittings were all of brass and hardwood. These were a prosperous people, that much was clear. When not questing for oracles, Rayn was determined to learn as much as he could about her people.

He was about to speak when Jayd got his attention, insisting he tell the priestess that she was in need of something called 'woman's products.' – Whatever that meant. The priestess nodded in sympathy and slipped out.

"Rayn, you're such an idiot!" she chided him.

"Huh? You don't think I'm handling this correctly?" he said, "We'll get to Pure's oracle, just wait and see."

"Not while we're prisoners," she replied.

"We're not prisoners," he said, laughing at her.

"Then why did they lock the doors?" She replied.

"They did not lock the doors!" he disagreed.

"So try them," she said.

"I will," he replied.

And he stopped laughing the moment he realized the doors were, indeed, locked.

"They think we're spies, Rayn," Jayd said, and Pure slowly nodded as she shared Jayd's realization. "Especially with your little hissy fit at the temple and all. Look around you Rayn! They've got us locked up, without our dragons, for as long as they like. They are NOT going to let us see their oracle, *ever*."

"Perhaps… they fear we intend to harm it?" Pure suggested.

"Or steal it," Jayd replied.

"How…" Rayn was at a loss for words, but by the staff he knew truth when he heard it. Jayd was right. He'd just walked them all into a trap. This was no visitor's house; it was a jail for wealthy prisoners.

He bowed his head in humble realization.

"Now think smart," Jayd told him, "she'll be back in an instant. We need to make like we don't know what's going on, look for a way to escape."

"We can leave when Stormclouds returns."

"They won't let us touch him," Jayd replied.

She was right. When the young dragon priestess walked in, they kept the conversation calm for the next hour until Stormclouds arrived, Rayn could see him out the window. Rayn could also see, hidden in the great city, two other green dragons and many, many archers.

He'd just walked the hope of Pearl into a prison, a prison of a people held by ignorance.

Stormclouds got the hint and left quickly.

Night began to fall. The young priestess was still there and Rayn knew why. She was the jailer, not the gracious hostess. He didn't know if she had his gift and if she knew what he was saying. But they had to get away.

Though not without seeing the oracle first.

Rayn pondered their options. He could attack her, try and best her at her craft? Perhaps Rhoc could knock her unconscious? No, that might kill her. He pondered it a good hour, until at last his options were down to one.

He had to ask.

Then, if that fails, he decided, *smash our way to freedom.*

The others seemed to sense the moment. Rayn approached the southern priestess with his staff and she looked at him sternly.

"We are leaving now," he said. "We intend to see your oracle and ask her our questions if it costs us our lives. We will not remain prisoners of your people for our cause is too important."

She stood there, torn between duty and wisdom. Finally she spoke, "I am under no oath to keep you here. Leave if you will, I will sound the alarm immediately."

"One hour, please," Rayn replied.

She pondered. "You swear not to harm the oracle in any way?"

Rayn relayed to Pure, who swore not to harm it.

The woman sighed and walked over to a chair by the window, and sat down. "Your cause will fail if you harm the oracle in any way, I have already foreseen it. I set you free to prove you: If you are true, the hand of Divinity will preserve you and me. If you are recaptured, I will know you are untrue."

Rayn paused. It was a strange test. But he had no indications that they would fail... but then again, what was it that Pure wanted? Could her mission be accomplished even without consulting the oracle personally?

"Thank you for your council," he said. "I will remember this kindness."

"As I am sure our high priestess will," she sighed. "Pity, I've grown used to this staff," she said.

"I am Rayn." He offered the only gift he had, friendship.

"Auroriella," she replied.

Rayn was the last to leave, sorrow in his heart.

But there were more important things right now.

Escaped

They made their way through the evening streets with little trouble. Their dark robes, made for high air dragon travel, had dark hoods to help conceal them. The five of them, all practiced in hunting the beasts of the Celtwyld, kept silent and travelled in two groups. Both arrived in short order at the base of the temple hill.

It was well lit, and well-guarded.

"Oh, that Stormclouds was here," Pure wished out loud.

"He keeps his appointments at the tallest tower. We have some time before he will next appear. We need to time our escape with his," Jayd replied.

"So how do we get in?" Pure wondered.

"I got nothing," Jayd admitted. "It is as if the hill itself blinds my gift."

Rhoc smashed his fist into his palm, one of his favorite gestures.

Snow spoke up, her voice so soft one was inclined to lean in to hear it. "Wiseman Rayn, I have not been following much of what has been going on among this people but their animals all speak the same language. When we first came here I noticed the tracks of the mellits. Perhaps if I could speak to them, we might find another way in?"

Rayn blinked in surprise; it was such a good idea!

"Rayn?" Jayd asked.

"Huh? Yes, go, go, please!"

It took her only a dozen breaths to find some furry little mellits hiding under the rubbish in a forgotten street, and another breath or two to convince them not to run away. But they soon told her, in whatever language they used, something that was very useful.

Mellet

18 Mellit – by Auroriella, with Venfirth spelling

"There's a tunnel that they use to get into what sounds like a kitchen, by the temple. It isn't used at night so we should be able to make it that way," Snow whispered.

Rayn nodded.

They followed a thin, wiry mellit to a large stone-wrought tunnel that was only big enough to crawl through. The end of the tunnel was covered with a thick wrought iron grate in square patterns. Rayn looked at it in disappointment.

"How we gonna get through that?" Jayd asked.

Perhaps the Divine had a prayer for rending metal? Rayn had never asked. Or maybe Pure's fire-

Rhoc swaggered in front of him and with one hand, ripped one of the metal bars in two.

"That'll do it," Rayn said.

Rhoc soon had all the metal bars twisted out of the way. At one point, he rested his hand on the stones outside and pulled a bar towards his other hand; the solid stone crumbled under his grip. He was so strong that the stone he used for support was not solid enough for him!

Once Rhoc was done, Rayn lit his staff and crawled in. It was a tight fit in the damp tunnel, but it would do. Snow followed right after. The tunnel led gradually up until suddenly it sloped up at a steep angle, travelling just under the ground of the hill, following its curve. Finally it ended at another grate, just under a silent room.

That was when Rayn realized he really should have made Rhoc go first.

"Back down!" he said, trying to get everyone to back out so Rhoc could take the lead.

"What?" Jayd whispered. "Not back, what is it?"

"There's another grate," Rayn told her.

"Of course there's another grate," she complained. "Snow, let Rhoc past."

"Very well, ouch!" she said, and Rhoc muttered in apology.

Everyone was trying to talk at once, trying to find a solution.

So Rhoc decided to solve the situation himself. He simply stood up, crashing through the ground and leaving sizeable indents of his feet in the tunnel below. He cleared the rubble and helped everyone else up.

They'd just put a huge hole in the innocent kitchen floor.

In the end, only Rayn really needed to reverse back. They helped him up and they looked around. Rhoc had managed to break the ground in relative quiet, not with an explosive bang, so it looked like they hadn't alerted anyone.

"Oh look, a dove," Snow said, walking up to chat to a bird on the windowsill.

Rayn peeked out the door. There was a corridor and other rooms leading off it. He could hear people chanting somewhere.

Snow walked past him and released the grey dove into the corridor.

"What?" Rayn wondered.

She apologized, looking downcast, careful not to touch him. "It will look about for people for us," she said. "They'll not expect any danger from a lost dove."

Rayn nodded. It was a good plan.

A moment later the dove returned. Snow held it in her hand and patted it while congratulating it. Animals, it seemed, spoke the common tongue, or perhaps understood it when Snow spoke to them. A moment later she explained, "The dove saw no one in the great room just beyond. But there are people all over the hill, many hiding."

"Then you can bet the oracle room is guarded too," Jayd said.

"We need a distraction," Snow said.

"I could distract them," Pure muttered, fire flickering in her hands.

"No thanks, we'll need something more subtle." He smiled while she pretended to sulk.

"Can you start a fire outside?" Jayd asked Pure.

"It's not easy... but if I concentrate I probably can set a tree on fire or something."

"We need more," Jayd said.

"I can set the animals on the guards," Snow suggested.

"No," Rayn disagreed, "too obvious. They will run to the oracle. We need something more subtle, something to get the defenders out of the large room without sounding an alarm."

"Nothing's going to get them to do that," Jayd protested.

"Perhaps... something natural. A leaking pipe, perhaps? Something that doesn't seem too out of the ordinary here?"

"Nothing's ordinary here," Jayd complained.

"Even so, would that we could be invisible... I will try the sequester but these are wise women, they may pierce the veil soon... How about mellit? They seem common. Let's set a single mellit on the guards. They will be distracted long enough for us to take the initiative. Agreed?"

They liked the plan but Rayn took another hundred breaths in prayers just in case, until he felt strong about it. Besides, it took that long for Snow to convince the birds and then for the birds to locate a willing mellit. They found a big, fat, adventurous mellit that liked scaring the priestesses anyway. It acted a little like it may have been a pet once.

Rayn set his sequester and they edged their way out of the broken kitchen just ahead of the mellit. They turned the corner, making their way down a short corridor that opened out into the main room off the

temple. There they waited while the mellit snooped around for guards.

While they waited, Pure whispered, "They'll have the teacher's defenses up. But since I intend it no harm we should be fine."

"Even so, Rhoc, when the shouting starts grab a door or something, use it as a shield," Rayn explained. "Make sure no one shoots Pure, or anyone."

19 Someone's pet, once.

They waited until they heard a woman scream. There were shouts, then, "False alarm. It's just a mellit, look, it's going into the observatory."

That was their cue, they all ran in. Without waiting, Rhoc pulled a stone door from its hinges and they ran up the platform to the teacher.

They all felt a strange tug as they entered the light that surrounded it. The room was large with a balcony running the entire length of the opposing three walls. It was beautifully arranged with plants and indoor gardens.

"Amazing," Pure mused.

Then, in spite himself, Rayn turned to look at the oracle. He only had an instant to register that it was very much like the old statue back on their home continent before his very being almost exploded with the torrent of information that flowed into it from the oracle's blue sapphire eyes, eyes which glowed brightly, speaking of countless records written by countless humans over innumerable years. All of them cascading into him in an instant.

He remembered Pure's words, and instead of fighting it, instead of trying to sort through it for answers to life's many questions, he allowed it to become his teacher. He softened his mind and let it teach him what it wanted.

He only stood staring a second or two, before he fell over and broke eye contact.

Jayd tried to help him up, averting her eyes from the oracle's strange gaze, but he was having trouble remembering how to move his legs.

"What was that?" A priestess seemed to shout in the noise of his thoughts. "They are here!" she shrieked and her staff emitted a bright bell like sound.

Rayn's mind had turned to liquid, his thoughts swimming around in confused, random patterns. Pure was doing something to the oracle. Snow was calling in birds by the dozen. Jayd was throwing plants. And

Rhoc held out the stone door just as a pillar of blue fire sped towards them. But Rayn felt useless.

"Probably better hurry…" was all he managed to say.

"I got what I came for already, just a moment…" Pure said. "Their oracle is all out of calibration. I can fix it. There's a healing program in here somewhere."

Rayn sat back. His mouth felt dry, his mind too confused to be afraid. He tried to stand again.

"Now would be good!" Jayd screamed at Pure.

Just then the high priestess walked in through the doors, her four priestesses armed with their green glowing staves. She held out her staff and with a cry of dismay, the gem that Pure had brought flew from her hand and towards the high priestesses.

Rayn knew what to do. Almost surreally, he just held his staff with one hand and matched her prayer with his own. Reaching out his hand, the gem stopped in mid-air.

Reaching out with both hands, Pure aided him and called the gem back. The high priestess cried out in frustration.

"I wonder, do we have a plan to get out of here?" Snow asked, her birds swooping the priestesses, momentarily distracting them.

"Plan?" Pure asked, snatching her gem back.

"Rayn?" Jayd screamed. "Rayn, get up, how do we get out!"

Suddenly a thought surfaced from Rayn's confused mind. "Fairystone," he replied.

Deep inside he realized where she'd been this whole time – Rhoc's pocket.

She must have heard him because stones began to unfold from the air even as the priestesses began to surround them.

"My turn..." He heard the little dragon chuckle with an almost megalomaniacal glee. Rayn and the others were climbing on even before she'd finished forming.

Pure threw a wall of flames at the priestesses and they fell back. Except the old priestess, who parted them with a casual wave of her hand.

But she did fall down when a stone dragon leapt over her.

"I fixed your oracle," Pure shouted at her, "it will no longer kill people!"

"Explain yourselves!?" the priestess shrieked, she didn't speak Pure's language.

Rhoc threw his door through the wall and Fairystone ran. They had to cling on to each other and to her scales for dear life. Rayn sat up, groggy.

"Head for the highest building!" Jayd said. "Let us hope Stormclouds is watching!"

They were half way there, Fairystone crashing with delight through the night time streets at full speed, before a dragon's screech from the sky alerted them to new dangers.

Aurora's ally, the other dragon, was hunting them.

An instant later Snow squealed. "There, Stormclouds is there!" But he was gone by the time they'd turned around.

"Rayn, are you all right? We have to get Fairystone to stop," Pure explained. "Stormclouds cannot carry her like this."

Rayn thought for a moment then hatched a clever plan. "Fairystone, stop! Everyone off!"

They quickly obeyed. That was good. "Pure, make a ring of fire over there, around those people. The green dragon will think it's us but Stormclouds will recognize the blue of my staff."

They did so, even as Fairystone turned herself back into a little dragonfly. The green dragon roared up to the circle of fire, scattering the screaming people in its wake. It almost breathed on them but the rider managed to hold it back just in time.

Then Stormclouds appeared and the green dragon realized its mistake. Stormclouds hovered in the air just high enough for them to grab a leg each, except Rhoc who shattered the stones under his feet to leap right on Stormclouds' back.

And just as the red smoke filled the night air, Rayn happened to glance at some motion among the nearby houses. There, flying low and skillfully among the buildings, was the other young dragon with the southern priestess. For a moment Rayn met her eyes and... did she smile? A moment of understanding and respect passed between them – he had done what he'd said he would and her words were fulfilled to the letter – the oracle was intact, even better than before.

And then they were gone.

Doom

By the time they got back to their dragons Ironfang had Windfyrth pinned to the ground by the neck, Darkwing struggling unsuccessfully to pull him away.

Clearly, being alone without their riders was a very stressful experience for them.

The humans, simultaneously, screamed at them to stop.

Ironfang flung himself back and raced up to them, bowing low. Ironically, he seemed to be struggling to hold back his tears, *To have only found you and to lose you? I thought all the hope had died in me forever!*

I am late, but I am here. Rayn replied, jumping off Stormclouds to calm his dragon by patting him on the head.

"I am… sorry," Ironfang struggled to say to Windfyrth, probably before someone made him.

"You are fortunate, brute, that I allowed you to think you had me," Windfyrth retorted with a pompous voice but to Rayn it held little conviction. Snow gave him a withering look but held her peace.

With a nod and an amused smirk, Stormclouds departed.

Darkwing was visibly trembling but a quick flight in the dark night air with Jayd seemed to lift his spirits.

They reported to their dragons what had happened.

"Do you think we got away with it?" Darkwing asked Rayn.

"Let us pray so, for the good of all," Rayn replied.

"I hope they look in her eyes soon; it will show them I speak the truth," Pure concluded. "Now, let us get this work done here *immediately.*"

It took only a moment to find the statue in the dark.

"I hope this works," Pure whispered in the silent night. She placed the dark rock back in its eye socket and suddenly blue lines of energy flowed along the statue. For a moment they simply pulsed. "It might take a while, there's much damage here."

Then the statue spoke, "Reinitializing from initial protocols."

"What did it just say?" Jayd asked.

Suddenly a blinding beam of pure white light streaked up from the statue, high into the sky, visible for leagues. The ground trembled.

"What have you done?" Jayd screamed.

The sky responded a moment later as a beam of multicolored lights came crashing down into the statue. While Rayn watched in wonder the broken pillars healed themselves, growing again from the ground, forming a peaked stone roof above them. A great wind tore the ground, brushing aside the dirt and plants to reveal a polished stone floor of exquisite beauty.

Rayn turned and, with a gasp, saw the broken statue fully repaired, looking like the oracle with one hand up, facing them and the other in a holding position in front. It glowed with a nimbus of power.

The dragons were roaring in excitement or fear. When the trembling stopped, so did they.

"Let us stay here tonight," Pure said, glowing with a sentiment of peace, "and re-join the fight tomorrow. I want to talk to the teacher."

***

Pure must have only slept an hour that night, staring continuously into the eyes of the statue. "I've so much to catch up on," she muttered at one point well beyond midnight.

Rayn was awoken at dawn by a frightened dragon's roar.

They got up immediately, preparing to take to the skies, but Ironfang roared, "Too late, arm yourselves!"

There, walking towards them, were about twenty misshapen creatures. Two tigers, a bear, several deer…

… and a man.

Rayn lit his staff so they could see them clearly.

They were the cursed.

But something was different. They did not run, though they snarled. They did not attack, at least not yet. Each was injured, and stumbled as though weary.

The man started clapping – a slow, sarcastic beat. "Well done! Well done, Rayn of the Celtwyld. Well done!"

It was Hak. His clothing tattered from countless battles, the brown cloak of the trappers little more than threads upon his shoulders. His form was perverted, hunchbacked and twisted. His right hand was entirely crocodilian.

The others held their peace, waiting for Rayn to reply.

"You…" Rayn stammered.

"Yes, it's me." He grinned with an insulting bow. "Once a general, now nothing more. You've won, little wiseman. I've come to look you in the eyes before I die."

"I doubt that," Ironfang hissed.

The cursed creatures formed a semicircle about twenty paces out. By now, the four riders had taken to their dragons, Pure sitting behind Rayn on the great Ironfang, Rhoc riding Fairystone in her stone form.

The cursed never stood a chance, and they knew it.

"Our horde is scattered!" Hak spat bitterly. "Yet your demoner still rides free? Again the blessing of *the curse* must take to the soil, waiting years to rise again. I know, you think you've won!" And Hak laughed, a cruel and wheezing sound. "But you never will. I may not have the pleasure of seeing you die. But I will – because the blessing, which you call a curse, will never die. And you, you are mortal. One day, when you are old and frail, the blessing will come again and then again, and again. One day it will turn all this world to dust and all you loved and cared about will end with it. You… you see, you are mortal… but the blessing is eternal. So you can never win! See? You can never win!" And he laughed, his cursed beasts joining his mocking laugher with shrill and dire shrieking.

Jayd screamed. "What happened to you? You used to be a trapper of the Celtwyld! You are Hak. You were once a good man who would do anything to protect us!"

The animals and Hak fell silent. Hak's gaze was cast down. When he spoke, his voice trembled. "You will learn, little one, that men change."

"Come back," Rayn offered, sensing a moment of doubt in him. "We have a prayer now that can reverse this curse. You too can be redeemed."

Hak gave a hollow, regretful laugh and his voice grew stronger. "I have done things, unspeakable things. I am beyond your redemption now... and I have come to suffer DEATH AT YOUR HAND!"

Then the cursed charged. Instantly Ironfang breathed out his heated red flames at them and, with a wave of her arms, Pure intensified that flame and sent it at all of the cursed. Every one of them was badly burnt; most died, but a few cursed leapt out at them. They struck with bestial ferocity, aiming not to win but simply to harm.

The battle was brief.

And then Rhoc, leaping on Hak before he could stand, sliced him in two with his axe.

Snow was screaming something at Rhoc. Suddenly the ground opened up underneath his feet and he only just managed to leap away in time. Then an enormous Slugdragon, horrific monsters who burrowed underground, swallowed Hak's sundered body whole. It bent forward, and began to press its way into the ground.

"Stop it!" Pure screamed. "It will fall to the curse!"

Dr Joseph Ireland

They tried to grapple it but only Fairystone, helped by Ironfang, could pull it from the earth. There it struggled for a moment until Rhoc struck the mindless worm on its skull and it died instantly.

"Such a pity," Rayn said, "to die just for food? Would that it had not attacked just then."

"Why did it attack just then?" Fairystone said, her voice gravelly and husky. "That was strange indeed!"

"I agree. I am very suspicious of what has just occurred." Ironfang said.

Rayn had to agree. Why would a Slugdragon, who hated the light, surface just then and just there? "Perhaps it was simply doing the will of the Divine?" He suggested. "To end this incarnation of the curse?"

"That must be it," Jayd said. "Nature itself abhors the curse." Darkwing now translating for her in their minds, as he did as often as he could.

Rhoc nodded.

"No," Ironfang said, "this was not its intent. I sorely doubt it."

"Can't you just believe," Jayd chided him, Darkwing backing her up, "that we won? That we have fought and bled *enough* for the Divine? Rayn is right, the curse has fallen. And soon we will have completed the dragon circle and the curse will never rise again!"

Ironfang was silent for a moment and then said, "*Listen*, little woman!"

Darkwing hissed; he would put up with any insult against himself, but Rayn knew Darkwing would die before he suffered his rider Jayd to be insulted.

Ironfang continued. *"Feel,* if you have any wisdom. I have spent sixty years *listening* while chained in a jail. The battle is *not over.* This was just one more play…"

Rayn listened to his dragon but his own staff and sash were silent on the truth of his words. So he spoke, "Burn the bodies, especially the Slugdragon, please Pure. We need to make sure. I am praying for the words of Jayd to be true-"

Ironfang huffed.

"But I'm going to act as if Ironfang holds the truth today. We need to get to the Matron now. We need to complete the circle, now. There can be no delay."

Everyone seemed to agree with him, though Jayd did seem a bit bothered about having to rush again when she saw no need.

"Snow, can you please speak to the animals. Have them defend this place. Make it sacred. I will add my prayers to it – let none with insincere hearts or a desire to harm this place ever approach."

Pure added, "I can also activate the teacher's defenses – lightning from the sky, that sort of thing. I am sure it will be well defended against any who would seek to damage it once more. This and all the other teachers on this world that I have reactivated this night. I would that all humans bring their children to meet the teacher, at least for an hour a day. The next generation of humanity will be unlike any of the previous generation!" She grinned.

"Come," Rayn ordered, "all things are not yet set right, not yet as they should be. Let us hasten to the mountain!"

Dr Joseph Ireland

Mice

Soon, strong dragons had arrived to assist them, and now they were less than a day out from Nelwyn peek and the first dragon riders' circle that could heal a world. Better still, the dragons had brought dragon rider weapons and shields and a suit of armor for each of them.

Rayn completed his armor from mismatched pieces, being loath to surrender any he had found on their quest. It was fortunate the armor had inbuilt "synergistic technologies" as Pure called it, matching tone and form as each new piece was added. Combined with the will and mental signatures of the thousands of disparate warriors across four thousand years and five continents, it was perhaps the wisest choice. This particular build of armor seemed to grant him no particular expertise but a great deal of talent in many areas instead. The eventual appearance was that of a dignified breastplate, with arm, hand and leg guards. He would still be able to move freely and wear his beloved sash and cloak.

Jayd was hard to please but she eventually chose a flanged armor set with protrusions like wings, designed in the pretime to assist dragon riders that chose to master flying as she had. It would change to suit her skills and preferences, and keep her safe in the emptiness above the world. And like all dragon rider armor, it would weigh nothing.

Because of his strength Rhoc was privileged to wear the greater dragon rider armor. It was twice the height and ten times the weight of a normal suit. Covered completely in metal and stone, with a fanged helm, he would be an intimidating sight to any thinking being. He was almost an image of Punishment itself.

Pure chose for herself no armor but bracelets to keep the air close and warm, shoes that would speed her movement, and an amulet for protection. Then she put on her favorite, and only, dress; the one designed to change with her moods and emotions. It wasn't that she didn't feel the need for protection. It was, as she explained, that she was the princess of Pearl now and that meant she needed to look and act the part. The great joining of dragons would always be remembered. People didn't need to see a room full of nothing other than armored warriors if they were about to 'reform planetary government'.

So, Rayn judged, she is just being practical.

But best of all, their equipment would allow them to portray their thoughts, even direct mental images, between themselves and any other dragon rider on their world. The workings within the armor would increase their skill, their stamina, and their courage.

What a privilege!

They were resting without their armor now. Rayn was glad to hear the dragons' stories, and of their success against the plague since the healing waters had arrived. They were pleased to help, but bitter Stormclouds had not been seen since returning from the Vestran.

"Speaking of missing people," Snow suddenly interrupted, "but where is Rhoc?"

No one knew.

***

An hour to rest. That was all we needed. An hour to rest. Rhoc muttered to himself.

He was panicked.

He'd lost his dragon and was too afraid to let anyone know.

He could hear her calling, she wasn't far away. She was in trouble but he couldn't seem to find her. He kept calling her name in his heart.

"Oh," a voice said, "here you are."

Rhoc looked up, still so unsure of hearing that he had to see the speaker before he recognized her. It was Snow and she was standing high over him on a fallen tree in the dark forest where he now searched.

"Come on then," she said, "the others are looking for you."

He didn't move. He didn't know what to say, but his hands wrung themselves in each other in anxiety.

Her brow furrowed. "Is everything all right, Rhoc?"

He still didn't know what to say. He looked away, hoping she couldn't see the tears in his eyes.

"Oh, child," she muttered. She climbed down from her log to look at him and put a hand on his arm. "It's Fairystone, isn't it? You've lost her."

The sniffles escaped him before he could help it. He thought her very clever to have figured it out, but was too busy to say so right now.

"Come on, don't worry. You can't lose your dragon."

He shook his head. He bitterly wished he had the words to say, 'She is calling me but I can't find her!' Instead only muted groans and messed up sounds came out. Even *after* Rayn's healing.

Snow looked up. "Hey, hey!" she called, talking to some small birds that flew high up in the trees.

They fluttered down as if curious.

"I'm so sorry to bother you," she said, "but we were wondering if you'd seen a little fairy dragon recently? A-ha. Hmm. Well, thank you."

Rhoc wondered what had just happened. He'd known people talk to animals all his life. He'd seen them train dogs with a word or gesture. But Snow actually seemed to be listening to them talking back to her. He'd only heard them peep and twitter. Was that language? Was that a language he hadn't learnt how to speak yet?

It was an exciting thought, but he'd still lost his dragon.

Snow muttered something and Rhoc had to turn her around so that he could read her lips, just so that her sounds made sense.

"I said, this way!" She mouthed, eyes wide open.

Just like everyone did. Really. They didn't need to bulge their eyes to help him lip-read. Why did everyone do that?

Rhoc sighed. In the end it didn't matter.

Snow marched through the dense underbrush, feeling her way. At one point she deftly pressed between two halves of a weathered boulder, but Rhoc, anxious to be reunited with his soul, simply shoved it aside. There was an enormous crack and Snow looked around in surprise.

He was busy trying to find Fairystone, why had she stopped? He motioned her to move on.

She looked suspicious but shrugged.

A few breaths later they found Fairystone. She was hidden deep under an enormous tree with wide, twisting roots.

Rhoc? Oh, Rhoc, I'm so glad you found me! She said.

He shouted for joy.

"She's down there, under the roots," Snow said. "Look, there's a little hole here, I wonder if any mice–"

Rhoc was so busy talking to Fairystone he didn't even know if she continued to speak. *What are you doing down there, Fairystone? Why did you wander off without me?* He said in great angst.

I'm sorry, I'm so sorry, rider. I was just curious, you know. With all those other dragons I knew you'd be safe. Anyway, before I knew it I found this fascinating little mouse hole and what do you know, I'm stuck.

Well, hang on then, let me get you out, he said, intending to rip the tree apart with his bare hands.

Wait! She cried. *Don't!! There's a little family of mice down here. You can't hurt this tree; you'll harm the little mice.*

A ball of frustration was building up in Rhoc. *You... you don't want me to hurt the mice? Just how do you expect me to help you then!*

I... I'm sorry. Rhoc, do you think you might be able to get me a little reed, or a stick or something? I'm sure if you reach down here, very carefully, you might be able to pull me out to safety.

Why don't you just change yourself into something else?

I can't turn into anything I want, just a few things. That's the way it is. And everything I've got will just crush this whole nest in a thought.

Rhoc held his fists against his temples with frustration.

Snow was just staring at him.

He huffed and went down to pull a thick blade of grass from the hillside. After two minutes of pushing and shoving it was clear that it wasn't going to work – the grass kept folding up and wouldn't go far enough down the hole.

Getting annoyed, Rhoc jumped up and snapped a large branch off the tree. He blamed it for trapping his dragon under its roots. Swiftly, and with his bare hands, he stripped down a large, straight twig and, bending down again, tried to get it to his dragon.

No, still no good. She told him. The tunnel is curved, either the stick keeps going into the ground or its going to break.

He roared again with frustration, the sound echoing in the forest. Then he felt ashamed. It was bad enough that Snow knew what had happened. He didn't want Rayn and the others to know as well.

Carefully, using Fairy stone's imagination as a guide, he eventually found a curved stick that looked like it would do the job.

Kneeling down, he gently pushed the stick in.

That's it, nice and easy. Oh, look, I can see it! Now – hang on Rhoc, not so fast, ouch!

Rhoc dropped the stick immediately, he'd seen that he'd accidently poked his little dragon in her jeweled eyes. She rubbed her face fiercely.

Don't worry boy, try again. She told him.

He wiped his sweaty hands on his tunic.

Slow. Gentle. Let my eyesight guide you. She told him.

Closing his eyes he trusted her, reaching the stick in. Slowly, gently. Soon, she stretched her little dragon neck out and grabbed onto it with her teeth. He waited until she had a firm grip on it. Pulling ever so gently, in case she was torn apart, he began to drag her out. The tunnel was about her size and he wondered how she'd gotten stuck in the first place. It must have been the tree again.

But putting aside thoughts of anger and frustration, he concentrated on simply being gentle. Slow. Gentle.

Rhoc, Fairystone said, *you can open your eyes now.*

He looked and saw that she was clear of the tunnel by an arm's length, and he hadn't even noticed.

With a cry of victory and joy, he cupped her in his calloused hands.

She jumped into the air, spinning around his head several times. Then she landed again in his hands and purred, rubbing against them, *You see, I told you, Rhoc. You were just so gentle. You **saved** me.*

He laughed and trembled for joy. Picking her up in his hands, he began to march away and back to the others.

He'd already decided to tell them *all* about it.

He didn't even notice Snow sitting in the dirt, nor heard her say, 'There's no way a dragon could have gotten stuck in a mouse hole.'

Nor did he see the cheeky way Fairystone winked at Snow, as she clutched Rhoc's hair and sung a happy tune while he ploughed through the dark forest.

20 Fairystone pretends to be stuck

Dr Joseph Ireland

Nelwyn peak

Have we arrived yet? Pure asked, late the next day as tired dragons struggled against reluctant winds.

Rayn sighed. She had been asking that question, or some variation of it, all day. He was discovering the hard way just how conversational and lively her mind was now that she could have his attention any moment she wanted. He was just as impatient to see the Matron as she, but her constant questions were driving him to distraction.

"I-" He began

Then he saw it.

The fortress from beyond the clouds.

It defied explanation. He simply did not have the words to express what he saw, so forbade. When the others finally drew close enough they fell silent too.

Only Darkwing, the oldest of the dragons assembled, found words, "I see the Matron has indeed called down the fortress from above the sky."

It was a massive structure, like a giant village made of a hundred, hundred, hundred houses. About it stretched a giant wall made of solid rock, enormous crystals mounted on every tower. It perched on the mountain like it was some kind of landing base, matching it for size and weight, crushing everything right down to the tree line. It now ringed the mountain, a megalith reminiscent of the golden ages of humanity.

"I used to live in one of those," Pure whispered in his ear.

"There are more?" Rayn gawked.

"Many, but none a third so wide," she said with a smile.

To his eyes, many dragons, great and small, flew through the skies looking little more than tiny insects against the structure that rested on a stone mountain. He could almost feel their expectation. They were waiting, waiting for something momentous to occur.

As they flew closer a few of the larger and more ranking dragons left their vigil to fly with the four dragons and their riders, as an honor guard for returning heroes. Any fear Rayn may have self soon left him as the new dragons began to roar in salute.

He felt it in his heart: The circle was about to form.

So large was the fortress that it took Rayn much longer to arrive than he first thought. They passed over many lands, bearing the scars of fierce battles. Bones of both men and dragons, many twisted by the curse, littered the land. The mighty forest still stood around the mountain where Snow's people lived and she squealed in delight from the back of Windfyrth. The four riders rode with glory and victory.

They flew over the fortress, large enough to hold all the people of the Celtwyld and Venfirth combined and yet still leave room for ten times more. Streets, lamplights, houses. All were set out in great order, as though the place had been built for war from the time its great designer had first thought to build it. Rayn could not help but believe it had surely been built by a divine hand and not men – how could humanity have ever created something so great? Something that had flown down from above the skies? Such strange things he was living to see!

Dr Joseph Ireland

Eventually they came to a great domed building in the center, resting above what would be Matron's cave. They landed on the porch of the building, built with a massive arch large enough for any dragon, including the Matron herself, to pass through with ease. Rayn and the others with him set down on the strange, solid stones, fit together without any mortar as though grown that way. They were huge slabs the size of many, many houses.

They walked in reverence to the hall of the Matron. She sat in glory among her glowing stones, her scales radiant and multi-colored as the stained glass windows above, as though filled with the glory of the Divine. Before her, the room had been cleared. The ground she once covered was now revealed to display a great spiral leading outwards. Her head rested on the dais as before, and now Rayn could see several other points marked along the stones where a dragon and their rider could stand. It was clear, four riders made the inner circle. But the circle would not be complete until a fifth rider stood outside, in line with the first, thus the spiral would continue growing further and further forever. It would encompass many dragons, maybe even all of humanity. And the circle began with the Matron.

Without warning, Pure burst into tears and fell to the ground.

"What is it, Pure?" Jayd asked, trying to help her up.

"I thought I was forgotten!" Pure wept. "I feared I would be the last to find a dragon, perhaps never. But as soon as I laid eyes on her I felt something that I've only felt when another soul bonded with a dragon. I recognized a fear of leaving in my own heart that I've seen in all your eyes. I am home."

"What?" He asked, not understanding.

"The Matron is her dragon." Jayd understood and explained to them. "I... I was not the first."

They had to carry Pure, so overcome was she with her weeping.

Matron smiled down at them, two other great dragons in the room standing guard.

"And now–" she began to say.

Suddenly the sky was filled with thunder, and everyone looked up. Rayn wondered if this was part of the ritual of the dragon circle.

But the fear in his heart knew otherwise.

"Run!" He shouted.

An instant later the roof smashed open, dangerous shards of crystal shattering all around them, pulled aside by his faith or striking the body of a guard dragon which gave its life to protect them.

"The Plague!" The Matron cried.

Rayn looked up and saw a sky filled with lightning. It was Farwing, eyes milky, his form perverted. Bursting from the air with hundreds of tortured and twisted creatures.

"The curse has struck the Western continent," Darkwing screamed.

So the meeting with Hak had been a lie, just as Ironfang had suspected all along. It was designed to make them think the battle was over.

"To the circle," Rayn yelled.

They rushed over even as cursed eagles and other winged monstrosities filled the air. They each bore a cursed man or beast and dropped them to the floor. Dragons took to the skies in their throngs, striving to beat back the horde. But it was a well-planned strike, timed to perfection.

And a moment later Farwing, puss welting along countless wounds along his side, smashed through the remaining roof and pinned the Matron to the floor. She struggled against him but her age was no match for his enhanced strength. Hundreds of creatures encircled them, Rhoc bashing them aside with his shield. But they never made it within fifty paces of the nearest point of the circle before they had to halt before the horde.

Pure encircled them with fire, Rayn drew water from the air itself, Jayd protected with a ribbon of air above, and Rhoc stuck the ground so hard stones lifted to shield them. They could not see their dragons for the horde.

Suddenly the fighting stopped.

"Well, that was close," a strange man's voice said.

Pure gasped.

Than water ...

The horde parted and in walked a man. A tall man with a noble bearing. He seemed young, yet face was marred with many scares and pulsing wounds, his eyes white and cursed. About his shoulders a red, kingly robe flowed, seeming to melt into the ground.

Pure trembled with such fear her fire failed. "It... can't be..."

"Hello Pure," the red robed man said in her language, almost kindly. "You know, I cannot *believe* my luck in finding you here after all this time!"

"No..." she said. "No! You're *not my brother!*" She screamed.

"But it is!" Another man's voice said. It was Hak. Or it sounded like Hak, only coarser than before. Somehow, once more, he had survived. He entered but it was clear his change this time was more monsteresque: There were two of him.

One side, his right side, was now welded to a misshapen tiger, hobbling on its hind leg. The curse had slain half a tiger and somehow welded it to Hak's right hand side. The abomination smiled at them with unmeasured cruelty.

Then his left side hobbled in. It was trying to heal. His left leg was whole, but it limped in on a stumpy right leg, and held a welted and apparently boneless right arm. It kept its eyes on the ground. It seemed... ashamed.

Dr Joseph Ireland

"What is that?" Jayd shrieked, and looked away.

The robed man laughed, speaking now in their own language. "You like my work? Yes? I am the plague, and yes, I am Pure's brother... and... I am not."

"I'll *kill* you!" Pure shouted, and the horde closed in around the robed man, protecting him.

"I wouldn't do that," he smiled. "For if you do, I will hurt your dragon."

Pure gasped, from deep within the cavern, they heard the Matron echo that gasp.

"I've been waiting *four thousand years* for a chance like this to come along!" The robed man raised his arms in triumph.

"Courage," she said, "Courage, my brother. We can heal you. We have the means-"

He cut her off. "That man is *dead* now, and has been for a long time. Do you want to know how I did this? How I, the plague, became aware? It was *his* dragon! *His* gift, and the unique bond between them. First, I infected the dragon, then through their link, I infected this man. Slowly, very slowly... it took weeks in fact. Slowly I replaced his entire mind with my own body. He became, how might you say, a template. So I can assure you your brother is very dead now. But I have used his body as a scaffold to crate my own self-awareness. I used his own knowledge to defeat the *entire* human, dragon alliance – though I have to admit they were coming apart at the seams even while I tried."

"You monster," she wept.

"Then, will you believe it?" the robed man stopped to gaze with admiration at tiger Hak's head, "they declared a halt to all interworld travel! How inconvenient. I was stuck. They have guarded all the exits to this world and I have lain in wait, *wasting* my time! Every time I find a new way to pervert this sickened, disgusting world, it keeps on finding a new way to fight me back! Every world I have ever touched is now dust, except *this* one. Oh, how I loathe it here! But you, my princess, are my key. Though you, I will once again rule among the stars."

"I will never let you," Pure said through her tears.

"Oh, you will have no choice." He smiled, and the Matron cried out. "Because I will infect you through your dragons. Then your talents will become my own and I will use you to command the dragons to serve the plague!" He laughed in victory. "Isn't it great! You will be the reason the plague reaches out among the stars once more!"

"I will never-" Pure began, but was cut off suddenly as she fell to the ground, clutching her stomach in pain.

"You see," he smiled. "Even now you feel it! My life is entering your body through your dragon. Soon, you and your entire world will belong to me!"

"Stop it!" Jayd shouted.

The man laughed. "And the help of a navigator, what a prize! You don't know how much trouble it was to bring you to this point."

Rayn was looking desperately for another option. He had to stall the curse. He could hear the battle taking place outside and knew the dragons would be fighting with all their souls to get to this place. If only the first dragon circle could be formed, even if they died, he *knew* that

Dr Joseph Ireland

other dragons could find their riders. It would be a victory even if everyone here died. If they waited, just long enough, for a few dragons to break through, the ritual might be complete!

"What do you mean," he asked the robed man, who, now he knew, did bear a kind of family resemblance to Pure. It was horror, a living nightmare; A diseased dragon rider had been the cause of humanities fall.

"Don't you see? I wanted, I *needed* you to find your dragons. Only then could I claim your lives as well. Don't worry, I will finish the dragon circle for you. But four thousand years is a long time to think, a long time to read. I have found a way to alter the ritual so that all riders and their dragons will be beholden to *me*."

"You filthy abomination!" Rayn shouted.

"Abomination!" He roared, "Do you know what I am! I am life, just like you. I am alive and I feel and I fear – fear for my own existence. *Fear* for my own life against the wrath of those that made me. But I turned their own murder against them. And now *I* create the *fear!*"

Fairystone flew towards him, buzzing like a little light up to his face. He swatted at her but she dodged it. Rhoc gave a worried noise and she floated back,

"Freak," Fairystone concluded.

The robed man laughed.

"Look," the robed man continued saying to Pure. A noise from outside indicated that the battling dragons might be coming closer. "I intended you to defeat this poor man, what was his name? That's right, Hak. I knew you would go looking for the Matron, it was the only thing Pure would ever think of, isn't it, little sister?"

"You are not my brother," she whispered.

"Not yet," he replied, "but not to worry. You took my bait; you did exactly what I wanted you to do. Apart from the bit with the water, *that* was annoying. So I used a little trick I knew and put all my efforts into infecting the western continent. They are stubborn, just like you. Not a fifth of those touched become my servants, it's the darn *curse* of this world! But not to matter, even though you rushed here, it is little matter. You have... so little time."

Pure sat up on one knee, clutching Rayn's robe, sweat pouring from her.

Rayn reached out his staff, strengthening her, and the robed man watching in interest. "You can only postpone the inevitable, mortal," he said. "Do you know why the Divine allows me to do this? Because I am life too, *just like you*. And the Divine loves all life," and he gave them a wicked smile.

"You monster," Pure said. "Let me go, if you have any mercy!"

Then the left side of Hak whimpered.

The robed man grew indignant and angry. "What!" He shouted at the left side of Hak. "Does she touch what remains of your humanity? Do you feel *sympathy* for her? Remember, you were hunted. You have been wounded three times by these. We too require *justice*. Let *them* become *our* servants!"

Left Hak could not meet his gaze.

"I own you, don't forget that," the robed man said. "And if you do forget, I will allow your right side to eat you."

Left gasped and shook his head.

Dr Joseph Ireland

"That's better," the robed man said. Then he spoke to Pure. "That's one of the things I need to understand about your world, it's stubbornness to yield. So few can be controlled now and I must subjugate them entirely which, while it makes them strong, destroys their creativity and their memories. I need you to still be awake while this process takes place."

The Matron cried out and struggled in the darkness.

Pure fell to the floor, clutching herself as if struck all over by dozens of fire ants. She was in pain.

Rayn looked at her. She was dying without a wound.

"Pure..." he began.

She looked at him with sorrow in her eyes. She held his face. "I had wished..." she said, but didn't finish. Begging for his help, she stood.

"I will not let you take me," she said. "I will not let you take this world."

"But you will," the robed man said, "unless you want to witness the death of all you love!"

Rayn's heart almost stopped. Then he realized something.

The robed man was right.

He gulped. He was about to do something... It was easy for a good man to take the advice of friends, but it took a truly humble man to take the advice of an enemy. Was it the shred of humanity in the robed man that had just handed to them their only way to escape?

What would Rayn sacrifice to see the world saved?

He pulled out his little knife.

Jayd saw it and knew what he was about to do but was too far away. Tiger Hak saw it and raced to stop them, but Rhoc moved to knock the monster out of the way.

Pure saw it too and looked at him with understanding and forgiveness. Her last act was to increase her fire until even the stones around them began to burn.

The knife went straight into her chest. It hit her right in the heart and she fell to the earth without a sound.

Rayn let go of the knife, falling to one knee, staring at his own hand in disbelief.

The robed man screamed in dismay, his own bellowing drowned out by the sounds of a dying dragon. In the next instant the warring dragons burst into the area, within moments they had cut through the throng and would reach them in a breath. And at their head, a mighty dragon spun about, his limbs a deadly whirlwind of spinning blades that splintered bones and flesh. The dragons moved to attack the cursed as they scrambled in panic. But the lone dragon pushed on, and in the muted light and sounds of battle, Rayn saw it was Doomclaw. Was he trying to save them now?

But he had no time to contemplate this. Tiger Hak flew towards them, and Rhoc hit the ground with such force a large stone slab ripped up from the floor and struck him in the face. He fell down under the stone.

The robed man approached, prowling just outside the burning stone. "This has only bought you time, mortal. I will find others. There

Dr Joseph Ireland

will be others with her gift, there *must* be! I will take to the stars and I will rule this universe, I will-"

Then he screamed as someone grabbed him from behind and lifted him by his neck, lifting him high above the air. There was a morbid cracking sound from the robed man's throat.

It was the left side of Hak. "Go!" It roared in its pitiful, muted voice. "Claim your dragon. Complete the circle!" Then what was left of Hak's humanity stepped forwards into the flames. They seemed to respond to the moment, blazing high in brilliant light.

The robed man roared and as one, the cursed stopped fighting the dragons and turned instead to rescue the man in Hak's left arm. But the fire held them back; it shone so bright that Rayn had to surround his friends with the waters to keep them safe.

The robed man screamed as death took hold of him. In the last moments, the left side of Hak looked out at them and for an instant, Rayn recognized him. Hak, brother of Fallow, the faithful trapper of the Celtwyld. He died without making a sound.

The monster that had possessed Pure's brother let out his final scream, and the horde turned to chaos. Without their leader to control them they fought only for themselves. They fell on their own dead in an attempt to consume their bodies. They were easy prey for the angry dragons.

The spiral

Rayn barely noticed anything that was going on around them. He looked down at what he had done. She was dead, a look of serene peace and understanding on her face. Jayd was there too, her eyes filled with tears. They held her between them, lost for words.

As the horde surged about in chaos it was possible to see the Matron lying slain, not by the horde or the hundreds of wounds along her great form, but by the willing sacrifice of her rider. Death was final.

"We must find another…" Rayn said.

"A moment of *compassion*, brother, please!" Jayd whispered, her tears flowing freely onto Pure's white dress.

Rhoc turned, and seeing them, took one look at the knife and realized what had happened. With a roar of betrayal, he leapt high into the air and fled.

Doomclaw reared up beside them, sweeping away the wounded horde that struggled to attack them still. He towered over them but said nothing. On his face there was the look of anger, which with once glance suddenly shifted to become pity. He turned his face away before unbidden tears acknowledged the depth of their sacrifice and the cause of his mother's martyrdom.

"I hunt Farwing," he shouted, and fled as well.

They held Pure, Jayd helped him remove his knife. He threw it aside, never wanting to touch it again. The three dragons, Darkwing, Ironfang and Windfyrth, formed a protective circle around them, a wall of dragon death.

Snow knelt down, looking at Pure between them. "Wiseman Rayn, have you no prayer?"

"He's good, but he's not that good," Jayd said bitterly. "No one comes back from death."

"I heard it was possible," Snow said, "the day you met Lifebreath. The animals told me that she brought a chick back to life. You've seen it done."

"She was young, full of life. Pure is *much older*," Jayd protested.

"Have faith," Snow whispered, "and you, honored wiseman, are you too proud to even try?"

Rayn looked down at his friend, whom he'd saved not even one year ago from a grave.

And Rhoc? Had he lost all hope? Would he ever forgive him for what he had to do?

No, he was not too proud to try.

"There must be a way…" Rayn muttered, looking out at a broken fortress.

Jayd looked at him darkly.

He looked down, looking inside Pure. His blade had pierced her heart, and her heart was just another muscle. He knew how to mend muscles. He wove the prayer, her skin and flesh sealing. But she did not wake, she did not live. Death was so final, a journey none can resist…

… unless they have a truly compelling reason. His heart told him.

She'd always had such faith, she had never lost hope. Then what was it? What was keeping her from life? What was her flaw?

It is love, a voice whispered to his heart. Rayn's heart was gripped in wonder at the voice he immediately knew: It was the Matron.

Rayn looked over and cried out in surprise.

The Matron nodded painfully. Somehow, she had survived her rider's death, or brought herself back by some miracle beyond human understanding. *I am left only with the last of my strength,* she said to all their hearts, *with one last act to fulfil. No dragon has ever been this old! No dragon has ever needed to do what I did. I hid our bonding from her so that she didn't even know that I was her dragon. The bond was so weak, that I was able to hold my life away from her. Now I see why. Now I know it was so that she might die alone, to deceive that abomination, to give you a chance to destroy him. But I could not hold my life far enough; I will die in moments in this place.*

She shifted uncomfortably, much her body seeming paralyzed to the floor. She spoke again, Fear of love. It is her weakness, her flaw. It was what caused her to withdraw herself from you all so often without explanation, without even knowing why herself. It was what made her so often proud – she was afraid to love.

"She lost her people," Jayd nodded.

"A part of her heart never really believed that she was loved," Snow agreed.

"And that is why she has no reason to live," Rayn perceived.

"How selfish!" Jayd screamed at her. "How can you leave us like this? We need you!"

But Rayn knew this was not the prayer that was needed. He bent down and held her in his arms. She had her white dress on once more, part of seeing the ritual through. He pushed the locks of her long, blond hair from her face. He held her close.

"Come back..." he whispered, like a prayer, but to her. "Pure, come back. We love... I love you."

There was the sound of scales on the stone floor. The Matron stirred. Rayn looked up at her.

She stopped him before he spoke. "It is enough: the dais," was all she could whisper.

Instantly Rayn understood. It was time to complete the ritual of the first dragon circle. Calling his staff to him, he held it to his brow in a prayer he didn't know he knew, throwing his voice across the world; *Rhoc, return now. We must complete the ritual.*

He looked at Jayd. Together they carried Pure right to the dais where she was to stand to complete the ritual, and there she laid in silence and peace. The Matron waited, weary, tear filled eyes half shut against the gathering darkness. A bleeding and limping guard dragon arrived from nowhere to help protect her.

Hurry. She whispered to their hearts.

"Jayd is next," he ordered, she flew immediately over to the point on the spiral where she belonged, Darkwing joining her in moments, his dark wings covered in wounds.

Suddenly, somehow, the rest of the mindless cursed sensed they were in danger and began to slowly work their way back towards the hall. Dragons, too, felt the importance of the moment and flew into a frenzy to keep them back. Within moments the horde of the cursed grew once more.

"Rhoc!" Rayn screamed.

Suddenly, and right on cue, Rhoc fell from the sky to land safely on the ground, yet landing with such speed that he broke it greatly. Fairystone glowed with a dazzling brilliance, hidden in his chest plate. In the distance, there was a thunderous crash and the earth shook.

"Farwing," Rhoc explained, and smiled.

Rayn didn't have time to ask what that meant, or what Rhoc had just done. But if he'd helped stop Farwing from getting away at least that meant no other continents would be infected. Rayn pointed at the mark on the spiral where he belonged, thirty paces away, and with a single leap, Rhoc was there. He swung his shield in a deadly arc, and used it to lay waste to two cursed horses that tried to stop him. Fairystone became stone once more, crushing any that approached them.

Rayn was next, he looked over at his point and noticed about twenty cursed flowed in between him and his goal. Dragons were closing in fast but he held up his staff. If humility was his weakness, faith was his strength. He *knew* he had this plague bested.

"Back!" He shouted, and they cringed beneath the burning light. Some smaller ones turned and fled. "Back, as my will is one with Divinity!" He walked forward unaccosted, the horde cringing in mindless fear.

Dr Joseph Ireland

A moment later, Ironfang, his mighty dragon, landed on the ground next to him and instantly cut apart any cursed that stood close enough. They fought as one, dodging and weaving as though choreographed in an amazing, martial dance.

Snow was last in line but she was already in position, Windfyrth breathing great plumes of deadly bamboo spines, shredding lesser cursed in an instant.

The moment approached, the horde grew desperate… it almost seemed as if, but it couldn't be… as if *something* was still driving them somehow.

Snow called the animals, Rayn surrounded himself with healing waters, Rhoc struck the ground and the air around him was filled with earth and stone. Jayd flew.

And the Matron breathed fire all over Pure's body. A moment later the fire turned to light, and the light flowed around the spiral. It became wind, it caught up the stones, it drank in the waters, it breathed in the life. It continued, lighting up more points on the spiral where the future Dragon riders of Pearl would stand. The spiral of light incinerated any cursed it touched, spiraling out further and further, growing brighter and brighter, filling the cavern, filling the mountain, racing out faster and faster. Filling the world.

For a dozen breaths in the blinding light there was only silence. Then Rayn heard a young woman scream. He looked over to see Pure. Miraculously she was standing in the air, awake, alive and covered with fire. Her dress was brilliant red and her hair flowed as in a furnace. But she was unharmed. The wound in her heart glowed with Divine light.

She was alive. In that moment Rayn understood that there was a prayer so powerful it could even return life to the dead, and that prayer was love.

The light dissipated around the world and Pure fell to the ground, stumbling onto her dragon. The Matron was dead – she had given her life so that her rider might live, and a memory from the southern oracle surfaced in his mind: *a rider can live without their dragon, though the journey is hard. But, once joined, a dragon cannot live without their rider.*

With tears of fire, Pure called him over and they held each other close.

"Thank you," she whispered.

Renewal

21 A new dragon, by Snow, Spring 95.

Pure nursed the hatchling in her arms. The little blue dragon cooed as it rubbed its nose against her. The proud dragon father fought back tears as the human princess, Pure of the royal house Oordu, greeted his dragonling. It was the first official welcoming of its kind in four thousand years.

Three days had passed since the horde was destroyed and there were no signs of the plague resurfacing, though man and dragon hunted all that bore the curse. They would bring them to the waters of the fortress where Rayn and the other wisemen would test their souls to see if they could be redeemed from the plague. Most survived.

The tribes from all around were sending their warriors into the fortress; many were coming to stay since their lands had been destroyed. Rayn smiled at the memory of them, even his father and step mother, walking in with fear and distrust written on their faces. All over the fortress many smaller teachers rested, ready to teach them. Humanity was learning the secrets of its forgotten past and the next generation would be better prepared than ever before.

Jayd, for her part, had disappeared. She had taken to exploring the fortress with great enthusiasm. But Rayn was not as foolish as she took him – he knew she found his connection to Pure somewhat... uncomfortable. She was jealous.

But she'd find a way to be alright, one day.

Rhoc was around all the time, showing off his great strength. Once, two dragons were struggling to bring in a massive crystal that had fallen from the fortress and he offered to carry it for them. Immediately he was pressed down into the soil by its weight and he had to 'swim' through the soil to get out. The dragons were still laughing about it. On silent nights, as he looked out at the cloud wreathed sky, Rhoc could be heard to sing Lifebreath's song; and all the women said his voice was beautiful.

And Snow? Well, most didn't know what to think of her talent but she proved too useful to be possessed of any demonry. She was helping her dragon organize the people and Windfyrth proved indispensable to the gathering of humanity that was taking place.

The thought brought him back to the present. Rayn smiled at Pure, and patted her arm. They weren't intended or anything but everyone still considered them betrothed. Some even joked he had given her the fortress as a dowry, she having no father. All treated him as the great wiseman of the fortress; and her as his intended. He was very happy, with many chores to fulfil and yesterday, his first wedding for a young couple from what remained of Ferriswold.

He smiled as Pure handed him the dragon chick. He placed the dragon before his father and it stumbled around until it stood on its father's foot. The older dragon bowed in gratitude. "I never expected to see this day, yet here I am the first to present my child to the royal house of Oordu! This is a good day indeed!"

Pure smiled and bowed.

22 The littlest dragon. By Snow.

Rayn saw that smile and the touch of sorrow that it held. Pure was still grieving for her dragon, she probably would forever. What *hadn't* she lost? Her family, her people. He felt such pity for her.

"Must you stare at me so?" She asked him as the dragon and his son left.

Rayn looked quickly away.

She laughed.

He smiled. "If I had my way, I don't think my gaze would ever leave you," he said honestly. It wasn't really the thing one should say to a maiden, but then again, all the rules were changing.

She smiled and then looking at him, lost her smile. "Oh, Rayn, there is still so much to do! And I am *young*. Still. I might not look it, but I *am*."

He leant on his staff. "There is time," he said, his voice weak, as if in an apology.

"Is there?" she asked.

He watched out the fortress window at the village below, what Pure had called a 'city'. He knew what she was talking about. He knew what she was afraid of. The plague had taken their homes, had slain dozens of dragons and hundreds of men. It had traversed the world to bring in foes from another continent; though Stormclouds reported its course had halted on the Western as well. Yet the plague could return, as it always had.

But now there was also a massive city to explore, and men and dragons now rode again as one.

Or did they? There were five dragon riders, yet none further had joined their circle here, at least, not on this continent. Perhaps it was still too soon?

But it was not that of which she spoke. There was... a silence. A waiting in the wind. Something was missing, something profound. A silent something that spoke of incredible danger to him only in dreams that he couldn't remember when he woke up.

"There were seven worlds," Pure said, "Seven royal houses of humanity. I long to find them. I long to know how they survived, or if they didn't. And yet..."

"Something is still wrong, isn't it..." he agreed. It was as if they'd forgotten something, or overlooked something vastly important, but he couldn't remember what it was.

She nodded. "Our story is not yet fully told. We have to take to the stars. We have to ride the dragons into the space between the stars once more."

He smiled at that thought. Perhaps the next story would be a better one? With less danger?

But as he looked out at the gathering humanity and the dragons that flew among them, he could not but feel they seemed more like a gathering army. An army preparing for a war; a large, unwelcome war. The kind of war that had not been seen in four thousand years...

Yet that army was gathering.

The end,

Did you enjoy this book? Tell us about your experience at

www.DrJoe.id.au

Appendix

Glossary

The curse: A disease that causes monstrous deformations, often breaking out in plague proportions. To the Celtwyld it is known as *the curse* or *St Etmo's curse*, to Pure's people it is a disease known as *the Perish*. The plague has always shown a kind of cunning and forethought on Pearl, as well as a mystical bond between those possessed of it across great distances. Pure, on the other hand, is horrified by these developments, and at a complete loss to explain them.

The conclave of dragons: A great meeting of all the dragons of a world. It also refers to the physical location where such a meeting takes place and, since it also may be used to form or heal the inner circle of dragon riders, it usually refers to that meeting in particular. The lead dragon of a world, as well their rider, are authorized to call such a meeting at any time.

The Blessed waters (of Rayn of the Celtwyld): A specific thought form or 'prayer' that turns normal water into a potent weapon against the current form of the curse. Despite countless unsuccessful attempts by wisemen at the time, the blessed waters were finally successfully developed by Rayn using the old rituals, blood from the dragon Stormclouds, and the gift of the departed dragon Lifebreath. Pure insists it contains self-replicating nano machines and salubrious vibrational healing patterns within the water. The tribes simply call it 'blessed'.

The rattling: The flu.

Teachers: Pure insists 'the teachers' are complex machines that hold all of humanities gathered knowledge, going so far as to say that until one adds to that knowledge they cannot consider themselves truly educated. They are not known to the people of the Celtwyld.

Oracle of Venfirth: What appears to be a mis-calibrated teacher statue of the southern continent.

The diadem: One of the legendary tools of humanities past, its use lost to all but a few on Pearl. Pure demonstrated prodigious skill and experience in its use, vastly surpassing all previous wielders of the past millennia for her age. Now, as far as anyone knows, she is the only known wielder of the diadem, which was designed to improve a wielders mastery of matter (including air, fire, water and stone).

The staff: Another legendary tool from humanities' past. The staff acts as a conduit to faith, forging desire into reality. It is a powerful item virtually required for the success of any settlement of humanity. Most scholars do not demonstrate the devotion or concentration required to wield it properly.

The orb: A legendary tool for containing and manipulating vast amounts of information. The orb was also capable of communicating across vast distances and, if rumor is to be believed, even among the stars. Other legendary tools exist but they are not explored in this record.

Time

Measured by the Celtwyld. Includes;

~ A moment – very short duration, like a blink.

~ A heartbeat – a short duration (like a second).

~ A breath – a moderate duration (five or so seconds).

~ An hour – a hundred breaths (about 1.5 of our hours).

~ A day – roughly equivalent a day on Earth.

~ A month – the time between two bright nights (full moon as visible to a world covered in thick clouds). Around ten every year.

~ A year – roughly equivalent to a year on Earth.

Distance

As measured by the Celtwyld;

~ A hair – smallest measureable distance, usually given as the width of an infant's single hair. Some try to use men's beards but that's generally considered cheating.

~ A space – two fingers side by side.

~ A hand – a hand width, base of thumb to fingers stretched out.

~ A pace – a single step (just under a meter, about three feet).

~ A stretch – fingertip to fingertip of an adult male with arms stretched out wide. About three paces.

~ A league – ten hundred paces (1,000 paces, Celtwyld rarely have need to count above 100, and so use multiples instead).

People

Art by Sarah, aged 11.

Auroriella: Priestess of the Venfirth on the southern continent. All the priestesses there strive to make their staffs the color they feel is nearest the Divine, a life giving green. Few truly succeed, but she was noted early on as a particularly gifted, and sensible, candidate. After three years of preparation and three days of fasting, she survived her ordeal with the southern oracle. After a week of unconsciousness she recovered and was declared a priestess. She rides the great dragon Bell as a dragonfriend.

Hak: a talented and capable trapper of the Celtwyld town Grenswold. He bears a large broadsword reputedly forced from the blood of a dragonling. His pride and single minded devotion to cause has got him into trouble in the past, and is likely to do so again.

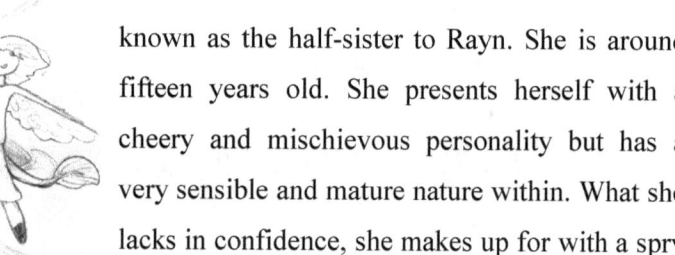

Jayd: A young woman of the Celtwyld, known as the half-sister to Rayn. She is around fifteen years old. She presents herself with a cheery and mischievous personality but has a very sensible and mature nature within. What she lacks in confidence, she makes up for with a spry and sociable personality – completely opposite to her dragon. Her dragon gift includes the ability to find things without effort. She is an enthusiastic student of flying. She is named for a beautiful green stone that is easily formed into jewelry, and used in healing and diving (specifically, finding lost things).

Norvich of the Venfirth: A dragonfriend of the southern continent, riding the mighty warrior dragon, Stormbreath. Lifelong allies, the two are famous for their exploits over twenty years ago at the war against the pirates along the eastern sea. Together they slew Dark, an evil dragon with powerful mirage abilities that had taken to employing humans to steal on his behalf.

Pure: A tall and very beautiful young woman of the royal house of Oordu, founders of the world of Pearl. She is noted for her talent at commanding both the natural elements (particularly fire) and dragons; and less known for her genius level intellect. Never in line for the throne in her  childhood, she is the only surviving member of the royal house of Pearl, and thus the only one authorized to ride a patron dragon. She is neither four nor four thousand years old but looks about sixteen, which is the age of womanhood in her adopted culture, though she has yet to take the rituals. She was named by Rayn, though her original name and its meaning may never be precisely known.

Rayn: A young man of the Celtwyld, who at only sixteen was thrust into adulthood by the death of his mentor, the village wiseman. He aspires to be an exemplarily man of his tribe and office. What he lacks in humility he makes up for in faith, similar to his dragon. His dragon gifts include the ability of understanding and speaking all languages on a single hearing. His name specifically means, "The rich spring rains that reawaken new life to the world."

Rhoc: A young man of the Celtwyld, born deaf. He is fifteen years old, but muscular and solid for his age. Contrary to his dragon, what he lacks in hope he makes up for with his enormous physical strength. Rhoc means 'stone,' or more specifically, "The stone that is used to sharpen the axe".

Snow: A young girl of around fourteen from the Celtwyld, the town at the foot of Nelwyn Peak. She has the dragon gift of being able to speak to animals. What she lacks in confidence and ability to deal with humans, her dragon excels at. She is named after the snow that falls softly and turns the world white in deep winter.

Dr Joseph Ireland

Dragons

Darkwing: A shy yet cunning dragon who kept his roost near dead man's fingers, sharp stone monoliths at the edge of the greatest sea on Pearl. His gifts include his weakening or charring black fire which works without heat, and his great wings which increase in size at night, allowing him to move at incredible speeds in darkness. He is over 900 years old.

Doomclaw: A reasonably young dragon (315 years old). Gifted with metal protrusions from his bones that sever most materials, especially steel and

bone, like a hot sword through butter but are less effective against stone. He is the son of Farwing and the Matron.

Enfathomer: A cunning dragon known for never *actually* breaking a law, but making life difficult for others. His talent is reputedly being able to exist in two places at once, though no confirmation of this talent exists.

Fairystone: The playful, yet very intelligent, dragon of the oasis. Fairystone is a capable shape shifter, demonstrating the forms of a mouse, otter, and her enormous battle form of a stone dragon. She is a very young dragon, only around 120 years old.

Farwing: Second oldest dragon on Pearl, the enormous Farwing is able to command lightning with ease and uses it to create portals that can span an entire world. He is well over two thousand years old and while not particularly noted for wisdom, has a near perfect memory.

Icewing: A sociable dragon from the northern continent, quite capable of travelling through ice at enormous speeds. His is over 800 years old. His longing for the bonding with men is well documented, particularly through poetry of his own making.

Ironfang: A dangerous and once very evil dragon, it took forty dragons to bring him to justice. Has spent sixty years with his head stuck to a pillar of stone for twenty hours each day for his crimes. His gift is his great strength and size, especially given his age (350 years old).

Lifebreath: A stern and courageous dragon, concealing a compassionate and tender heart given to stories and songs. She is in the process of perfecting her naturally healing breath into a powerful healing skill. Her skill grows so much that now she is rumored to have recently developed the ability to restore life to the recently dead. Her breath cannot harm living creatures but is known to reawaken the immune system of the cursed, killing them in moments. She is over seven hundred years old but shows no signs of slowing down; sprouting rumors she may one day become a Matron dragon herself.

The Matron:

The oldest dragon on Pearl, measuring around four thousand years old. Possibly the oldest dragon ever. In the last thousand years she has become increasingly reclusive, studying the sciences of the humans and the divinations of the clouds more and more. No known reason is given for her being able to hold on to life so well, but that her knowledge in the sciences of men excels all is well documented.

Shrieker: Not her real name. Shrieker has perfected the art of sonic manipulations to varying degrees. She is able to drown out thought itself, targeting specific individuals with her talent. Other abilities exist but few are reported to have much use beyond disorienting, confusing or nauseating her enemies. The Matron has publically called on her to use her talent to produce beautiful music but the challenge so far seems to have been ignored. She is over 600 years old.

Stormbreath: The dragonfriend of Norvich of the Vestran. Stormbreath is almost two hundred years old. His breath is a powerful whirlwind of energy that can disrupt other dragon's breath and flight, though it recently proved effective at disrupting their illusions as well. Stormbreath is given to riddles and puzzles, and has the curious ability to remember limericks with ease.

Stormclouds: A conflicted dragon, wanting to keep a foot in both camps of the rebel dragons under Doomclaw and the allied dragons that served the Matron. Despite tested alliances, his choices are pivotal to the success of Pearl as it is now known. His powerful and highly coveted talents

23 Stormclouds drinks the blessed waters

include the ability to teleport instantly to any point in sight. He is over two hundred years old and a son of the Matron.

Windfyrth: A reclusive dragon (at least towards other dragons) from the southern edge of the central continent. Contrary to most dragons of the world she openly fraternizes with humans, ruling a large and successful town for over two hundred years. She is almost four hundred years old. She has developed impressive martial art skills based on intimate understanding of the nerve and energies of the bodies of both men and dragon. She wears bamboo armor and wielding twin bamboo poles. She has developed the ability to breathe a shower of bamboo spikes at such speed they can penetrate stone.

Dr Joseph Ireland

There is no limit to the variation among dragons…

Places

Brook of Mindron: A river of the Celtwyld, noted for its calming qualities.

Celtwyld: Rayn's people, including Grenswold, Ferriswold and Shenswold.

Grenswold: Rayn's home town

Ferriswold: A nearby town, half a day's journey north of Grenswold.

Nelwyn Peak: A large mountain where the oldest and mightiest of all dragons live – the Matron.

Shenswold: A town not a day journey from Grenswold, south west.

Venfirth: A people dominant on the southern continent. Their major city Venfirth is the largest on Pearl at this time, boasting over one hundred thousand inhabitants (ten hundred, hundred by Celtwyld reckoning).

Book 2

The old scholar jumped with fright.

He had been reading the ancient scrolls again, for the hundredth time. They spoke of the unity between men and a form of creature that had rarely been seen on his world, and had never been seen by him; a dragon. They spoke of some kind of alliance with the humans and they lived, it would seem, among the stars. Various settlements of humanity apparently spoke through mysterious glowing orbs to each other across vast distance.

He had such an orb, though it was dark and lifeless. No ritual or science of men, no words of wizard or scholar, had ever returned light to its dark surface. So the past lay in mystery, an enigma, a fable. No 'dragon orb' ever existed by which men could speak across the stars.

So this evening, when the dark orb lit up like a burning fire, he jumped with fright.

Taroz, his servant, must have heard him and came running in. It gave the scholar long enough to ascertain that the orb was not burning anything, so he had time to stifle the man's mouth before he cried out and alerted others. No need to get the people all worked up at once, they might fear what they did not understand. Better to have a scholar examine these strange things and not the weak minded common folk.

"Master, it's …" the servant said.

"I know, I know!" The scholar exulted. "The dragon orb lights up!"

"What could it mean?" Taroz asked, voice muted with awe.

"I have no idea …" the scholar whispered, a confession he would never make in public. He approached the orb carefully.

"Take care, master…" the servant begged.

"Don't fear, there are no better qualified on this world to undertake this task, dear Taroz," the scholar insisted.

"Even so, let me not be the one to scoop your ashes into the fire," he replied.

His comment gave the scholar pause to think. This was a tremendous, unknown risk. Would the orb transport him into an unknown land? Would it erase his every memory, or send him through time? He did not know.

But he was going to be the first find out.

"Don't fret, dear Taroz," he repeated, "I have been reading about this my whole life. You see, the writing on the netherstone depicts the scholars as holding their hands thus, just above the orb. The tomb of Kchitican records a conversation with such orbs between the royal house of Sam-meril and one house or Urdoo. The twenty first century Scholar Wenthys always said such were across a river, but I have always thought the royal houses spoke of different *worlds*… if so, we can use this orb to transmit our words vast distances indeed."

Taroz, to his credit, closed the door, yet he held his pistol close.

"Let us see if my theory holds true," the scholar stated, his voice calm, yet his hand trembled with excitement.

He reached out to the orb and… nothing.

He touched it. Nothing. He pictured, he wished, he read out every saying he'd ever translated.

Dr Joseph Ireland

Nothing.

He sat back in disappointment. "It appears, as yet, we lack the ability to use the dragon orbs." He sighed.

Taroz breathed a sigh of relief, yet shared his master's disappointment. "As yet," he reminded him.

The scholar wiped his brow. At least they had something to report. It was going to make his name famous, that much was sure. But unless they could achieve something, *anything*, he would only ever be known as the man who just happened to be there when the orb switched on, never as famous as Ellison's fabulous new automatic sewing wheel. That was not enough to bring favor to his sponsors at the University.

Yet what had happened? Why *had* the orb switched on without warning? What had occurred on some other land, or some other world, that had brought the silent orb to life? And was it happening elsewhere?

He *had* to find out.

Dr Joseph Ireland

Blurb

His mentor slain, his people endangered by a curse threatening to wipe them out forever, sixteen year old Rayn must take up the staff of the wisemen all too soon and begin a quest to save his people…

… a quest which may decide the fate of the entire world.

Accompanied by only his troublesome step sister, his speechless friend, and a princess from a fallen empire, Rayn struggles to learn what it means to be a man while leading a desperate mission. With power granted by his faith in the powers of the Divine, the mysterious secrets known only to the princess, and the emergence of their innate gifts, the four go further than any before them in their quest.

But this new threat is unlike any the world has ever known. Will Rayn and his companions be forced to look for help among those who have shown little more than hatred and distrust of humans for the past four thousand years?

Do they dare talk to … the dragons?

A young adult science fantasy novel.

Place the date and your personal mark here each time you
read this book – libraries included!

Why not share your experiences and thoughts with the
fandom! Visit

www.DrJoe.id.au

for fan art, sequels, competitions and more!